VITAL MISSION

A JAKE FORTINA SERIES

LOVE STORY

Also by

Award Winning Author

Ralph R. "Rick" Steinke

***

The Jake Fortina Series:

MAJOR JAKE FORTINA AND THE TIER ONE THREAT

JAKE FORTINA AND THE ROMAN CONSPIRACY

CHANGE OF MISSION: A JAKE FORTINA SERIES NOVEL

***

NEXT MISSION:

A MEMOIR FROM THE DAYS OF PUNISH FRANCE, IGNORE GERMANY, FORGIVE RUSSIA

(To be republished late 2025, early 2026)

PRAISE FOR
VITAL MISSION

"*Vital Mission* is the latest installment in the Jake Fortina series, and it's both gripping and deeply moving. Steinke captures with chilling accuracy the harsh reality faced by families devastated by Russia's brutal invasion of Ukraine in February 2022. The novel's portrayal of children orphaned, abducted, or killed is stark and unflinching—but also necessary. Over the past few years, I've had the privilege of mentoring extraordinary Ukrainian women. Many have shared stories of unimaginable heartbreak—some as they unfolded in real time.

What sets Vital Mission apart is not just its raw truth, but its humanity. Through characters like Jake, Hennadiy, and Marco, Steinke spotlights the multinational efforts of those fighting to protect and care for these children. And, in Margarita—a Russian soldier wrestling with her growing moral outrage—we see a rare and complex glimpse of conscience within a system built on lies. *Vital Mission* doesn't shy away from horror—but it also honors the courage, compassion, and solidarity that persist amid the darkness."

—Lauren C. Anderson, former FBI Executive and Global Women's Advocate

"5/5 Stars! *Vital Mission* is another gripping thriller from award-winning author Rick Steinke. The story follows Jake Fortina as he finds himself in extreme danger in Russia and the Russian-occupied Donbas region of Ukraine and Russia. The author's masterful storytelling brings Jake and a cast of memorable Ukrainians, Italians, and Russians to life, making it easy to become fully invested in Jake's mission and those of his allies. Steinke's writing style is fast-moving and suspenseful, with unexpected twists and turns, and a must-read for anyone looking for a gripping story. *Vital Mission* is a great addition to the Jake Fortina series that will not disappoint fans of Jake's exploits, moral character, and sense of duty!"

> **—Brigadier General Steven M. Anderson** (US Army, Ret.), Iraq veteran and frequent CNN military contributor

"In his most powerful and emotionally charged mission yet, Jake Fortina comes out of retirement as Russian forces invade Ukraine, and innocent children are torn from their families. Rick Steinke delivers a gripping and gut-wrenching story rooted in today's brutal realities. This tale of courage, sacrifice, and redemption pulls on every heartstring; especially for those who have served, are parents, and who love their country. It's storytelling with purpose, and Fortina's fight has never felt more real or more urgent."

> **—Command Sergeant Major Daniel Pinion** (US Army, Ret.) Multiple Deployment Iraq War Veteran and award-winning author of *Chop that Sh*t Up: Leadership and Life Lessons Learned While in the Military*

"*Vital Mission,* the fourth book in Ralph R. "Rick" Steinke's Major Jake Fortina series, is a military thriller with exceptional heart. It goes beyond combat tactics to explore the traumatizing impact of war on those who wage it. *Vital Mission* confronts the true cost of war, not in headlines, statistics, and maps, but in kitchens, schoolyards, and the private corners of people's minds. Vital Mission is brisk and cinematic with frequent shifts of perspective. Its tight pacing constantly engages readers with the narrative while still allowing room to bring in great emotional depth.

Steinke strikes a masterful mix between urgency and empathy, utilizing simple yet powerful words to draw each scene. Whether in a darkened gym where children whisper into their covers or along a frostbitten tree line where Ukrainian soldiers lie in wait, the language Steinke uses is visceral and immersive. 5/5 stars; highly recommended!"

> **—Best Book Chanticleer Book Reviews**, Excerpt, August 6, 2025

"Another thriller in the Jake Fortina series from acclaimed author Rick Steinke, but this time our restless hero takes us to Ukraine. In a supercharged story to rescue two young boys caught in the complexity and viciousness of the Ukraine battlefield, Steinke once again draws on his own unique experience and knowledge to weave a story that seemingly fluctuates from non-fiction to fiction and leaves the reader in suspense from start to finish. Warning: Another Steinke book that will captivate you to read in one sitting!"

—**Colonel John E. Chere Jr.** (US Army, Ret.), Security Cooperation Instructor, Joint Special Operations University, Tampa, Florida.

"With literary brilliance of riveting storytelling, Steinke crafted fictional characters with exquisite sensitivity. Each chapter unfolds with irresistible intensity, weaving together emotion and keen insight into the risks associated with present-day European affairs. He also captures the complexities of the human spirit with such grace and authenticity. This work leaves a lasting impression, stirred with deep admiration, and aspirations for the international stage."

—**Dr. Corinna Balderramos Robinson** (U.S. Army, Retired)

"In *Vital Mission,* Rick's characters once again leap off the page. His writing is evolving with every new novel, and I have found all of them to be gripping and adrenaline-filled, while maintaining a realism sometimes missing in the genre. Some scenes in the book were 'triggering' but handled with dexterity and empathy. These were not just for shock value or to trigger action, as some writers use them, and enhanced the story by expanding the breadth of his characters. A captivating read and one that I will definitely be picking up to read again."

—**Ruth D. Noble**, Award-winning children's book author and cover designer.

VITAL MISSION

A JAKE FORTINA SERIES LOVE STORY

RALPH R. "RICK" STEINKE

Vital Mission: A Jake Fortina Series Love Story

By Ralph R. "Rick" Steinke

Copyright 2025 by Ralph R. "Rick" Steinke

Paperback:

ISBN: 979-8-9880754-3-1

Published by: *Steinwald Productions, LLC*

Book Cover by: Miblart (Miblart.com)

AUTHOR'S NOTES

THE VIEWS EXPRESSED in this publication are those of the author and do not necessarily reflect the official policy or position of the US Department or the US government.

While this book references historical facts, events, and names, this is a work of *fiction*. Except for those individuals obviously referenced in history, all the characters, even though some names may be the same as or approximate living individuals, are completely fictitious, as are some commercial businesses.

To place readers in a general timeframe, each chapter's heading states the month and year. Roughly, if the chapter's events occur in the first ten days of the month, it will, for example, state "Early February" and the year. If it's within the last ten days of the month, it will state "Late February." And if it's the middle, it will state "February."

Trigger Warning for Readers

This book contains scenes that might be difficult for readers, one of a sexual assault and two of physical child abuse. Other references to these events are also present. As these scenes may trigger traumatic experiences for the reader, the reader's discretion is advised.

DEDICATION

To Sofia, Isabela, Elena, Gonzalo, Luis Riccardo, and
the children of Ukraine

ACRONYMS AND NAMES

BRDM-2   "Boyevaya Razvedyvatelnaya Dozornaya Mashina" (Russian); Combat Reconnaissance Patrol Vehicle. The BRDM-2 (also BRDM) is an eight-wheeled amphibious Russian Army vehicle. https://www.youtube.com/watch?v=JGt6PGUJd6Q

BTR-80   "Bronetransportyor" (Russian); Troop Carrier. The BTR-80 is an 8×8 wheeled amphibious armored personnel carrier (APC) designed in the Soviet Union. It was adopted in 1985. https://www.youtube.com/watch?v=NzjaqPRiBO8

FSB   The Federal Security Service of the Russian Federation (FSB). It is the principal security agency of Russia and the main successor agency to the Soviet Union's KGB. Its immediate predecessor was the Federal Counterintelligence Service (FSK). The FSB is considered a combination of the US Federal Bureau of Investigation and the Department of Homeland Security.

mm   millimeters; 10 mm equal .394 inches; 155 millimeters equal 6.1 inches.

Schengen

| Zone | A zone in Western and Central Europe, where twenty-nine European countries have abolished border controls at their shared borders, allowing for free movement of people within the area. |
| T-72 | The T-72 is a Soviet-designed main battle tank that entered production in 1973. It replaced the T-54/55 series as the workhorse of Soviet tank forces. At the link is a modernized T-72 version, being operated in Ukraine by the Russian Army.
https://www.youtube.com/watch?v=0R-Y69asNmA |

"We demand that Russia urgently returns children who have been abducted from occupied territories, as well as prisoners of war and civilian prisoners."

—Excerpt, **Swedish Prime Minister Ulf Kristersson** from a joint statement by the **Leaders of the Nordic Baltic Eight*** on Ukraine, August 16, 2025

*Denmark, Estonia, Finland, Iceland, Latvia, Lithuania, Norway, and Sweden

PROLOGUE

February 24, 2022

ANGER BORDERING ON RAGE FILLED JAKE FORTINA. And then, a deep empathy and sadness for Ukraine and its people. Every Italian and many major international news outlets were covering the trauma and violence happening in Mariupol, Ukraine. Jake had served in the US Army for more than twenty years. Some of that time was spent as a military attaché in Paris and Rome. So, he kept a close watch on potential threats to US national security and threats against US allies.

Dammit, Jake thought as he watched the newest report from his, Sara's, and their young Giacamo's home in northern Italy, *I knew this was a possibility. But I fervently hoped and prayed that power-hungry Russian dictator wouldn't go through with it.*

"It" was the beginning of a major Russian military assault against innocent and defenseless civilians living in the Ukraine-Russia border town of Mariupol. On this somber morning, Jake had no idea where Russia's brutal attack would lead. Jake knew that Russia, shortly after hosting the 2014 Olympic Winter Games in Sochi, had already attacked Ukraine. By the end of 2014, Russia occupied major chunks of terrain in Ukraine's Crimea and Donbas regions.

How far will (Russian President) Puchta go? He asked himself. *Is he seeking to take more of Ukrainian territory . . . or all of Ukraine? And when he's finished subduing Ukraine, who is next? Finland? Sweden? The Baltic states?*

During his time in the US Army, Jake made a dear friend in Ukrainian Air Force Colonel Hennadiy Kovalenko. Kovalenko still served his country and would now be in another fight for his life and the life of his country.

No longer in a US Army uniform, Jake wanted to help, to be "in the fight." But he knew that in addition to Sara, he had their young son to consider.

Dear God, I wish there was some way I could help my friend Hennadiy and his wife Mila, prayed Jake. *Please protect the people of Ukraine and let them survive whatever attacks and dangers come their way in the next weeks and months.*

As Jake would learn in the next months and years, the Almighty answers prayers based on His timeline, not on the timelines of the faithful.

CHAPTER 1

TAKE CARE OF YOUR BROTHER
Late February 2022

THE "BOOM" RUDELY AWAKENED OLENA KOZLOVA-LEVEDEVA. Within seconds, another boom, this one sounding more like a loud thump and more distant. Over several seconds, more booms and thumps came from outside her house, shaking its foundation.

The boys! Olena thought, panicked.

As she moved to sit up in bed, a Russian Army-fired 152 mm (about six inches in diameter, twenty-eight inches long, and weighing 110 pounds) artillery projectile passed through the top side of her home's A-framed, concrete ceiling and its heavy stone-coated, steel roof tiles. Dense metal chunks from the shell's shrapnel struck the ceiling between her room and the room where her boys slept, just twelve feet away.

More artillery shells exploded within 50 to 100 yards outside her house and in the extended neighborhood.

Then darkness, dust, smoke, and silence.

Olena tried to open her eyes. She could only open one. Looking into the dark void above her, she could barely make out a few stars. They appeared intermixed with smoke and darkness.

Or are those clouds? She pondered.

Immobilized and not understanding if she was in a nightmare or reality, Olena was covered in chunks of concrete and what was left of a five-by-five-inch, 14-foot-long ceiling timber.

Pieces of cement-coated steel roof tiles (common in Ukraine) blanketed her.

Olena blinked her uninjured eye.

This is no nightmare, she thought. *I'm alive.*

She tried moving her legs and arms. They did not respond. Olena realized that her throbbing head, unlike the rest of her body, was free, not covered in whatever covered and restricted the rest of her like a straitjacket. Any physical movement other than by her good eye was impossible. Through the mental haze, she could not comprehend why her prone body had no sense of feeling and would not respond to her thoughts—and the surging mental pleas—to move her legs and arms.

But I can breathe, she thought.

"Thank you, Jesus," she moaned aloud.

I can breathe.

"Sergiy!" she cried out, her strength and voice diminishing by the minute.

Silence.

As Olena's internal organs hemorrhaged, she again willed herself—with the help of adrenaline coursing through her veins and Divine presence—to cry out.

"Sergiy!"

A response pierced the silence.

"Yes? Mama, is that *you?"*

Ten-year-old Sergiy was lying on his back with his legs trapped under a piece of timber and partially pulverized cement and plaster. But much of his upper body and head were miraculously free. With his best physical effort, he could wriggle free.

"Yes, Mama! I'm *here!*" he cried out again into the darkness.

"Sergiy!" Olena cried out, her breathing now heavily labored, "Take care of your brother! Please take care of yourself and your brother! I love . . ."

Olena Kozlova breathed her last breath.

Several seconds passed by.

"Mama!" yelled Sergiy again. "Are you there? Mama!"

CHAPTER 2

SIX WEEKS EARLIER: THE COMMISSIONER

Early January 2022

POLINA GONCHAROV WAS ANXIOUS BUT EXCITED. She could not believe she was seated at the same office table with Russian President Vasily Puchta. Sure, Goncharov had been an ambitious and successful Russian politician who had successfully participated in local politics in the Penza *oblast* (region or province). But this felt surreal.

Joining the United Russia Party was the best thing I ever did, she thought.

She reflected on the day the Russian Prime Minister had personally given Goncharov her party membership card.

And being appointed to this position by the President is the greatest thing that has ever happened to me.

Four months prior, President Puchta had appointed the Senator as Russia's Federal Commissioner of Children's Rights. Her predecessor had developed plans for abducting tens of thousands of Ukraine's children who would one day be orphaned on the heels of Russian military forces violently conquering all of Ukraine . . . or so went Russia's grand strategy. It was now Goncharov's job to make sure her predecessor's plan and the organization behind it were effectively refined and executed. Since being appointed Commissioner, she had met twice with the Prime Minister, but never with Russia's President.

Before he addressed Goncharov, the Russian President looked at her as if to size her up. The Prime Minister had strongly endorsed her for the job. The President intended to make the weight of what Russia and Goncharov would soon be facing clear.

"You know that someday, we will have to liberate our Slavic neighbors to the west," said the President, not mentioning Ukraine by name nor giving any hint that "someday"—when Russian armed forces would brutally invade Ukraine—was less than six weeks away.

"And when we do," he continued, "we will face what might be a years-long struggle in making sure Ukraine's youth understand the full privileges and responsibilities of becoming citizens of our great Russia. Is your organization fully prepared to make those children understand that?"

Goncharov was prepared for the question. From the moment she had been appointed as the Children's Rights Commissioner, she had worked feverishly to make sure Russia would be able to "save" tens of thousands of Ukrainian youths . . . from their parents, who would either be killed or physically separated from their children during the Russian military's onslaught deep into Ukraine.

"The Ukrainian children have been severely tainted by the corrupt and hollow Western ideas of individual liberty, freedom, and democracy," the Russian President had said to his closest advisors.

Well before Goncharov came to this rigid meeting with the President, the Russian Prime Minister had also made her mandate clear.

"Your mission is to ensure that Ukrainian children will be fully integrated into Russian society," the Prime Minister had told her on her first day on the job, "and you will have much work to do in ensuring the children understand and internalize just how superior the Russian people and society are to Ukraine's. Not to mention, those of the West."

Goncharov responded to the President's question with conviction.

"Yes, Mr. President," she began, "my people are more than ready. With the full support of our great army, I am sure that we will be able to process, from day one, tens of thousands of young boys and girls and bring them into the loving arms of Russian mothers and fathers. Their inoculation against Ukraine's morally bankrupt society and those of Western so-called democracies will be complete not long after that."

CHAPTER 3
DAWN
Late February 2022

LITTLE SERGIY DID NOT HEAR ANY RESPONSE FROM HIS MOTHER. He desperately cried out "Mama!" nine times more over the space of fifteen minutes. He wondered if she had fallen asleep, and, if he just shouted a little louder, he might be able to wake her. He cried "Mama!" six more times. And then he dozed off.

Almost two hours later, darkness gave way to dawn. The brisk thirty-seven-degree-Fahrenheit woke Sergiy. Covered exactly where he lay when the ceiling materials fell on the lower half of his body, he realized his arms, upper chest, and head were uncovered and free. The wool blanket and cotton sheet that covered him when the artillery shell hit the house were still there, too. The blanket and sheet covered him up to the middle of his rib cage.

Fortunately, the concrete remnants partially covering him were mostly pulverized. None of the potentially deadly cement-covered, steel roof shingles had struck him, either. The walls in his bedroom were mostly still intact. Much of the ceiling above him was intact, too, providing a respite from a barely discernible but chilly morning breeze.

Sergiy remembered what his mother had told him when he was eight years old.

"Sergiy, when you are alone and feel afraid, cry out, 'Jesus, help me!' And He will. You can think it, but it is better if you say it out loud."

"Jesus, help me!" he cried, tears forming in his eyes.

He waited. Jesus did not appear.

"Jesus, *please* help me!" he called out again.

Nothing happened.

A Divine thought entered his mind.

Try to move. You are able to get up.

Sergiy tested his body and realized he could sit up. After sitting, he began to push the crumbled concrete and stucco pieces off the lower half of his body. On top of the crumbled cement covering his ankles and feet was a twenty-six-inch-long, two-by-four-inch splinter of wood, lying at an angle to his lower legs. Sergiy was surprised he was able to push that off, too. Feeling the chilly morning air through his thin cotton pajamas, he wrested the remainder of the blanket out from the rubble and wrapped it around his shoulders.

Sergiy glanced across the ten-foot-wide room toward his five-year-old brother, Gleb. Curled up under his blanket, Gleb was asleep in his single bed. Gleb would turn six years old in one week. Miraculously, other than a thin layer of stucco and cement dust on his blanket, Gleb had been unaffected by the damage surrounding him. And he had slept through all the violence. Or so it seemed.

"Gleb, are you awake?"

Sergiy heard no response.

Sergiy located his slippers, which he had placed under his bed the evening prior. He grabbed the slippers, shook the dust out of them, and put them on. He gingerly took three short steps over small pieces of rubble and dust to Gleb's bed.

Gleb was sleeping on his side, facing the wall away from Sergiy. Sergiy reached out and shook Gleb by the shoulders. Sergiy was surprised when Gleb immediately turned his upper body and head toward Sergiy. Fatigue, fear, dust, and tear stains streaked Gleb's face.

"Gleb, are you OK?" asked Sergiy. "Were you awake?"

"Yes, I was," responded Gleb. "When the noise happened, it was dark. I was afraid to move. I thought I was having a bad dream. And then it was cold, and I did not want to take my blanket off and get out of bed. And then I heard something moving. But I did not want to look."

CHAPTER 4

DIMA AND IGOR

Late February 2022

"DIMA!" SHOUTED IGOR. "COME HERE!"

***

Two days prior, Igor and his soldier buddy, Dima, were part of a large Russian Army training exercise inside Russia. The training occurred less than twenty miles from the Russia-Ukraine border. Dima and Igor thought the military maneuvers, involving over 100,000 Russian soldiers, might conclude in a week or so. After that, they would head back to their military base located in Russia's Southern Military District, roughly 400 miles east of the Russia-Ukraine border and Mariupol. With any luck, after cleaning and putting away their vehicles and equipment, and cleaning their weapons, they might get a day or two of leave. Or so they hoped.

But just thirty-six hours earlier, their sergeant searched them for cellphones a second time. Igor had left his phone at the base, thinking it would be "a pain" to keep it charged in the field. Besides, his senior sergeants and officers had said that cellphones "were absolutely forbidden" from being brought on this military exercise. Their Russian Army superiors did not want to take any chance that Russia's massive assault, planned to reach across all of Ukraine, might be compromised because some 18-year-old Russian soldier put a video on social media.

Dima brought his cellphone anyway. He was severely reprimanded after his platoon's senior sergeant found it in a side pocket of his rucksack. Dima knew that he would never see the cellphone again.

Several hours after the cellphone search, their platoon leader, a lieutenant, told the entire platoon that their "training" mission had changed. There had been rumors circling among the troops, but now the worst of the rumors was about to be confirmed.

"We are about to liberate Ukraine from its evil Nazi leadership. Combat operations will begin tomorrow morning," the lieutenant told his soldiers.

The lieutenant and his soldiers visualized—hoped, perhaps—that the "operations" might start after 6 A.M. at the earliest, thereby allowing for a full night's sleep. But it was not to be. Operations would commence at 3:30 A.M., not 6 A.M. That is when the first artillery rounds and rockets would launch.

The lieutenant continued.

"Your job—our job—is to go into Mariupol and find abandoned Ukrainian children. Do not worry about the civilian adults. Somebody else will take care of them. Your job is to find the homeless children and bring them *here,*" he said, pointing to a crude map and a gymnasium east of Mariupol.

"Do not harm the children in any way," he continued. "If they are lightly injured or bruised, bring them. If you are in doubt about their physical condition, tell your sergeant, and he will call me on the radio. I might tell you to bring them . . . or not. If they are severely injured, however, leave them. Someone else will take care of them."

The lieutenant knew that unless local Ukrainians found, treated, and evacuated the severely injured children, they would be left to die. The lieutenant did not know, however, that the top military officer in the Kremlin had directed that "children needing more than superficial medical aid will place far too much of a burden on our military forces as they conduct our combat liberation operations" and "should not be brought back to Russia."

"Up to what age should we capture them?" asked a young sergeant, the boldest of anybody in the platoon who dared ask the lieutenant a question.

Unlike in the US Army, US Marine Corps, or any other US military service, this question was not welcomed. In the Russian Army, those in leadership roles subjugate rather than empower, inspire, and lead soldiers. Junior and mid-level sergeants are mostly sidelined and have little leadership and decision-making discretion. The center of gravity for frontline soldier leadership is principally held by the officers. It's rarely a young soldier's or sergeant's place to question an officer.

"You are NOT capturing them!" the lieutenant shot back. "We are *saving* them from their corrupt Nazi government and immoral and corrupt Ukrainian society. We will bring them back to Russia, take care of them, and make sure they grow up to be honorable Russian citizens."

The lieutenant was proud that he had added the part about the "Nazi" Ukrainian government. After all, that is what Vasily Puchta had explained to his Russian generals and Russian people as the reason for "liberating" the Ukrainian people: to save them from the Nazis, who led the country. The generals knew it was a bold-faced lie.

But they also knew that labeling the Ukrainian government as Nazis would be easily understood by the relatives, friends, and offspring of the more than twenty million Russian and Soviet citizens who had perished fending off the German Wehrmacht and Nazi formations in eastern Europe during World War II. And it was a *narrative*—once referred to as *propaganda* by the West during the Cold War—that could be easily controlled by the massive and ubiquitous Russian state media apparatus.

***

"Dima, get over here!" Igor repeated.

Dima came running at the concern in Igor's voice. Igor was pointing at the semi-crumbled house in front of them. Two walls were entirely intact. The other two were in differing states of destruction. About one-third of the home's ceiling was intact. Halfway inside the rubble sat two young boys, blankets wrapped around their shoulders.

The younger boy was sobbing; the older boy looked straight ahead. At the sight of the two soldiers, the older boy stood stoically, his shoulders squared. He faced the Russian soldiers directly. Young Sergiy did not know who the two young men were.

They approached the boys.

With roughly sixty percent word commonality between the Russian and Ukrainian languages, the two men—and their roughly thirty fellow platoon members—had been told by their lieutenant to "speak slowly, clearly, and non-threateningly" to the children. The two soldiers did not know it, but that guidance originated from a Russian three-star general who had met with Russia's Federal Commissioner for Children's Rights.

The general understood that the impetus for the entire "child saving" operation came from high up, if not the very top, in the echelons of the Kremlin. He could not afford to have his soldiers botch this "humanitarian assistance" mission. The general was told that this "child-saving" mission was every bit as important as destroying the Ukrainian Armed Forces and taking control of Ukraine.

"Hi, young man," said Igor to little Sergiy. "What happened? What is your name? Is this your *brother?*" he asked, nodding to Gleb, who sat in a surviving wooden kitchen chair, sniffling.

"My name is Sergiy, and his name is Gleb," responded Sergiy, nodding to Gleb. "He's my brother."

Sergiy either did not know what else to say or perhaps could not remember the man's question. He went silent. Sergiy was trembling and doing his best to follow his mother's pleaded request just over three hours earlier.

"Please, Sergiy, take care of your brother!"

Igor looked at Dima, wondering what to say next.

"What is your last name, Sergiy?" asked Igor.

"Levedeva," replied Sergiy.

"Is there anybody else in the house, Sergiy Levedeva?" asked Igor.

"Yes. Our mother. She's right there," said Sergiy, pointing down and about six feet to his right.

"She's under that log and pile of junk."

Igor took two steps and looked down. He could see a dirtied head with its face turned on its side. The face was more than half visible through a twenty-inch-high pile of ceiling chunks, roof tiles, and part of a ceiling timber. The woman's dark hair was filled with coarse dust. Blood stains ran down from one corner of her mouth. The Russian soldiers could not see it, but there was about a four-inch gash behind her ear. Next to her head on the cement floor was what looked like a dark spot about nine inches in diameter, where blood, dust, and grime had mixed.

Igor bent over to listen for breathing. Nothing. He reached through the rubble and touched the woman's forehead. Igor was surprised at how cold it was. The young soldier shuddered. It was the first corpse he had seen or touched in his life.

Igor looked at Dima and shook his head. Sergiy looked on; Gleb just looked blankly at the rubble surrounding his feet.

CHAPTER 5

DISGUSTED

Late February 2022

JAKE FORTINA WAS DISGUSTED. He could not believe what he was hearing from the "military expert," a retired US Army general, on CNN. The retired general was expounding on Russia's invasion of Ukraine, launched just a few days earlier. It was Jake's habit to check at least three news sources for major events and stories, whether from print or televised media. He changed the station to Fox News. What he was hearing there from another retired Army general, this one who had been out of the Army for at least twenty years and who had made other "expert" news appearances, was even worse.

Seeing Jake's troubled look, Sara had to ask a question.

"What is wrong, *cara mia* (my dear)?" she asked while seated next to Jake on the couch.

"These so-called experts have no freakin' idea what they're talking about," responded Jake.

Sara saw the revulsion on Jake's face. For Sara, it was a rare sight in the several years since she had met Jake at the George C. Marshall European Center for Security Studies, located in Garmisch-Partenkirchen, Germany. It took a lot for Jake to show that kind of negative emotion on his face.

"American generals are pontificating about how the Russian Army will overrun Ukraine within sixty days. One general just said it would be completed in much less time than that. I've never heard any so-called experts be so damn *wrong* about anything before in my life!"

Sara, sensing the strength of emotion in Jake's demeanor and voice, decided to give it a few minutes before engaging again. After the retired Army general on Fox News wrapped up his interview and his "strategic analysis," she thought it OK to ask Jake more questions.

But Jake spoke first.

"Strategic analysis, my ass," said Jake. "This guy has overlooked so many things."

"Such as?" asked Sara.

Knowing he needed to calm down, Jake inhaled deeply and exhaled slowly.

"Well, for one," said Jake, feeling a modicum calmer, "I think I know the Ukrainian people. And I guarantee you they will fight to the death—to the last soldier alive—to protect their country. Puchta's brutal and naked aggression is so egregiously wrong for so many reasons. In his early years as President, he seemed to be reasonable and approachable, at least from an international relations perspective. But then something changed. It soon became clear that he wanted to restore Russia to its Cold War international standing, before the Soviet Union, with Russia as its hegemon, collapsed. He longs for the days when Russia was feared as the major superpower in the east, backed by the Soviet Union and its Warsaw Pact, with its communist ideologies. And were Puchta to be successful in taking down Ukraine, other former Soviet countries like Poland, Estonia, Latvia, and Lithuania would be next on his 'conquer and subdue' shopping list."

Jake paused to take a drink of his *Ripasso* red wine. He had first tasted it during his days of serving with the 173rd Airborne Brigade Combat Team in Vicenza, Italy. Made from the Valpolicella wine blend, the *Ripasso's* double fermentation vinification gave it extra body. It was Jake's kind of wine.

"While the majority of Europe and the world think the 'mighty' Russian Army will overpower Ukraine and its people, the Europeans and many others are wrong, too. The Ukrainian military is better led and trained than Russia's. Like most countries in the West, Ukraine has learned to empower its frontline leaders, and by that, I mean its *sergeants.* The Ukrainian sergeants, many of them trained using US, UK, and other NATO countries' small unit leadership principles, based on actual standards of performance and effects-based outcomes, will lead with courage, creativity, and initiative. Why? Because they know their cause is right and that Russia's unprovoked aggression is completely indefensible."

Sara nodded her head, encouraging Jake to continue. She knew, once again, that Jake had to get his thoughts and emotions off his chest.

"Russia tried to subdue Ukraine in 2014 when it forcibly occupied territory in Crimea and Ukraine's Donbas region. Those land invasions—by Puchta's so-called little green men— were completely illegal by international standards. General Eisenhower once said that 'the most critical factor in winning a war is *morale.'* The Ukrainian military knows their government and the Ukrainian people have their backs, all the way up to Ukraine's president. We—us Americans, I mean—recently offered Ukraine's president safe passage out of Ukraine. And do you know what his response was?"

"No, sweetie, I do not," replied Sara.

"I don't need a ride, I need ammunition!"

CHAPTER 6
HOLDING CENTER
Late February 2022

MARGARITA ROMANOVA'S EYES WIDENED AS SHE OBSERVED ANOTHER GROUP of children enter the gymnasium. The gym, with a large team handball court at its center, had been quickly transformed into a temporary "holding center" for Ukrainian children seized by Russian soldiers.

Romanova, a 23-year-old field medic holding the junior Russian Army enlisted rank of *yefreytor* (private first-class or E-3 for the US Army, R-4 for the Russian Army), was thankful she had not been assigned to one of the combat divisions now seeking to invade deep into Ukraine. But she knew that day was coming.

"You will be assigned to the child-saving operation in Ukraine for the next ninety days," a junior officer told her. "And then you will be assigned to the 10th Armored Division to do the job you have been trained for."

Romanova accepted her "child saving" assignment gratefully, having no idea—other than it would be a very male-dominated environment because her Russian Army was only five percent female—what experiences might later await her in the 10th Armored Division.

Besides, she thought to herself when she was given her new orders, *anything is better than being back home with an alcoholic father and a submissive mother who he completely controls.*

Romanova had attended Moscow University for a year as a health and medical administration studies major before realizing she was not cut out for it, nor did she have the ambition to continue her university studies. After three years of wandering through a handful of service jobs, including as a paltry-paid store clerk and then waitress, she decided to join the Russian Army. It was her attendance at a May 9 Moscow Victory Day Parade and seeing the proud faces of the few surviving veterans of World War II, as well as the Russian citizens' adulation for those soldiers, which motivated her to join the Russian Army.

As Romanova eyed the first group of a dozen kids who entered the gymnasium, her eyes caught an older boy, *maybe ten or eleven years old,* she thought.

The boy was holding the hand of a younger boy, *probably half his age and size,* she assessed.

The younger boy was sniffling and appeared very afraid. The older boy possessed an almost stoic confidence about him that exceeded his years.

Margarita instantly thought of her brother. When he was five and Margarita was eleven years old, he had died from "hitting his head on the floor after falling off the kitchen counter." Or so her parents had said when Margarita had returned from school on that terrible day.

But Margarita could never bring herself to believe her parents. Since that dark afternoon when she had returned from school, she had carried years of doubt about a vodka-fueled and violent father, whom she had seen brutally beat her younger brother on at least three occasions.

Romanova immediately approached the two boys.

"Hi boys," she said, kneeling on one knee and first looking the older boy in the eyes, followed by the younger one. "What happened?"

"Our house was bombed," said Sergiy, not fully comprehending why or by whom. "And our mother died."

Gleb, hearing his older brother's words while staring down at the tarp-covered gym floor, finally had the courage to look up at the pretty, kind lady with blue eyes. Perhaps because of Divine design, Gleb couldn't feel the weight or the long-term implications of Sergiy's words, "And our mother died." But he felt sad—very sad—nonetheless.

"I am so sorry that your house got damaged and that your mom will not be with us anymore," said Margarita. "But please, do not worry. I will take *good* care of you. C'mon, let's go over and see where you will sleep, shall we?"

She reached out to take each boy by the hand and led them to the rows of cots arrayed on the gym floor. She found two cots that were parallel to each other and toward the center of the gymnasium floor. Each had been equipped with a wool blanket, a small pillow, and two bottles of water placed on the floor underneath the cot.

Fortunately for Sergiy and Gleb, one of the soldiers who had found them had taken the time to find the boys' overcoats before leaving their bombed-out home. The coats were still hanging in a hallway armoire cabinet, unscathed. When they arrived at the gym, the boys were wearing those coats on top of their t-shirts, pajama pants, and tennis shoes. The shoes had been pulled from the rubble where the front door had once been by the second soldier. As the boys had left the house with the two soldiers, Gleb had asked Sergiy a question.

"What about Chestnut?"

Chestnut was the family's seven-year-old Corgi. He was born a year before Gleb came into the world. The Corgi had protected and fussed over Gleb since the first night that Gleb was in his crib. After Gleb fell asleep, Chestnut always returned to sleep on the floor next to Gleb's crib. Once Gleb left his crib, Chestnut moved to the master bedroom.

Olena's husband, Roman, while he loved the little Corgi, was not a big fan of sharing the bed with the family dog. And to keep things simple, Olena helped ensure Chestnut did not come into her side of the bed, either. The little guy always slept on the floor, next to Olena's side of the bed.

Sergiy had seen a bloodied Chestnut lying partially buried under rubble, and about one yard on the other side of his mother. But Sergiy did not want Gleb to know that.

"I heard Chestnut barking outside when he ran away last night," Sergiy replied carefully. "I think the noise scared him. I'm sure he'll be fine. OK?"

Still looking down, Gleb nodded his head.

"Listen, boys, you should only be staying here for one night, maybe two at the most, OK?" interjected Margarita. "I will watch over you tonight and every night and day after this. Don't worry, OK?"

"Where will we be going?" asked Sergiy.

"It will be a good place for you. Don't worry." Margarita repeated.

Gleb nodded his head in hopeful and innocent acknowledgment.

CHAPTER 7
DYMER, KYIV OBLAST, UKRAINE
Late February 2022

LYING STOMACH DOWN ON THE FROSTY GROUND, *Starshiy Serzhant* (senior sergeant) Roman Levedeva observed the long, ducks-in-a-row line of Russian T-72 tanks. The tanks were mixed in with a few BTR-80 armored troop carriers. Levedeva kept his focus on a single BTR-80. The wheeled, lightly armored vehicle held a crew of three Russian soldiers and seven infantrymen in the main troop compartment. The BTR-80 was Levedeva's designated target.

Lying on the cold ground to Levedeva's left was a rifleman and much more junior paratrooper from the 95th Airborne Brigade (also known as the 95th Separate Polesian Air Assault Brigade). The Brigade had earned its stripes and an exceptional reputation with the rest of the Ukrainian military after a daring raid behind Russian lines in the Donbas region of Ukraine in 2014. In 2022, the 95th Airborne Brigade was considered one of the most prestigious and capable units in the Ukrainian armed forces.

The young paratrooper's job was to help Levedeva spot his target and provide additional security. Levedeva settled in, his right hand on the trigger mechanism of the individually fired Javelin anti-tank missile launcher, and his extended left arm and hand supporting the launcher tube from underneath.

On this chilly February 25 morning, the brigade's paratroopers knew they constituted the critical—and *final*—line of defense for Kyiv, Ukraine's capital. If the unsuspecting Russians got past the 95th Airborne Brigade, they could make a fast and relatively uncontested dash for the capital.

The Ukrainian brigade's mission was to stop the Russian armored column before it reached the streets of Kyiv and achieved a huge psychological victory for the Russian Army and the Kremlin. In short, the 95th Airborne Brigade's success or defeat would reach well beyond tactical and into strategic implications for the direction of the war.

In thirty minutes, it would be dawn's "first light." It was that grey period when night's darkness begins to yield to the morning's first hints of light. Levedeva knew the slumbering Russian soldiers inside the vehicles were at their most vulnerable point in a 24-hour period.

Two hours earlier, the Russian armored vehicle convoy had passed through the Ukrainian village of Dymer, located just six miles to the north. Because the Russian troops were exhausted, the convoy's lead vehicle had surprisingly stopped, shortly after emerging from the woods, in the middle of a clearing. They should have stayed in the wood line and ensured 360-degree security for their vehicles and soldiers. But, due to a combination of poor troop leadership, poor discipline, and exhaustion, they didn't.

This left about half the convoy exposed in the open darkness, with no forest coverage surrounding them. This also gave the Ukrainian paratroopers excellent fields of fire for attacking the convoy, with no trees or thick brush obstructing their vision or that of their about-to-be-fired Javelin missiles. The back half of the Russian convoy was in the darker woods, with its experienced soldiers thinking they were safer than the exposed troops ahead of them.

Levedeva understood that if his team of fellow paratroopers could destroy or render inoperable more than a third of the vehicles—especially the lead vehicles—in the fifty-four-vehicle convoy, the rear vehicles would be blocked from advancing further. And the Russian leaders and soldiers manning them would be shocked and demoralized since almost half of their formation would be destroyed within seconds.

At that moment, another company of 95th Airborne Brigade paratroopers, commanded by a Ukrainian captain, would ambush any survivors in the woods who might try to exit their vehicles and run into the darkness for cover and concealment.

For the past thirty minutes, Levedeva and the hand-picked team of mostly experienced sergeants had the resting convoy under observation. As one of the best units in the Ukrainian Army, the men were fortunate to have night vision goggles, a special piece of equipment that ninety-eight percent of the Ukrainian Army did not yet have.

Thanks to the United States, twenty-one of the forty-five Ukrainian soldiers were carrying individually launched Javelin anti-tank missiles. The missiles were lethal against Russian Army tanks and armored troop carriers.

In military training areas in Western Europe, ten of the sergeants had been trained by American noncommissioned officers (sergeants) on the use of the shoulder-mounted, individually fired anti-tank weapon. Those back in Ukraine who did not have the opportunity to train directly with the Americans were trained by their fellow Ukrainian sergeants upon the return of their comrades to Ukraine.

Levedeva and the line of Ukrainian soldiers lying prone on the frosty ground kept a low profile. Each sergeant assigned a Javelin was propped up on his elbows while keeping the convoy under observation. The adrenaline coursing through their veins boosted their alertness and warmth.

For additional security in the event of a close-in attack, a rifleman was positioned beside each Javelin firer. The distance between each two-man team and the flanking teams was about fifteen to twenty feet.

In observing the convoy at a range of about 250 yards, Levedeva realized the Russians had only put out a few token security guards to secure their sleeping comrades inside the tanks and troop carriers. Those that *were* pulling security were no more than twenty-five to thirty yards away from their vehicles, not a sufficient distance away from the convoy to provide early warning in the event of an attack. Furthermore, almost all the battle tanks and troop-carrying, lightly armored vehicles had left their motors running so that their heaters would keep the soldiers inside the metal structures warm.

Their security sucks. And so does their self-discipline. Must be mostly draftees, thought Levedeva as he observed a soldier urinating not far from his tank and without his personal weapon.

A low, barely audible voice came through Levedeva's radio headset.

"In twenty seconds, mark the ten-second countdown."

The voice was that of a Ukrainian major who had also volunteered for the ambush on the Russian tank column. He'd gained combat experience as a junior captain when he and his fellow paratroopers parachuted behind Russian lines, some eight years prior.

Located about three hundred yards north—and positioned between the Javelin element and the ambush element—was a thirty-nine-year-old lieutenant colonel. He and his senior battalion sergeant had picked their location to best be able to guide both the Javelin element and the ambush element during the heat of battle that was about to erupt. The lieutenant colonel and senior sergeant were accompanied by two radio operators and two additional riflemen.

At the precise second, the word "mark" came over the radio. With their luminescent watches, this started the ten-second silent countdown. Levedeva would be the first in the group to fire, followed instantly thereafter by everyone else carrying a Javelin.

At the zero-second mark, Levedeva pulled the trigger. The Javelin tube ejected its armor-penetrating missile with a slight "pop" sound, followed by a longer and stronger "swoosh" sound. The Javelin missile followed its precisely programmed flight path to the target, where Levedeva had set his crosshairs before he pulled the trigger.

What made the weapon so deadly against tanks and other armored vehicles was that it didn't strike its target at the aimpoint—on the vehicle's front or side—where the heavier armor was. Instead, during the last half of the missile's flight path, the missile rose in a high arc above its target. Then, like a pelican plunging from the sky straight down to attack a fish underwater, the Javelin's missile plunged and penetrated through the tank or armored vehicle's top. The top was the tank's "softer"—less armored and most vulnerable—spot. For the soldiers inside the tank or vehicle, their fates would be a violent—and hopefully for them, quick—death from fire and molten shrapnel.

CHAPTER 8

FIRE AND FORGET

Late February 2022

JUST AS HE WAS TRAINED, Levedeva knew he didn't have to hold a steady bead on his target until it was struck by the missile. After he pulled the trigger, the Javelin's "fire and forget" engineering and software did its work.

With all missiles hitting their targets, the men quickly crawled back behind the slight rise in the ground from which they had launched their Javelin missiles. They stood up and peered over the natural earthen berm. The horizon was full of bright flashes of white, yellow, and occasional orange. Secondary explosions from ammunition occurred every few seconds. A few panicked shouts and screams could be heard from the handful of Russian guards who had been outside the tanks. Their tanks had instantly become infernos of bright flashes, extreme heat, and muffled human screams.

Just to the north, the weapons' fires from Levedeva's comrades in the airborne company were causing chaos, death, destruction, and shock among the convoy's back half. Knowing they could be next to receive the mortal wrath of the Javelins, the convoy's Russian Army survivors were trying to exit their vehicles and run for cover. As they did, the Ukrainians shot all but a handful down.

"Team Javelin, move out," came the calm command over the radio from the battalion commander.

Lebedeva walked quickly and deliberately to the front of the group. Because of his experience and legendary nighttime land navigation skills, the senior sergeant had volunteered to lead the large platoon-sized group (about thirty to forty soldiers) as safely and quickly as possible back to their rendezvous point, some three miles away. There they would find their camouflaged vehicles, hidden off-road in a darkly wooded area.

To ensure 100 percent soldier accountability, a quick headcount was taken before the paratroopers began to move. In the event of an attack on what was now essentially a robust Ukrainian patrol, the major located himself about two-thirds of the way back from Levedeva. If an enemy attacked the unit, this was the best position for the former company commander to quickly assess the situation and issue orders.

After about 300 yards, the rear guard, a Ukrainian captain and a handful of senior sergeants, turned to visually sweep the area. The twenty-one burning and exploding Russian Army tanks and troop carriers continued to light up the night sky, while the 95th Brigade's airborne company farther to the north was taking care of business with the remaining Russian survivors trying to run for cover in the woods.

The Russian tank convoy's march to Kyiv, with only twenty miles to go before reaching the outskirts of Ukraine's capital, had been thwarted. And so had Vasily Puchta's goal of quickly decapitating the Ukrainian national government in Kyiv and subduing the Ukrainian people shortly thereafter.

***

Dimitry, without night vision goggles, was straining his eyes. No more than three minutes prior, his sergeant had told the Russian Army draftee to "take up a security position in front of the BRDM and watch for the enemy."

After their route reconnaissance mission was completed the evening prior, Dimitry, his sergeant, and two other soldiers had parked their BRDM-2 combat reconnaissance patrol vehicle deep in the wood line and about 600 yards forward of the now-burning convoy. When the fireworks started, the sergeant tried to establish radio contact with his lieutenant, who was back in the convoy. There was no response from the twenty-four-year-old lieutenant.

The Russian sergeant did not know that all that was left of the lieutenant, who was in the fifth vehicle from the front of the convoy, were charred remains. The sergeant also tried to contact his captain, but received no response from him either.

"We must go back to the convoy," the sergeant told his three soldiers, "and help the survivors."

"Dimitry and Vasily, stay on security while the two of us get our sleeping bags, mats, and water cannisters put away and prepare to move. There may be enemy in our area."

The two young soldiers did as they were told, moving to positions at opposite ends of the BRDM. With approximately sixty years of existence in the Russian Army, the wheeled, lightly armored BRDM vehicle was among the oldest in the Russian Army. It had also been in use by at least forty other countries around the world, many of them in or aligned with the former Soviet Union.

Dimitry took up a position about twenty yards in front of the vehicle. Within three minutes, he could not be sure, but he thought he could see dark figures lightly silhouetted from the half-moon and intermittent starlight. He was exhausted and wondered if he was hallucinating. But then he realized the dark figures were becoming ever larger and were clearly heading in his direction.

Dimitry swallowed hard.

The enemy! He thought.

Struck with fear and too panicked to warn his sergeant, Dimitry slowly squeezed the trigger on his AK-47. Three seconds earlier, the "enemy's" point man, spotting the BRDM through his night-vision goggles, had raised his right arm to signal "stop and get down" to his fellow soldiers. And then, for an added measure, he turned around to the soldiers nearest him to whisper, "Get down!"

As the patrol's point man was half-turned around to warn the soldiers behind him, the Russian soldier's AK-47 shot echoed through the forest. The 7.62 mm round penetrated the left side of the patrol's point man, and he immediately dropped to the frozen ground.

Dimitry fired three more shots, all missing any target, before his alarmed Russian sergeant could get his bearings and locate his weapon.

The Ukrainian patrol immediately went to the prone, face-down position. Radio transmissions of "Levedeva has been hit!" and "there is a BRDM about seventy yards in front of us" immediately reached the Ukrainian major and other leaders in the group. The major quickly called for a five-man fire team to maneuver to the right side of the BRDM, while calling for the patrol's forward element to put down a base of direct weapons fire on the BRDM. Meanwhile, a medic and two paratroopers crawled forward to assess Levedeva's condition and render medical aid.

With intense Ukrainian fires directed at the BRDM, the Russian sergeant and his soldier in front of the BRDM were pinned down. Without night vision goggles and severely outnumbered, they did not yet know their chances of surviving against a Ukrainian Army unit with night vision goggles were next to zero. The second conscripted Russian soldier who had been pulling security in the *back* of the BRDM began quickly crawling away from the BRDM and away from his buddies. The suppressive Ukrainian weapons fires continued to terrify the remaining Russian Army trio, preventing their return fire.

Within minutes, the five-man Ukrainian fire team spotted two Russian soldiers near the front of their BRDM armored vehicle, and the Ukrainian airborne professionals quickly eliminated them. The soldier who had been keeping security behind the BRDM quickly low-crawled on the frosty ground and away from the kill zone as fast as he could. When he got to about forty yards away from the BRDM and the mayhem and death surrounding it, the Russian Army draftee took the chance of his life . . . and got up to run. A few trees protected his fleeing form from the Ukrainians, and he kept running before eventually turning toward the light of the burning convoy some five to six hundred yards to the north.

The Ukrainian medic checked Levedeva's pulse and breathing. Nothing. Assisted by a junior sergeant, the medic quickly removed Levedeva's anti-ballistic vest. By feel, the medic located the bullet's entry wound along the side of Levedeva's rib cage.

The medic soon realized the bullet had struck Levedeva right on the very side of his upper rib cage, where there was an open space of about three inches and no ballistic armor protection.

Fucking unlucky shot for Levedeva, thought the medic.

The medic immediately began CPR but thought twice about doing chest compressions, at first fearing they might make Levedeva's wound worse. But then he felt he had no choice other than to continue. He performed CPR for five minutes before switching with the rifleman next to him. The medic knew that in "normal circumstances," CPR should be performed for twenty minutes or longer. But staying in this spot for longer than a few more minutes could put the Ukrainian patrol in jeopardy of being discovered by any surviving Russians from the convoy, or any other Russian soldiers who might be in the area.

After eight total minutes of CPR, the medic checked Levedeva again.

"He's gone," he said to the three soldiers nearest him.

"We have to move now," said the major, knowing the patrol had a long way to go before reaching a safer place.

Two of the patrol's strongest men, both known to their fellow soldiers as serious weightlifters, stepped forward and volunteered to carry their beloved comrade, Roman Levedeva. Two more Ukrainian soldiers instantly volunteered to help. Rather than using a poncho to be held on each of its four corners by a soldier to support Levedeva's corpse, one of the biggest men in the platoon stepped up and threw the 160-pound Levedeva over his right shoulder like a sack of grain.

"Let's go," he whispered.

Each patrol member softly placed deliberate but efficient steps on the frosty ground. The big man traded off carrying Levedeva every ten minutes with two comrades as the men moved through the darkness toward their pre-designated rally point.

CHAPTER 9
THE TRANSFER
Late February 2022

MARGARITA ROMANOVA BARELY SLEPT ON THE STIFF COT. Located among the other Russian soldiers' cots, it was positioned along one of the gym's longer interior walls. The gym had been noisy throughout much of the evening. Caused by a few whimpering or talking kids, or by kids being taken to the bathroom, or by bright lights emanating from the bathrooms, or by adults occasionally passing by, some level of background noise or light was ever present.

Getting good sleep on the cot and in her Russian Army sleeping bag was hard for Margarita. Somehow, she ended up with a sleeping bag intended for Arctic conditions. On top of all the distractions, Margarita had been too warm, even with the sleeping bag partially unzipped.

By midnight on the first day of the shelling and bombing of Mariupol, thirty-two children had been brought to the holding area. So far, Margarita had been officially assigned to control and escort eight of the children, two short of the number she would be responsible for at the gym before escorting them to their next location. But for most of the evening, there were two kids she could not take her mind off: Sergiy and Gleb.

Sergiy seems like a tough cookie for a ten-year-old, thought Romanova, *but I do worry about little Gleb.*

For most of the evening, the last image of Margarita's five-year-old brother, whom she had kissed goodbye before walking off to school, kept tormenting her.

If I were home, would he have died—however he died—that day?

Of the twenty-four female soldiers and two male sergeants assigned to the gym, it was the ladies' job to be in contact with and serve the children, including taking them to the bathroom. The two male sergeants were there to supervise the overall Holding Center operation, with a medical service corps captain and a lieutenant serving as the two senior officers on site.

Four large cardboard boxes filled with children's clothes and shoes of varying types and sizes were positioned along the gym walls, in the event that an orphaned child needed one of the items.

The basic operational concept for "the transfer" operation was that once the gym contained enough children, they would load onto a bus and be transported east into Russia, to Rostov-on-Don. An over six-hour bus ride almost due east from Mariupol, Rostov-on-Don was an industrial city with over one million people. Each bus would carry forty children and four adults, one for every ten children.

At the beginning of the "child saving" operation, the Federal Commissioner for Children's Rights had no idea how many kids would be "saved" in Mariupol. Much of it would depend on the pace of the military operations in capturing and subduing the city. But in any case, the Commissioner had planned for "saving" at least a couple of thousand children from the city, just to be sure.

At 7 A.M., the children who were still sleeping in the gym were awakened by their guides. The thirty-two kids dressed, put their shoes on, and went to the bathroom. They were then led outside the gym to a large military tent, adjacent to the Russian Army mobile kitchen trailer.

Inside the kitchen trailer were two busy Russian Army cooks, finishing up preparing two large pots of *kasha*. Much like oatmeal, the warm porridge and Russian breakfast staple was made from buckwheat.

The kids formed a line and passed by the cooks, dispensing the *kasha* into white plastic bowls. After receiving their steamy bowls, the kids were seated at the wooden picnic tables inside the tent. Margarita's heart warmed as she noticed what she thought was an ever-so-slight hint of calm from Gleb. He was consuming his breakfast while sitting on a bench, close to his brother Sergiy.

Within two hours, fourteen more kids were brought to the gym. Within an hour after that, Margarita boarded a commercial bus with her ten children, ranging from ages three to twelve.

CHAPTER 10
THE SEA OF AZOV
Late February 2022

MARGARITA LED THE TWO BOYS, with her other eight assigned children right behind her, one-third the distance down the bus's aisle. She stopped and seated the young brothers together. She ensured that Gleb got the window seat, with Sergiy taking the aisle seat.

Margarita placed her army hat down to reserve the aisle seat just across the aisle from Sergiy for herself. She then seated a single seven-year-old girl beside her, next to the window. Margarita directed the other seven children to quickly fill the seats behind her.

Within minutes, the fifty-passenger intercity bus carrying forty-four passengers was on its way to cross into Russia at a Ukraine-Russia border crossing site southeast of Luhansk. The roads and highways were better than the direct easterly route out of Mariupol, making the route to Rostov-on-Don a clockwise semi-circle from Mariupol. With due north being 12 o'clock, it was a route from the 9 o'clock position in Mariupol to the 3 o'clock position in Rostov-on-Don.

For the first twenty miles or so, the bus took a directly easterly route paralleling the north shore of the Sea of Azov, before heading north. The sea did not go unnoticed by Sergiy.

"Look, Gleb! I think that's the sea where Mommy and Daddy took us in the summertime! Do you remember how much fun we had on the beach? Do you remember that big plastic green crocodile we played with? You loved that thing!"

In his first display of a hint of enthusiasm and joy since the artillery attack, little Gleb responded.

"Oh, yeah, I do!" he replied, nodding his head vigorously and bravely attempting his best smile.

"And do you remember the sandcastles we made with Mom and Dad?"

Again, but with no verbal response, Gleb nodded his head enthusiastically.

Margarita smiled at their conversation. But upon hearing Sergiy trying to cheer up Gleb, she fought back tears. Margarita felt embarrassed and angry as she lay her head back on the headrest. *I haven't even asked their mother's name, or anything about their father,* she thought.

Sergiy kept up his conversation with Gleb. Margarita looked past the two jabbering boys and out their window toward the glistening Sea of Azov.

Another unavoidable thought floated through her mind. *I must be careful, or I could fall in love with these kids.*

During the almost-seven-hour, roundabout drive to Rostov-on-Don, Sergiy told Margarita that his mother was a wonderful lady who always made sure the boys had "nice clothes and good shoes" and that his favorite meal from his mother was *Deruny* (potato pancakes), "always with sour cream."

"She also made very good *Holubtsi,*" said Sergiy, referring to a cabbage (or vine leaf) rolled with rice filling and sometimes meat and caramelized onions.

"But Gleb didn't like the *Holubtsi* so much," he added.

Gleb didn't hear a word of it. He had fallen fast asleep in the corner of his seat.

"What about your father?" asked Margarita.

"He's a soldier," answered Sergiy, "and he's gone a lot."

"What's *a lot?*" asked Margarita. "How often do you get to see him?

"Usually once about every two months, for a few days, but always for Christmas and Easter. In the summer, he comes home twice a month, which is great, because he and Mommy would then take us to the beach, and we would stay there all day long!" said Sergiy, joy glistening in his eyes.

"What's his name?" asked Margarita.

"Roman Levedeva," replied Sergiy.

"And your last name is Levedeva, too?" asked Margarita.

"Yes, Levedeva," replied Sergiy. "I am Sergiy Levedeva."

CHAPTER 11
NO CONTACT
Early March 2022

THE UKRAINIAN MINISTRY OF DEFENSE CIVILIAN was frustrated. It was his job to make sure that whenever a death occurred among military members of Ukraine's Armed Forces, the service member's designated next of kin was notified as soon as possible. Before the war had started, the standard for notification, once the Ukrainian soldier was officially certified by a competent medical authority as deceased, was twenty-four hours.

In the past week, however, given the Russian Army's multiple illegal border crossings and assaults on not only Ukrainian soldiers but also on Ukrainian civilians, the notification goal had been moved to seventy-two hours. The number of deaths had grown too large to handle the notifications more efficiently. Although the civilian official did not know it yet, his office would soon triple in size and then triple again. And the notification time would be moved back to five days.

During the relatively static fighting in the Donbas region before the February 2022 invasion, death notification was handled by two members of a military unit located near the deceased soldier's designated next of kin, typically located in or near the soldier's hometown. But now, with Ukraine's heartland under assault and the country's very survival at stake, every Ukrainian military member was needed to stop the Russian aggression. Death notifications would have to initially be made by cellphone and followed up by an official letter.

"Sir, I'm very frustrated with a couple of death notification cases we need to do in Mariupol," began the civilian, speaking to his supervisor. "In this case, I've been trying to contact a soldier's wife, Olena Kozlova-Levedeva. If she's still in Mariupol, she is not answering her cell phone. And I've tried for three days to contact her."

"It could just be that she is not answering her phone, but as you know," replied the supervisor, "much of Mariupol is under attack by the enemy. Hundreds—maybe thousands—of civilians have died. She may be among the dead, or she might have safely gotten out of the city with some of the fleeing local citizens. We are going to need to get creative on finding out who the soldier's other surviving next of kin are, where they are, and how we can contact them. This surely won't be the first case that will present these kinds of challenges. It might be weeks or months before we know. With the name you have, I'd begin searching social media and whatever else you can think of to see if she or her parents or siblings might be alive, and make the notification— again, if she is still alive somewhere in Ukraine—through them."

"Will do," replied the civilian.

CHAPTER 12

IN A FUNK

Early March 2022

JAKE FORTINA WAS IN A FUNK. His close friend's country was getting bombed, burned, and terrorized at the Russian president's direction. Millions of Ukrainian lives were being traumatized by the unprovoked Russian invasion. NATO and many Western countries were deeply concerned about the massive violence in Eastern Europe. This was all because of Vasily Puchta's megalomaniacal and perverted idea to return Russia to its former Soviet "glory." Several Russian political allies, like Belorussia, had bowed in obeisance to Puchta and Russia's hegemony.

Jake knew that sharing his anxious and concerned thoughts with his best friend, lover, and the mother of his son was the best way of dealing with the ache he felt inside. On this night, he would bounce it all off Sara.

"Vasily Puchta has spewed outright lies to the Russian people and the world, including that Russia needed to 'put down' the 'Nazi regime' in Ukraine." When and how this war will end is anybody's guess, but I don't believe for a minute it will end anywhere near as fast as many people predict that it will. Nor will it end in the way they predict. Although Ukraine has been in a static war in the Donbas region and Crimea with Russia since 2014, I believe the Russian bear has awakened a slumbering Ukrainian lion," began Jake.

"I know we have dear friends in Jake and Hennadiy Kovalenko," replied Sara. "But why else do you feel so passionately about this?"

It's about a lot more than our friendship with Hennadiy and Mila. It's also that the Ukrainians—a nation of over 44 million people—just want their freedom. They suffered when Puchta and his 'little green men' invaded Ukraine in 2014, and they are once again being subjected to wholly undeserved suffering by this maniac, his minions, and what is practically his private army. Puchta is the oligarch of all oligarchs."

"I know it's terrible, Jake, and I get that. But this war seems to be affecting you in a deep personal way. *Perche* (why)?"

"I guess part of it's because I'm no longer in uniform and part of it is because I feel uncomfortable and—to be completely honest—somewhat down at not being able to somehow participate in this war's outcome. And I can't believe the number of my own citizens who don't understand what ceding Ukraine to a brutal dictator like Vasily Puchta would do to overall peace and stability, not only for the trans-Atlantic alliance and our European allies, but the world."

CHAPTER 13
THE PROCESSING CENTER
Early March 2022

TO MARGARITA, THE FIVE-STORY BUILDING looked like an old Soviet boarding school or military barracks. But the building had clearly been renovated, with a coat of fresh white paint evident on the outside.

Standing on the top step just outside the front doorway, ready to meet the kids and soldiers, was a stout Russian woman in her late forties. A woman and a man who appeared to be in their mid-thirties stood in the doorway behind her. The Federal Commissioner of Children's Rights hand-picked these three from a city of over one million people to run the local "processing center" for the "child saving operation." That operation was being conducted in Ukrainian cities currently under attack by the Russian armed forces.

Margarita, her ten children following behind her, approached the doorway. The robust Russian lady, her greying black hair tied in a tight bun and wearing a blue smock over a grey, below-the-knee skirt, immediately motioned for Margarita to stop with an outstretched hand.

"Stop right there," she said. "Once everyone gets off the bus, I will make an announcement."

"Yes, ma'am," replied Margarita.

After a couple of minutes, the remaining three female soldiers and thirty kids got off the bus. With the lady standing at the top of the steps, the four soldiers stood below her, naturally forming a semicircle.

As the group quieted, the Russian lady spoke.

"My name is Mrs. Kuzmina. Welcome to your new home, the House of Hope. For a few of you, you may only be here for a few days. For others, it might be a week or two, or maybe longer."

Margarita wanted to roll her eyes at the "House of Hope" reference, also knowing that the kids five and under, and perhaps even six or seven and under, had no concept of what a "few days" might mean as compared to a "week or two." But she held her respectful demeanor.

"Outside, we have a playground," continued the lady, pointing to a playground about fifty yards from the structure that at least half the kids had already noted, "and inside, we have a nice cafeteria and real beds for everyone. Behind me are my two assistants, Olga and Aleksandr."

Olga and Aleksandr smiled and waved enthusiastically to the kids.

"They will show you your rooms in a minute, and then we will have dinner in the cafeteria in about thirty minutes, at precisely 6:45 P.M. The boys will sleep on the third floor and the girls will be on the fifth floor. There is a stairwell down the middle of the building, right behind me. The boys will never go up to the girls' floor and vice versa. I expect we will have more children joining us in a day or two, so please remember this."

At this point, the lady addressed the four female soldiers.

"The children's rooms have two bunkbeds, so four beds, each," said the lady, "and there are common bathrooms on the opposite ends of each floor."

The stern lady briefly paused.

"For you soldiers, we have two rooms on the first floor, each with two single beds, so two soldiers to a room. The showers and bathrooms are at the end of that hallway, too. When you take the kids upstairs, please fill each room at the end of the hallway before occupying the ones toward the center. Follow Olga and Aleksandr. Aleksandr will take the boys up to the third floor, and Olga will take the girls up to the fifth floor."

The lady stepped aside. The four female soldiers led the kids into the building, making sure the girls followed Olga and the boys followed Aleksandr up the steps.

CHAPTER 14
FIVE MONTHS EARLIER: POSSIBLE ADOPTION
November 2021

KIRA NOVIKOVA WAS BESIDE HERSELF WITH DELIGHT. She had met Polina Goncharov four years prior at a United Russia Party political convention. And even though Goncharov was nine years senior to Novikova, the two had hit it off. Novikova was a simple mid-level government functionary in Rostov-on-Don. Unbeknownst to both women, Goncharov was about to become a rising star in the United Russia Party. Within two years of their initial meeting, and because of a very ill parent, Novikova had to step back from being active in the Party. Her mother died within a year, and Novikova, at thirty-nine years old, was afraid that her marriage to the mercurial, 42-year-old Dimitry Novikov might die, too.

Married for eleven years, the couple had originally hoped to have children. But after nine years, it became clear the couple could not have a child. Meanwhile, Dimitry Novikov had steadily become more withdrawn in his relationship with Kira, and his drinking was getting worse.

When Kira learned in the fall of 2021 that the Russian government was about to increase its adoption numbers, and then heard about the great news that her good friend Polina had been appointed to the elevated position of Russia's Federal Commissioner of Children's Rights, she reached out to her friend. Novikova was convinced that adopting a child would help her save her marriage.

"Only one child?" Goncharov had asked her friend. "Or would two be better?"

Novikova was surprised and happy at the question's implications.

"You mean it's possible to adopt two?" asked Novikova.

"Yes, it very well might be," replied Goncharov.

Without the specifics of timing, country, or place, Goncharov, shortly after assuming her new position, had been informed that "in the future, Russia will likely launch plans to adopt children in massive numbers from other countries."

"Could be in three or four months, could be in three years," the Prime Minister had told the new Commissioner of Children's Rights. "But your job is to execute the plans your predecessor has left you, and to be fully ready four months from today to bring into Russia and process potentially thousands of children for adoption by Russian families. Single mothers or married couples can adopt them. Your predecessor has drawn up comprehensive plans, identified the necessary infrastructure and staff, and has begun training the identified staff of over 100 people to implement this. I approved those plans. Your job is to quickly become an expert on those plans and, when required, put them into motion. You should be ready to execute those plans as early as the first quarter of calendar year 2022."

"Yes, sir, Mr. Prime Minister," responded Goncharov.

"And by the way, this is not out in the media yet. You are to treat this as highly confidential information, only to be shared with your government colleagues on a need-to-know basis. Understand? Any questions?" asked the Prime Minister.

"Not at this moment," replied Goncharov. "I will be a quick study, Mr. Prime Minister, and will come back to you, sir, if I need more guidance. But I'm sure my predecessor, with your supervision, did a splendid job in putting the plan together."

"Indeed, she did," replied the Prime Minister.

Goncharov nodded in understanding. Within hours, she would begin to connect the dots for some of the scenarios that the Prime Minister was referring to.

CHAPTER 15
BIRTHDAY PLANS
Early March 2022

MARGARITA MONITORED HER ASSIGNED CHILDREN AS THEY CONSUMED THEIR BREAKFASTS of Kasha porridge and bantered among each other. After three nights in the Processing Center, she was thinking—more like hoping and praying—that the children, away from the horror and violence of Mariupol, might be feeling a bit more normal.

The playground is a Godsend. And so is that single soccer ball and the handful of children's books, thought Romanova.

The books were shared and rotated among the four soldiers as they read them aloud to each of their ten children.

"What day is it, Miss Margarita?" asked Sergiy Levedeva, looking up from his bowl of Kasha.

Margarita Romanova did not expect the question.

"It's Thursday, March 3rd," replied Romanova. "Why do you ask, Sergiy?"

"Because tomorrow is Gleb's birthday. He will be six years old."

After looking at Gleb, who paused eating his kasha to look at "Miss Margarita," Sergiy looked back at Margarita expectantly.

"Well then, we will celebrate tomorrow!" Romanova quickly responded, hoping she would raise the two boys' spirits.

Sergiy and Gleb smiled brightly. As their excitement spread, the other children smiled.

***

The children left the cafeteria to go to the playground. A few of the older boys and girls formed up around the soccer ball on the small nearby field. Margarita approached a fellow soldier, Katya Smirnov.

Margarita had gotten to know Katya better than the other two female soldiers. As two former disenchanted university students with vodka-bedeviled fathers, their common backgrounds helped bring Margarita and Katya closer together. Besides, Katya—a Muscovite—was the only one of Margarita's fellow soldiers in the Processing Center who also thought that a little birthday celebration for Gleb might be appropriate, fun, and uplifting. The other two soldiers had objected because it "might set a precedent too hard to follow" or was simply "too hard to do."

"Let's bake a cake!" said Katya. "And maybe we can convince Olga or Aleksandr—and give them a few rubles—to go into town and buy some paper, crayons, and pencils—so the kids who want to can make birthday cards for Gleb. Between our twenty kids, I'm sure we can find a few who would like to participate."

Katya mentioned the idea to Alexandr. He loved it and volunteered to go. He pitched in a few rubles himself and did not have to go far in a city with over 1,000,000 people to find a store that sold some basic school supplies. He also stopped by a supermarket to purchase the basic supplies for a cake.

Later in the morning, Margarita caught up with Katya.

70

"I asked my nine kids who aren't named Gleb," said Margarita to Katya, laughing, "and they all want to make birthday cards for Gleb!"

"My kids are all talking about it, too," replied Katya. "I say we make *Medovik torte* (honey layer cake). I'd be happy to make it. But perhaps instead of the typical fifteen or so layers, I propose we keep it to six layers or so and make *two* cakes."

"Sounds perfect!" replied Margarita. "And I will be your sous-chef!"

CHAPTER 16
TWO BOYS
Early March 2022

KIRA NOVIKOVA SLOWLY OPENED THE CERTIFIED MAIL ENVELOPE. The letter's official blue and red Russian government letterhead was *impressive,* thought Kira. But some key words in the text were more impressive to Novikova.

"Dear Mr. Novikov and Mrs. Novikova,

"We are delighted to congratulate you on your authorization to adopt two Ukrainian boys, Sergiy, age 10, and Gleb, age 5 (ages were self-stated by the children). You are authorized to proceed to the Federal Commissioner of Children's Rights Processing Center located in Rostov-on-Don, on March 10, 2022, at 10 A.M., to meet and take possession of the two boys. In the weeks and months ahead, additional instructions will be provided on required Russian citizenship training for the children, including Russian language training."

Novikova was suddenly overwhelmed with a potent mix of excitement, worry, and hope. The hand holding the letter shook. The other covered her heart as if to steady the wild beat of it.

"Furthermore, we are pleased to inform you that beginning on April 1, 2022, and the first day of each month thereafter until further notice, you will receive 95,000 rubles each month in support of each child."

Upon reading the last lines and salutation of the form letter, Kira Novikova's heart leapt with joy. She was thrilled about the prospect of being a mother to two young boys.

While she had expected to receive a Russian government stipend for each child, she did not think it would exceed 20,000 rubles (approximately $200) per month. The quoted amount was almost five times that much. Since the average Russian salary was 1,240,000 rubles (roughly $15,000) per year, and since Dimitry was bringing home about $19,000 per year from his butcher shop, earning an additional $24,000 total from both children seemed to Kira like living in a different economic stratosphere.

I can't wait to tell Dimitry! she thought.

CHAPTER 17
THE PARTY
Early March 2022

SERGIY LEVEDEVA COULDN'T BELIEVE WHAT HE WAS SEEING. Margarita and her friend Katya brought two large honey-layered cakes into the dining hall. Each cake had six candles.

Gleb's birthday party is really going to happen, he thought, smiling.

Gleb's face lit up as Margarita started the Russian "happy birthday" song. She was delighted—if a bit uncomfortable—that the three older kids took the lead in singing, but in Ukrainian. All the other kids immediately and loudly joined in.

Ms. Kuzmina, listening to the singing from her office just down the hallway from the cafeteria, could not believe she was hearing a Ukrainian song being sung in "her" cafeteria.

This is ridiculous, she thought, a scowl forming on her face. *Where do these kids and so-called Russian soldiers think they are?*

With the song complete, "You have to blow out the candles!" said Katya.

Gleb happily obliged, enthusiastically blowing until all the candles on the two cakes were extinguished.

The excitement of tasting the cakes and the chatter among the kids is beautiful. Their bright and smiling eyes say it all, thought Margarita, fighting back a tear.

Margarita and Katya made eye contact with each other and smiled.

"I'm happy we made that second cake!" said Katya.

Margarita nodded and smiled.

Feeling at once happy and sad, *Mama would be proud of me,* thought Sergiy. *I'm doing my best to take care of Gleb.*

CHAPTER 18
KONSTANTINOVSK, ROSTOV REGION
Early March 2022

KIRA NOVIKOVA WAS EXPECTING A MORE ENTHUSIASTIC RESPONSE from her husband, Dimitry.

He knows how much I want to adopt, thought Kira.

"We will get to adopt not one but *two boys.* Isn't that wonderful, Dimitry?"

"That's great," Dimitry replied.

His flat tone and stiff demeanor belied his positive words.

Dimitry knew for at least a year that Kira wanted to adopt a child. And when she'd told him they might be able to adopt more than one a few months back, he was unmoved.

Kira Novikova was in denial about Dimitry's increasing bouts with heavy drinking. And for the past months, she wondered whether Dimitry had begun an affair with a younger woman. But Kira had chosen not to investigate further. If it were true, she didn't want to confirm it.

The two boys will be better for our marriage, she kept reminding herself.

They will be brought to our house in one week. We need to prepare their room . . . the one with the two single beds. I'll need to buy some linens for their beds, and once they arrive, I'll need to take them shopping in Rostov for some clothes and shoes and toiletries, she thought.

"How expensive is this adoption going to get?" asked Dimitry.

"It will cost several thousand rubles," responded Kira, intentionally vague about the exact sum. "But we will be paid 95,000 rubles to take care of each boy. Can you believe it?"

"*How* much?" asked Dimitry, thinking he had not heard correctly.

"Ninety-five thousand rubles . . . *each month*," responded Kira, enunciating each syllable.

"That can't be true," responded Dimitry disbelievingly. "Are you sure? The total for both is almost twice what I bring home each month from my butcher shop."

Kira chafed at the "*my*" in reference to the butcher shop. She had invested half of the cost of the shop from her own savings. It was not long after that she and Dimitry had married. It was just another sign that Dimitry was keeping his distance.

"It *is* true," replied Kira. "And I have the letter from the Kremlin to prove it. We will receive the first payments at the beginning of the next month."

CHAPTER 19
"WE REGRET TO INFORM YOU."
March 2022

MILA KOVALENKO PRESSED THE RED PHONE SYMBOL ON her cell phone. She felt her stomach tighten, the blood drained from her head, and her breathing became labored. Tears welled up in her eyes. She quickly turned toward the kitchen table, sat, and put her head down on the table. A minute later, tears streaming, she raised her head and called for Hennadiy, who was in the living room.

Hennadiy had known Mila for many years. So, when he heard her cry, "Hennadiy!" he knew it was nothing good.

Hennadiy entered the kitchen and saw Mila, her tears, and her white-knuckled grip on her cellphone. Hennadiy moved to the table, bent over, and hugged her. After a minute or so of holding her and letting Mila cry, he sat facing her in the closest chair.

Empathy etched on his face, "What *happened?* What's *wrong?*"

Mila slowly shook her head, sniffling, still weeping.

"What's wrong?" Hennadiy repeated.

"It's Roman," came the halting reply. "He's dead. He was killed defending Ukraine against those fucking criminals." Her grief was now tinged with anger.

"What? *When?*" asked Hennadiy.

"On the first night of the war." The anger strengthened her voice. "He was involved in that special unit that stopped the Russian tanks from entering Kyiv. The captain on the phone said Roman died heroically, leading his fellow troops during a battle. He said a formal letter would follow explaining more about what happened."

Hennadiy knew about the crucial battle that Mila was referring to. Virtually everyone in Ukraine's Armed Forces knew about it, as did many Ukrainian citizens—at least those who still had access to cable or satellite TV.

"Our brother-in-law did something that our fellow Ukrainian citizens will honor forever," said Hennadiy.

"I know he did," replied Mila. "And now I just pray that we can find something out about my sister and those boys. I'd rather know the truth than be stuck in this terrible state of doubt and fear. I feel so bad that she didn't get out of Mariupol earlier." Another sob threatened. Hennadiy grasped her hand holding the cellphone in both of his.

"I feel terrible, too, Sweetie. I know our government is working hard through NGOs (non-governmental organizations), the Red Cross, and diplomatic contacts with the Russian government, to find out about all of the people who have gone unaccounted for and the hundreds if not thousands of adults and children that have either been killed, taken into Russian hands . . . or just gone missing," replied Hennadiy bracingly. "It's unbelievable that this is happening in the twenty-first century . . . in Europe!"

CHAPTER 20
OFFICE MEETING
March 2022

MARGARITA ROMANOVA DID NOT KNOW WHAT TO EXPECT FROM HER OFFICE MEETING with the "hair bun lady." That was the nickname the four Russian female soldiers had given her. It was a name they used frequently, always making sure the Director of the Child Processing Center was not within earshot. Earlier in the day, Aleksandr had told Margarita that she was again being summoned to the director's office.

I wonder what the hell she wants me for now, she pondered.

For Margarita's first visit to the hair bun lady's office, Ms. Kuzmina had expressed her displeasure at hearing Gleb's birthday song in the Ukrainian language.

"That will never happen again," Kuzmina had said.

After the meeting, Margarita had thought about how hard it would be to enforce the hair bun lady's order.

The kids can't learn Russian overnight, she thought.

As she again arrived at the Director's open office door, she knocked on the frame to signal her presence.

The poker-faced Director looked up from her desk.

"You wanted to see me, Ma'am?" asked Margarita.

"Sit down," said the Director, motioning to a stiff-backed wooden chair five feet from the front-center of her grey metal desk.

Romanova sat down, folded her hands on her lap, and awaited the news . . . *or the interrogation,* she wasn't quite sure which.

"It seems two of your boys, Sergiy and Gleb, must have some special connection to the Kremlin," said the lady.

"How do you mean?" asked Romanova.

"Well, as you have observed until now, all eighteen children who have been released to their adoptive parents thus far, including five of yours, have been picked up by their new parents here at the Center. But these two boys—Sergiy and Gleb Levedeva—they will be *driven* to their new home in Konstantinovsk. Granted, it's only a little more than two hours from here by car, but this is quite unusual, and not at all per our standard procedures."

Romanova nodded her head, not knowing what to say.

"So," hair-bun lady continued briskly after a brief pause, "the day after tomorrow, you will escort them to their new home and drop them off at Konstantinovsk. You will leave here at 3:30 P.M., which means you should arrive there by 5:30, 6:00 P.M. at the latest. Aleksander will drive you in the one car we have, issued to us by the federal government to run this place." Ms. Kuzmina considered Margarita carefully, "I depend on that car a lot, so don't get in any accidents. You should not stay in the boys' new home for more than fifteen minutes or so. The boys' new parents will be expecting you. And then I expect you both to drive straight back here before the roads get icy. Any questions?"

"No, madame, I have none at the moment," replied Romanova.

"If you do have questions, ask Aleksandr. He knows everything I do," said the lady. "You are dismissed."

As Romanova left Kuzmina's office, *Aleksandr and me being told to drive straight back here has nothing to do with icy roads or our safety,* Margarita thought icily. *She doesn't trust me, and I sure as hell don't trust her, either.*

CHAPTER 21
YOUR NEW PARENTS
March 2022

MARGARITA ROMANOVA FELT A KNOT IN HER STOMACH. She knew that it would not be as gut-wrenching as the moment when she would have to say her final "goodbye" to the boys, but she also knew that delivering the news to the boys would not be easy. As sterile as it was, the Child Processing Center—with its playground, warm beds, regular meals, and other kids to play with—had provided the boys a modicum of stability in a mad world where a war was raging just six hours away.

During supper, she had told Sergiy, who habitually took each meal with his little brother, to "please stay at the table after the other kids leave."

Given the otherworldly trauma that had already befallen the two boys, she didn't want to add more anguish to the boys' troubled souls. But she understood instinctively that was exactly what she'd be doing. Even remembering her pain at the traumatic loss of her brother at a young age, Margarita had fallen in love with both boys. But there was no way to change the course of events other than to deliver the news as softly as was humanly possible.

As she sat down at the table, she took a deep breath and slowly exhaled. She looked first at Sergiy.

"He is the strong one," she had told Katya.

Then Margarita smiled at Gleb. Looking back at Sergiy, she began.

"How was dinner, boys? Did you like it?" It was simple, boiled potato and a small cut of pork with a couple of carrot slices.

"It was OK," replied Sergiy.

Margarita wanted to ask about dessert, but there had been none that night, as dessert, thanks to the hair bun lady, was served only on Wednesday and Saturday nights.

"Well, boys, you know how some of the kids have already been picked up here at the Center by their new parents, right?" she began.

Sergiy nodded, not saying anything. Over the preceding days, he'd observed kids being met by their new parents. In a couple of cases, it had made Sergiy sad as he'd become friends with kids he'd likely never see again. It was clear to Sergiy that there were now fewer kids in the Center than when he and Gleb had first arrived. Gleb sat silent.

"Well, your turn to go to your new home is coming soon. It will be the day after tomorrow," said Margarita. "Isn't that great?" she asked, infusing her voice with more enthusiasm than she felt, knowing the boys might be thinking that it was not so "great."

The boys did not respond.

Margarita bucked herself up, telling the boys what she knew she had to tell them.

"The day after tomorrow, Alexandr and I will drive you to your new home. It's about two hours from here. I understand that your new parents are nice people, and I believe you will like your new parents very much."

Margarita knew that what she had just said about the boys' new parents being "nice people" was pure conjecture. But she wanted the boys to believe it, and, more, Margarita wanted to believe it too. For the upcoming trip to Konstantinovsk, she and Aleksandra had only been given the names "Dimitry and Kira Novikova," a house address, and a telephone number, if needed. That was it.

Before she could continue with her rehearsed spiel, Sergiy did something rare: he interrupted, "Miss Romanova?"

She paused expectantly.

"But what about our father?" he continued, "When do we get to see him? He will come here, won't he?"

The question was a bayonet to Margarita's heart. She paused and again nodded.

"As soon as he learns you are here in Russia, I'm sure he will come here to see you, OK?" she replied.

Margarita knew the chances of a Ukrainian soldier coming to Russia anytime soon were nigh impossible. But there *was* a speck of hope in what she'd said.

Perhaps, someday, when this war is over, he will be able to come to Russia, she rationalized.

It was the only thought that gave her slight comfort. She deeply *wanted* to believe it. Of course, she had no idea that Roman Levedeva's corpse had been cremated almost two weeks prior.

"OK," replied Sergiy, placing his full trust in the only person he could.

"OK?" Margarita repeated, this time smiling and looking at Gleb.

Gleb did not answer, but his hope-seeking young heart prompted him to nod in acknowledgment.

***

Little Gleb Levedeva, sleeping in the bottom bunk, was not sure what he was hearing. It *sounded* like crying. Knowing he was not dreaming, he tried hard to listen. It was coming from just above him and sounded as if it were coming out of the lamp.

Since the other two children in the bunk bed across the room had been picked up by their new parents the day prior, Gleb knew that the adjacent bunk bed was empty. For safety reasons, Sergiy had given little Gleb the bottom bunk, and Sergiy, the caring big brother, had taken the top one. Gleb soon realized that the top bunk was where the weeping emanated from.

Is that Sergiy? He wondered.

He crawled out from the sheets and ascended the five-foot metal ladder. After climbing three rungs, he peered over and into the top bunk. Sergiy's head, protruding from the bed sheets, was just eighteen inches from Gleb's. There was no doubt, it was Sergiy who was whimpering. The news of receiving "new parents" had awakened emotions and dark scenes that Sergiy had bravely tamped down since that horrible morning when he had found his mother and family dog dead, his home collapsed on top of them.

Gleb reached out to touch his brother's shoulder.

"It's OK, Sergiy. Don't cry. It's OK."

Gleb ascended the last two rungs of the ladder and got under the sheets with Sergiy. Sergiy welcomed his little brother's warm presence. Gleb placed his hand on his brother's shoulder but said nothing.

"Thanks, Gleb," replied Sergiy, smiling a smile little Gleb could not see.

CHAPTER 22
IT'S TIME TO SAY GOODBYE
March 2022

IT WAS 3:25 P.M., BUT IT ALREADY FELT LIKE A LONG DAY. The anticipation of parting ways with Sergiy and Gleb Levedeva made Margarita anxious and sad. Upon waking up from a fitful night of sleep, she'd vowed that after she dropped the boys off later in the day, she would *someday* see the boys again.

Margarita maintained what she called her "happy face." Walking between them, she held each by a hand as they departed the old Soviet-era dormitory and headed toward the six-year-old, government-owned, silver subcompact *Lada Granta*. Arriving at the car, Margarita opened the back passenger door for Gleb. Sergiy, without prompting, walked around the back of the car to the other side and got in.

Margarita made sure Gleb's seatbelt was secure, while Sergiy did that for himself. Aleksandr was seated behind the wheel, having started the engine when Margarita opened the back door to let Gleb in.

Once Margarita got Gleb situated and closed his door, she opened the front passenger side and got in her seat. She shut the door, secured her seatbelt, and Aleksandr drove away from the Center. As she looked out her passenger side window, Margarita could see fifty or so kids playing in and around the playground. Forty new kids had just arrived the day prior, while six more had departed with their new Russian parents.

Aleksandr, who had only marginally sensed Margarita's fondness for the two boys, could sense Margarita's tense mood. He decided to break the ice.

"I can't believe they allowed us to drive this beautiful Mercedes all the way to Konstantinovsk and back, can you?" he asked Margarita, tapping the dashboard with a smile.

Glancing at Margarita, he could see a smile forming on her face, too.

"I wonder if the bun-lady would allow us to take a spin to Moscow and back with this fancy car?" he asked.

Due to a slip of the tongue by Katya, Aleksandr had heard the "hair bun lady" moniker only once. But it stuck with him. He smiled again, a glint in his eye, and Margarita broke out laughing.

"Wait, did you know . . ."

"Of course, I did," he said, interrupting Margarita. "I'd heard it only once, but I have to say, even though I don't think she's all *that* bad, it sounded very funny when I heard it." Laughingly, he continued, "And don't worry, I won't say a word to her about it. Olga and I think you soldiers have done a good job with these kids. And of the four, we think you are the most attentive and caring. I don't think that matters as much as efficiency does to Ms. Kuzmina, though.

Margarita nodded her head in agreement.

Reaching into her purse, she pulled out two small, clear plastic Zip-lock-style bags. Each contained four Russian tea cookies. She turned her head and upper torso toward the backseat and Sergiy.

"Here is a little something for our trip," she said. "One is for you and the other is for Gleb."

Beaming, Sergiy answered with a heartfelt "Thank you, Miss Margarita." Margarita couldn't see it, but Gleb had a big smile on his face, too, as did Margarita.

It was the first time Sergiy had said "Miss Margarita" instead of "Miss Romanova."

***

Aleksandr made the last turn on the potholed cement road before he and Margarita spotted the grey stucco-covered, one-floor concrete home. The modest home was on the southeastern periphery of Konstantinovsk. The Don River was less than 500 yards to the south, bordering much of the southern half of the town's city limits and the town's 18,000 inhabitants.

As Margarita exited the car, she noticed a small yard of uncut grass in front of the home and that it backed up to a stand of tall mixed coniferous and deciduous trees, with no other homes or roads in sight behind it.

Should be a good place for the boys to play outside, she thought.

She also noted that there were other homes of similar build and size in the neighborhood, none of which appeared to be larger than 1,400 to 1,800 square feet in size, or so she reckoned.

Guiding the car toward the house and another parked car, Alexsandr slowed to a stop and set the handbrake. He turned off the ignition. Margarita got out of the car and opened Gleb's door. Alexsandr followed suit with Sergiy. Margarita held Gleb's hand while Aleksandr put his hand on Sergiy's shoulder. All four approached the front door of the house, with Margarita and Gleb in the lead. There was a lone window off to the left side of the metal front door. Just before Aleksandr was about to ring the doorbell, the simple front door swung open to the inside.

Standing before the foursome was a pleasant and beaming dark-haired lady of medium build with dark eyes and a pale complexion. Both Aleksandr and Margarita instantly thought the same thing: *the lady is perhaps only a few years older than Aleksander,* who was thirty-four.

"Hi! Welcome!" she began. "My name is Kira Novikova!"

Novikova reached her hand out, first shaking Margarita's hand.

"I'm Margarita Romanova," said Margarita, smiling.

"And I'm Aleksandr Vasiliev," responded Aleksandr.

"Good to meet you both," replied Novikova. She then turned her attention to the boys, bending forward at the waist as much as possible without getting on her knees.

"And are you, Sergiy?" she asked of the boy who was clearly older.

"Yes, I am Sergiy Levedeva," responded a stiff and anxious Sergiy.

Kira Novikova stooped and gave Sergiy an awkward hug, half-heartedly reciprocated by Sergiy.

"It's so wonderful to meet you, Sergiy," said Kira Novikova.

She then addressed Gleb in the same manner. Gleb was only slightly more receptive than Sergiy to the woman's hug.

"Well, please c'mon in," said Kira.

Kira offered to take everyone's coats, stepping forward as she spoke to help the boys get their coats off.

Aleksandr piped up.

"Thank you, Madame, but we cannot stay very long."

Margarita felt like a cold gust of wind had hit her soul. Aleksandr's pronouncement signaled that her departure from the two boys was not far off, if not imminent.

"I understand," responded Kira.

Margarita discreetly made a few quick glances around the living room. She was comforted by the fact that the home was clean and comfortably furnished.

As she finished her observations, a forty-something man of stout build, medium height, protruding gut, balding dark hair, and dark eyes stepped out of the semi-dark hallway leading to the back of the house.

"Hello, everyone," said Dimitry with a meager hint of enthusiasm. "My name is Dimitry."

Margarita immediately asked herself why the man was not at the door to greet his two adopted sons.

"Yes, everyone, this is my husband, Dimitry," said Kira, following up on Dimitry's awkward entrance.

"We are both so happy to adopt you boys," Kira continued. "Aren't we, Dimitry?"

"Yes, we are," responded Dimitry, forcing a nod and smile.

Dimity walked over to the two boys. Both sat closely together on a love seat. As he did, Margarita caught what she thought was the scent of alcohol emanating from the man. He looked to be at least ten years older than Kira, although there was only three years' difference between Dimitry and Kira. Margarita didn't know it, but Dimitry's bouts with alcohol were adding years to his physical appearance, especially apparent in his drawn facial features.

Margarita prayed that what she smelled was the scent of cheap cologne, not alcohol. A vision of her father flashed before her eyes, followed immediately by fear trying to force its way up from the depths of her soul.

"So, you are Sergiy and Gleb?" asked Dimitry clinically, while standing erect and looking down at the boys with his hands in his pockets.

At least he remembers their names, thought Kira.

"Yes, I am Sergiy, and this is Gleb," responded Sergiy.

"OK. My name is Mr. Novikova. You may call me 'Father' or 'Sir.' Understood?"

The boys nodded.

An awkward silence hung in the air for seconds, but it felt like minutes to Margarita, Aleksandr, and even Kira.

Kira broke the silence.

"Can I get you anything to drink? Some cookies or perhaps some bread for your trip back?"

"No, thank you," said Aleksandr. "We must leave soon."

Aleksandr shot a glance at Margarita, knowing those words would cause her anxiety. But he also thought that *it's better to rip the band-aid off sooner than later.*

Dimitry interjected.

"Would you like a shot of vodka before you leave?" he asked, looking only at Aleksandr.

Dimitry's words pinched Margarita's conscience and soul, almost making her wince out loud.

Aleksandr knew that several years prior, to decline such an offer in Russia would have been deemed ungracious or even disrespectful. But as far as he was concerned, times were changing, certainly among many of Aleksandr's younger adult generation. Much of his generation was observant enough to know that, due to alcohol addiction, many Russian men did not live to see their sixtieth or even fiftieth birthdays.

"No, sir, but thank you," responded Aleksandr. "I must drive, and we must be going. But thank you for your hospitality."

Thinking she had a little more time to linger with the boys and their new parents, Margarita understood the time for saying goodbye was upon her.

"Yes, thank you for your hospitality," said Margarita, while also looking at Kira Novikova.

Turning to the two boys, Margarita said, "Well, I guess it's time to say goodbye, boys."

With all her being, Margarita choked back tears.

She got on one knee and put her arms out to the boys. They leapt off the love seat and ran to embrace her. Gleb reached Margarita first. She soulfully hugged little Gleb. His lower lip was trembling, and he was on the verge of wailing. She then hugged Sergiy, who also fought back tears.

"Be good boys," she said. "Maybe we will see each other again someday, OK?"

Both boys nodded their heads vigorously, each barely eking out an "OK" above the sadness and weeping that was trying to subdue their throats and eyes.

CHAPTER 23
KIDNAPPED
March 2022

HENNADIY KOVALENKO HAD SEEN THE ALARMING MILITARY INTELLIGENCE SUMMARIES reporting that Ukrainian children were being abducted by Russian soldiers and civilians. He'd also heard rumors of sightings by Ukrainian citizens claiming that they had witnessed busloads of children being transported away from Mariupol, headed east toward the Russian border.

Still, the report by the United Kingdom's *Independent* news outlet came as a kick in the stomach to the Ukrainian colonel. The report strongly suggested what might have happened to his two nephews, who had been missing for almost a month. And there was still no word of what happened to his sister-in-law, Olena.

On March 22, the *Independent* reported that "thousands of Ukrainian children have been 'kidnapped' by Vasily Puchta's forces and taken to Russia."

Ukraine's Foreign Ministry said, "2,389 children have been transported across the border from the eastern oblasts of Donetsk and Luhansk."

"This is not assistance. It is kidnapping," the US embassy in Kyiv had echoed, citing the Ukrainian Foreign Ministry (the US equivalent of the US State Department) as its source. The Ukrainian Foreign Ministry called the abductions "a gross violation of international law."

Upon hearing the news, Kovalenko decided it was better to tell his wife, Mila, about the report when he got home, rather than on the phone. He wanted to be in her presence to comfort her when she heard the news. And truth be told, Kovalenko knew he needed to be there not only for her but for himself, too. He needed her support as much as she needed his.

***

As Hennadiy Kovalenko entered his apartment kitchen, his wife, Mila, seated at the kitchen table behind her laptop computer, cast a smiling glance in Hennadiy's direction.

"Hi, Sweetie," began Kovalenko.

"Hi, Honey," said Mila. "How was your . . ."

Seeing the troubled look on Hennadiy's face, she stopped mid-sentence.

Before Hennadiy could open his mouth, Mila asked, "What happened?"

Mila stood up from behind her laptop and stepped toward Hennadiy at the same instant Hennadiy approached her. They hugged each other as Mila braced for bad news.

"Let's sit," said Hennadiy, pulling out a kitchen chair for Mila and then himself.

"Today, I heard a report," began Hennadiy. "A British news outlet reported that 2,389 Ukrainian children have been transported across our border and into Russia. The US embassy backed up the report. I checked with our Foreign Ministry, and they confirmed the report, adding that it was a conservative number at best, meaning that many more kids have likely been abducted to Russia."

Hennadiy reached out to put his hands on Mila's hands.

They were folded together, resting on the tabletop.

Mila was quiet. She first looked down at the table and then looked back up and into Hennadiy's eyes.

"Hennadiy, do you think Sergiy and Gleb were taken to Russia?" asked Mila.

"We can't be one hundred percent sure," responded Hennadiy. "But yes, Mila. That is where I believe they are . . . in Russia."

Hennadiy prayed as much that it *was* true as he *thought* it was true. Because if true, it would at least mean they were still alive.

In one sense, because she'd had nightmares of the boys being buried under the rubble in Mariupol, Mila was relieved. The questions about the boys' well-being—if they were indeed alive and in Russia—flooded her thoughts. But there was one question that came to the surface.

"What can *we* do, Hennadiy? How can we find out if they are in Russia?"

"We can inform the Foreign Ministry of their being missing. I went through the standard procedures of reporting that Olena, Gleb, and Sergiy were missing a week after the fighting in Mariupol began, when it became evident that they were not holed up somewhere in Mariupol. But I also think our government is overwhelmed and just trying to survive while trying to track thousands of Ukrainian military and civilian dead and missing. And now these abducted children have been tragically added to the government's information challenges."

Hennadiy paused.

"I will follow up with the Foreign Ministry to make sure that they are aware that Sergiy and Gleb might be among those reported to have been abducted to Russia," he continued, "and that the Foreign Ministry should do everything humanly possible to determine where in Russia they are if they are, if they are not doing so already."

Mila nodded her head.

"But . . . Mila, it might take a while to receive a definitive answer. We are, of course, at war with the Russians, and they are not exactly going to be welcoming to our inquiries, nor anybody else's inquiries about Ukrainian family members, be they immediate family members or nephews. But I will do my best, honey. I know how much we both love those boys."

Mila fought back tears. It was all she could do to squeeze both Hennadiy's hands.

"And what about my sister Olena?" asked Mila.

Hennadiy sighed deeply at the question. Hennadiy had heard nothing through his military channels about Olena's fate. He was aware, though, that some three weeks after Russia had started the war, thousands of Ukrainians had already been murdered by Russian bombs, missiles, and Russian soldiers on the ground in Ukraine. The Russians had established several mass graves outside of Mariupol for many of them.

CHAPTER 24
MARIUPOL
March 2022

JAKE FORTINA SLOWLY SHOOK HIS HEAD. It was March 29, 2022, and he could not believe what he was watching on the Italian and international English news channels.

So much for the peace dividend. Damn Russians, thought Jake.

Jake commissioned in the US Army eleven years after the Berlin Wall came down and approximately nine years after the Russia-led Soviet Union officially collapsed on the day after Christmas, 1991. In the years immediately after the collapse, prominent Western politicians, political pundits, and the media were raving about a "peace dividend." The Cold War was declared "over," and Western democracies, including the United States, drastically began to cut their active military forces by twenty-five to fifty percent. For the United States, the cuts in the size of its overall active armed forces amounted to almost forty percent.

Sara watched her soulmate tenderly. She knew Jake was sadly incredulous at the events unfolding on the television screen.

"Penny for your thoughts?" Her tone was gentle, her voice quiet.

"How much time do you have?" Jake joked sardonically.

"Do I look like I'm in a hurry to go somewhere?" asked Sara lazily. She wore her "comfy" pajama bottoms and long-sleeved blue cotton t-shirt.

Jake, grinning, nodded. Chuckling lightly, Sara reached for her glass of Barbaresco wine.

"Watching this crap takes my mind back a few years," he sighed. "The Western politicians involved in the groupthink surrounding the so-called peace dividend were so cocksure that peace in greater Europe was 'guaranteed' that on December 5, 1994, representatives of the United States, United Kingdom, and the Russian Federation held a summit in Budapest, Hungary."

"What was the purpose of that summit?" asked Sara.

"To disarm Ukraine, then the third most powerful nuclear weapons country on the planet. And to assure the Ukrainian people's future security after the loss of their nuclear weapons, those three countries—the United States, United Kingdom, and Russia—guaranteed that *they* would ensure Ukraine's security in the future."

"I mean . . . what else did these countries tell the Ukrainians to convince them to give up their nuclear arsenal?" Sara probed, genuinely curious.

"Your nuclear weapons are no longer needed," Jake shook his head. Indignation colored his tone as he continued, "or so went the narrative and sales pitch to the Ukrainian political leadership. Not only that, all three countries pledged to guarantee Ukraine's national security for the future. The result? The *Budapest Memorandum.* It was signed by each of the attending countries, including Ukraine. It stripped Ukraine entirely of its nuclear capability in exchange for a life insurance policy underwritten by the United States, the United Kingdom, and Russia.”

“Actually, I had no idea about that,” replied Sara.

“Today . . . ,” said Jake, “today much of the free world has no idea about that, either.”

Jake’s mind flashed to the year 2000, when he was commissioned as a second lieutenant in the US Army, on a corner of the Plain at West Point.

What a helluva year 2000 was, thought Jake. *First, the Y2K scare on New Year’s Day. But then that became the least of our problems. In March 2000, that KGB weasel got elected Russia’s president, and he’s still in the Kremlin. Today, the international political situation seems more like 1922 than 2022.*

Refocusing on the TV, the news announcer was updating viewers on the situation in Mariupol. What Jake saw and heard made his gut roil with anger.

“The Ukrainian government estimates that over 3,000 Ukrainian citizens have been killed in Mariupol. On March 18, after seven weeks of battle, Mariupol was finally surrounded, with stay-behind Ukrainian military forces fighting for their city and their lives against the Russian Army’s onslaught. On March 20, an art school providing shelter for roughly 400 people was destroyed by Russian bombs. And two days ago, Ukraine’s deputy prime minister said that ‘over 85 percent’ of Mariupol has been destroyed.”

“Excuse me for a minute,” said Jake to Sara.

Jake went to his bedroom and shut the door. He got on his knees in prayer, placing his head and hands on the chaise near his side of the bed. He knew the Ukrainians would fight like lions, and he prayed for a quick and just end to the war. He also prayed that the Ukrainian people would be free, and their country restored, as soon as possible, to what it was before the Russians first attacked Ukraine in 2014.

CHAPTER 25
NEW ASSIGNMENT
Early April 2022

MARGARITA ROMANOVA SAT STUNNED. She'd only been back at the child "holding center" and converted athletic facility on the eastern outskirts of Mariupol for less than six hours when she'd been called into the bun lady's office and told to report to her new captain.

"Your time with us here has been cut short," her new captain had said. "I'm not sure what happened at Rostov-on-Don, but the rumor is that the lady running the place did not like how you performed your duties."

How I performed my duties? thought Margarita. *What does that mean? Was it because that old bitty didn't like me leading a birthday song in the Ukrainian language? Was it because she didn't like me using the kitchen to make a few Russian tea cakes for Sergiy and Gleb? What a bitch,* she thought.

Margarita did not respond to the captain. He continued.

"We have been told that you will receive official orders within three days. The orders will direct that you report to the 9th Armored (Tank) Brigade. The brigade is currently fighting in the Donbas region, north of Bakhmut. The brigade's mission is, like all of us now in our army, to subdue the Ukrainian Nazis. So, I guess you'll finally get to do what you wanted to do when you first joined our army: be a combat medic. Anyway, I'm sure you'd rather do that than run after a bunch of Ukrainian snot-nosed kids every day, wouldn't you?"

"Of course," replied Margarita, the pain of saying goodbye to Gleb and Sergiy still so fresh and so great that she vowed never to let herself get that close to orphaned kids again.

Despite that silent vow, the confidence in her tone, and the excitement about treating combat-wounded Russian soldiers on the battlefield, she knew she would miss caring for the kids. And underpinning these thoughts was the feeling of how strange—if not outright *wrong*—the Kremlin was in seizing Ukrainian kids from the combat zone and transporting them to Russia.

But all of that was last week—less than six days since she'd said goodbye to Sergiy and Gleb. Worry for them gnawed quietly at her heart as she had made her way to her new unit and signed in with the 9th Armored Brigade. It haunted the back of her mind while she worked at the brigade's aid station. The feeling of unease over the Kremlin's actions was an uneasy pool in her mind that grew larger every day.

CHAPTER 26
THE COMMANDER HAS NOTICED
Late April 2022

MARGARITA ROMANOVA HAD ONLY BEEN AT THE 9TH ARMORED BRIGADE medical aid station for two weeks when she got the news from the grizzled Russian Army sergeant. With seventeen years of Russian Army experience, he was the top sergeant in the forty-soldier medical platoon. It was the medical platoon's mission to staff the medical aid station and support the three professionally trained military doctors assigned to treat the injured, sick, or wounded members of the brigade's 2,600 soldiers, before they were either sent back to their units or on to a big hospital in Russia.

"You are doing great at your job, and you have a good attitude, Romanova," said the sergeant. "The Brigade Commander has noticed. He has selected you to serve as his orderly."

"He's noticed?" asked Margarita. "Noticed what?"

"Yes, he's noticed," replied the sergeant. "Word gets around quickly when soldiers do good work."

"What's an orderly?" asked Margarita.

"It's someone who watches out for the needs of the colonel when he is too busy or too heavily engaged in fighting these Ukrainian Nazi bastards. If he needs hot food, you get it for him. If he needs his clothes laundered, you do that. If he needs a message delivered to another officer within the field headquarters, you do that, too. Basically, you do whatever he needs done. But this means you'll be staying around the command post, which also means better food, warmer tents, and better sleeping accommodations than those poor bastards on the front line."

Margarita, at first, wanted to believe that she was indeed doing her best to be a good soldier and medic, and that her attitude and efforts *had* gotten her noticed. But as she thought about it, she could only remember three times in two weeks when she got called in to the aid station for an emergency to assist with soldiers who had been wounded or were involved in accidents. The front lines had been stable for the past three weeks. The fighting had not been too heavy, only a few light engagements against Ukrainians who were probing the Russian front lines. Margarita did not know it, but those military engagements would increase significantly in another month or so.

While the comments made by the old sergeant were not alarming, *his words rang kind of hollow,* thought Margarita.

CHAPTER 27
THE 9TH BRIGADE COMMAND POST
May 2022

IT HAD BEEN THREE WEEKS SINCE COLONEL IVAN SOKOLOV had first eyed the auburn-haired and shapely Russian soldier from behind. He'd spotted the voluptuous and bright-eyed beauty the first day she was standing in military formation next to a dozen other new and mostly eighteen to twenty-four-year-old soldiers who joined the brigade. Now she sat at an army field table (a bit smaller than a four-person card table) not ten feet from him. His smile was almost lecherous.

Life is good, he had said to himself. *I am leading a tank brigade of soldiers against a corrupt and worthless enemy. I have sponsors—all senior ranking generals—who think I'm the next Georgy Suvorov* (a Russian general once compared to Napoleon). *I've finally divorced that ugly, obnoxious bitch of mine, and now I can have whoever I want. In six months, I will be promoted to brigadier general.*

Inside the medium-sized Russian Army tent, converted to a field headquarters with maps, radios, field tables, and folding chairs, the colonel surveyed the large wall map. He focused on the ground locations of his three tank battalions.

"Margarita," said the colonel, turning around.

"Yes, sir?" responded Margarita Romanova.

"Would you mind adding a little more cream to my coffee next time?" asked the colonel.

"No problem, Colonel Sokolov," responded Margarita. "I will do so now."

"Thank you," responded the colonel. "I appreciate it."

Two other Russian brigade staff soldiers, one a young captain and the other a senior sergeant, were nonplussed by what most Western armies would view as an overly personal—not to mention chauvinistic—and unacceptable exchange between a senior Russian Army officer and a young female soldier.

After all, this is a man's army, the young captain told himself. *The only reason a woman would want to join this army is to find a man.*

The junior officer and his senior sergeant considered themselves loyal to the colonel under any circumstances, and they thought it normal for a rapidly rising Russian Army officer and commander to be getting "special" treatment. But in the majority, if not all, Western militaries, this kind of special treatment was not normal.

***

It was Margarita Romanova's fifth week being assigned to the 2,600-person tank brigade, with its 120 T-72 Russian tanks and 200 other vehicles. The brigade was engaged in fighting Ukrainian forces north of Bakhmut, in Ukraine's Donbas region. Margarita's new friend had been with the brigade since it had invaded Ukraine and launched operations against Ukrainian military forces and cities and towns on March 1, 2022. To make sure they were out of earshot of any prying ears, the female Russian sergeant, three years older than Margarita, walked

Margarita over to the afternoon shade of a large oak tree. It was about forty yards from the command post.

"Be careful," said Margarita's friend.

"Be careful about *what?*" asked Margarita.

"Don't become a field wife . . . *unless* you *want* to?"

Margarita gave the sergeant a perplexed look.

"What the hell is a field wife?" asked Margarita. "What are you *talking* about?"

"I'm surprised you have not heard the term. It's when a female soldier, especially an attractive one like yourself, either willingly accepts or is forced into a personal relationship with a senior officer in the brigade . . . in exchange for special privileges."

Margarita reared back in shock.

"I presume that by *personal* you mean . . . *sexual?*" responded Margarita, slightly aghast.

"Of course that's what I mean," answered her friend. "There is the occasional female soldier who consents to it and maybe even seeks it, either for personal *protection* from a few lurking sexual predators in this brigade, or for the privileges of sleeping in a warmer tent or eating better food. But of course, most women don't want anything to do with it. You haven't been here long enough—nor served close enough to the frontline troops yet—to realize how hard it is for women to focus on their duties when we are out among the ogling troops. In case nobody told you, the Russian Army is ninety-five percent men."

Margarita said nothing but nodded, listening closely to her friend's words.

"Before you arrived, I heard that one of the girls here, after resisting and then eventually being sexually assaulted by an officer in one of the battalions in our brigade, was sent back to Russia, practically in a straitjacket," continued the sergeant. "Her soul was crushed, and nothing happened to the criminal prick of an officer who assaulted her. It's like there is a special protective mafia among the senior officers. As for the rest of the so-called senior leaders around here, they just stay quiet. If women don't comply to be a field wife, I've heard they're sent to locations where the fighting is the most intense and where the casualties are the highest. You know, there are some frontline units that have it worse than us in terms of casualties."

"Well, I sure as hell don't want anything to do with what you described," replied Margarita. "I'd rather they send me home in a body bag than become a sex slave to some sick, warped officer."

"Well, just know this, Margarita: the rumors of you becoming a field wife started the day you rolled into camp with the other newbies. I don't mean to suggest that it might be your fault, so please don't take this the wrong way. But you are much more attractive than most ladies in this camp. I don't know if this is true, but this morning I heard a rumor that the brigade commander really has his eyes on you."

Her friend's words sent a chill crawling up Margarita's spine. For the first time in weeks, the thoughts about Sergiy and Gleb moved to the back of her mind.

CHAPTER 28
DINNER
May 2022

AT FIRST, SERGIY FELT FEAR. But then resolve grew inside his brave soul.

The next time he does that, I will do whatever I can to stop him, he thought.

Sergiy had no idea what "whatever I can" meant, but he resolved that he would do anything to protect Gleb from Dimitry, the man Sergiy now hated. Dimitry had backhanded Gleb so hard that the little six-year-old was knocked completely off his dinner table chair, landing a couple of feet away on the concrete floor.

Gleb's cheek and eye were swelling badly as Kira Novikova tended to the sobbing six-year-old on the floor.

"Dimitry!" she exclaimed to her husband. "What the *hell* is *wrong* with you? The boy says he doesn't like the meat, and you do this to him?"

"He deserved it," responded Dimitry. "He should be thankful he has food to eat, food that comes out of the shop that I own. He must learn to eat *everything* I bring home."

Sergiy shuddered at Dimitry's words, especially Dimitry's reference to "everything." Sergiy had already choked down cow lung and tripe (intestines), and now that dreaded word—"everything." It added another level of anxiety to what Sergiy had felt from being in two strangers' home, forced to obey their every command, and to eat the food put before them. Sergiy knew Kira was doing her best to tend to the boys whenever she could, but she couldn't always be there.

Just a week prior, in an alcohol-fueled rage, Dimitry burst into the boys' bedroom at night and severely beat them with his belt. Welts rose and red streaks stained their cotton pajamas. The neighbors could hear their screams through the boys' slightly open bedroom window. But, in Puchta's Russia, it was rarely worth getting involved in other people's problems.

"They had it coming," he had told Kira. "I told them to be quiet. When I say no whispering, I mean it."

It was all Kira could do to console the boys afterwards, beyond Dimitry's mistrusting, alcohol-induced, violent, paranoid earshot.

CHAPTER 29
JUST A FRIENDLY SHOT
May 2022

MARGARITA APPROACHED THE COLONEL'S TENT. Night had fallen about twenty minutes ago. She carefully placed each step, so she did not trip over a tent peg or rope securing the camp's tents to the damp ground. She carried a bowl of *borscht,* made by the army cooks in the nearby mobile kitchen trailer.

She'd tried the borscht and thought the common Russian potato and red beetroot soup was acceptable for human consumption. And she'd been in the field with the Brigade long enough to know that any warm food in the field tasted a heck of a lot better than any restaurant fare.

As always, she stood outside the tent entry flap and announced her presence. If the colonel had fallen asleep or was in some state of undress, she didn't want to just barge in. This was standard protocol in the brigade, regardless of whether it was a male or female soldier wanting to gain entrance to a tent where soldiers slept. It was almost common knowledge, though, that several men in the brigade were known to just walk into the women's tents anytime they pleased, without warning.

Those troops closest to the enemy, the soldiers manning the tanks and other vehicles at the front line, slept wherever they could. Very often, this meant inside a tank, half-seated in the cab of a truck, or on a bedroll on the ground and under the stars. But sleeping on the ground in front of a vehicle was never smart, because a frontline vehicle or unit might have to move quickly in the middle of the night, on short notice, and bleary-eyed drivers could easily run over a soldier in a sleeping bag.

In the rear area, commanders, senior staff officers, medical doctors, and some sergeants got shared tents. The brigade commander was the only one who got his own tent. The Commander's tent was a roomy one that could easily sleep four soldiers on cots.

Margarita was thankful that she slept in a tent shared with seven other female soldiers, mostly medics.

"Sir, I have your dinner," said Margarita as she stood outside the colonel's tent.

Several seconds passed before the 44-year-old, six-foot-tall, 200-pound, thickly built colonel responded.

"What is it?" he asked grimly.

"Borscht, sir." Margarita was getting used to this almost nightly routine with the notoriously gruff "old man."

"Is it any good?"

"Yes, sir, I tried it. It's good."

"Good. I don't want my cooks poisoning me," he only half-joked, chortling. "Bring it in."

Margarita did as she was told, stepping just inside the tent door with the steaming bowl of borscht.

Before taking the bowl of soup, the colonel stood from his seated position on his cot and thrust a two-shot glass of vodka into Margarita's free right hand.

"Take it. Drink it. You deserve it. I know it's a pain working for me. But if you don't drink it, I'll send you to the front line of troops tomorrow and make a tank driver out of you." The colonel chuckled at his wit.

Margarita handed the bowl of borscht to the colonel and took the glass of Vodka. She hesitated.

"Don't worry, it's just a shot of good ole Russian vodka. It will warm you up."

Margarita nodded and drank it in one go. Handing the glass back to the colonel, she mumbled a feeble "Thank you."

"You see, that wasn't all that bad, was it?" cajoled the colonel.

"No, sir, it wasn't. May I head back to my tent now?"

The colonel took a long and, for Margarita, uncomfortable look at her. It only lasted five seconds, but to Margarita it felt like five minutes.

"Sure," said the colonel. "I can't wait to see you again. See you tomorrow."

As she stepped back into the blackness, a touch of starlight peeking through the thick clouds, Margarita felt the hair stand up on the back of her neck.

CHAPTER 30
MARIUPOL
Late May 2022

JAKE FORTINA'S EYEBROWS ROSE AT THE NEWS REPORT. Sara Simonetti-Fortina was sitting on the couch next to him, scrolling through her phone, occasionally glancing at him.

"The siege is over, and Mariupol has finally fallen," said Jake. "Estimates are that over 8,000 Ukrainian civilians have been killed, and twice that number have been wounded. And now, the horrific news about missing children is also coming out with more granularity. Ukrainian government authorities and international media outlets are saying that tens of thousands of children have been taken back to Russia. Puchta has also apparently signed a decree today giving the children a path to citizenship. How *nice* of him," sarcastic anger thickened Jake's voice.

Hearing it, Sara comforted him, reaching to massage the back of his neck. "How *long* do you think this war will go on?" asked Sara.

"Could be months, could be years. It depends on how much the West—especially the United States, the United Kingdom, and other European allies—step up to help Ukraine, and how ugly the Russians are going to get."

"Ugly? It's already ugly, isn't it, *caro mio* (my dear)?" asked Sara.

"Yes, it is. I can't believe that, after the Balkan wars (in the late 1990s, after the breakup of the former Yugoslavia), we'd again be looking at a major land war in Europe. But by 'ugly' I meant the degree to which that crazy jackass in the Kremlin might use nuclear weapons. That would be, as we say in the US, a game changer. And who knows how horrific or long-term or widespread collateral damage from nuclear weapons might be to civilians or the environment."

Sara nodded in understanding. Jake looked at Sara and knew he didn't have to explain further. Sara understood the stakes and the threat to Europe and the world if nuclear weapons were involved.

"But as to the Ukrainians, I guarantee you this: they will not cede an inch of territory unless they have no other choice. And they will not go down in defeat. Vasily Puchta has no idea of the mettle of the people that he has picked a fight with."

CHAPTER 31
NEXT OF KIN
June 2022

MILA KOVALENKO STARED AT THE "GOVERNMENT OF UKRAINE" RETURN ADDRESS on the envelope. She called Hennadiy to "come into the kitchen" from the living room. Hearing the concern in Mila's voice, he was there within seconds.

Seated at the kitchen table, she opened the envelope while Hennadiy stood at the counter.

Mila intended to read the letter out loud. But feeling the first tears form in her eyes after reading the first sentence, she realized she couldn't keep reading the letter. She pushed the letter away, across the tabletop. Hennadiy immediately came over, took a chair by Mila, and grasped the letter.

"Please read it out loud," said Mila. "I could not read it beyond the first sentence."

"OK, my dear," responded Hennadiy, nodding his head.

"Dear Ms. Mila Kozlov-Kovalenko,

The Government of Ukraine regrets to inform you that your sister, Olena Kozlov-Levedeva, was killed in her home by a Russian artillery attack as Russian Armed Forces launched violent, brutal, and unprovoked attacks on the city and people of Mariupol. We cannot ascertain the exact date or time Olena Kozlov-Kovalenko's death occurred, as the area where she resided and most of Mariupol have since been occupied by Russian military forces. But we were able to assess that it was within a day or two of the initiation of hostilities by Russia on our homeland, which commenced in the early morning of February 24, 2022.

The Government of Ukraine was recently informed that Ms. Olena Kozlov-Kovalenko's body was identified in her destroyed home by local citizens fleeing the eastern edge of the city during the first days of the war. As best we can determine, you are her surviving next of kin."

Hennadiy stopped reading just before the salutary paragraph and signature block. He recalled the hundreds, if not thousands, of Mariupol citizens who had been buried in mass graves outside the city. Hennadiy reached out to hold Mila's trembling hands.

"She and the boys were within two days of leaving Mariupol before the firing started," Mila told Hennadiy. "I can't believe I didn't do more to convince her to leave earlier."

Hennadiy put a hand on Mila's shoulder. He, like Mila, also felt a bit of survivor's guilt, knowing it was a natural but mostly irrational feeling.

"Very, very few people thought those bastards would actually do what they did," said Hennadiy. "You had no way of knowing that it would actually happen, let alone the hour or day when it did. And I know it's small consolation, but at least we know somebody—a surviving neighbor, perhaps—knows where she died. We now have thousands of Ukrainians who don't know the exact circumstances of their relatives' deaths. And I've heard the Russians are bringing in cremation equipment to hide as many of their atrocities as they can."

Mila nodded her head in response. Unfortunately, she had fully expected that her sister had died this way. She and Hennadiy were quiet for several seconds.

"But what about the boys?" asked Mila. "What happened? What do you think happened to *them?*"

Hennadiy could hear anguish, fear, and desperation in her voice. It was the same question Mila had asked Hennadiy just a few days prior.

Hennadiy sighed.

"I don't *know* what happened to the boys," replied Hennadiy, "but I deeply believe they are somewhere in Russia. Until we receive an official report—God forbid—that they are no longer with us, we still have hope that they are alive and well."

Hennadiy felt terrible for Mila. And he also felt as sad as he'd felt since his father had died unexpectedly of a heart attack some six years prior.

Mila and Olena had been close; they loved each other. Each Christmas, Hennadiy and Mila would send gifts to Olena, her husband Roman, and their two boys, Sergiy and Gleb. They'd even sent along something for their family dog, Chestnut. In the summers, they met at an annual two-day family reunion with other members of the Kovalenko-Levedeva families. Between the family picnics, outdoor grilling, and storytelling, Sergiy and Gleb had come to call Hennadiy "Uncle Hennadiy," and Mila "Aunt Mila." Childless, Hennadiy and Mila had considered the two boys the sons they never had.

CHAPTER 32
TONIGHT, WE CELEBRATE
June 2022

IT HAD BEEN SEVEN WEEKS SINCE MARGARITA ROMANOVA BEGAN HER DUTIES as Colonel Sokolov's orderly. During that time, Margarita's friendship with Sergeant Anna Orlova, not in Margarita's direct chain of command, had grown stronger.

"Maybe my initial feelings were just a reaction to the rumor mill. He's not done anything but be kind to me. I feel quite comfortable around him now, and not at all like soldiers in the brigade paint him," she told Anna, as the two were seated on their cots, facing each other.

"But do you *like* him?" Anna asked, raising her eyebrow at Margarita.

Margarita recoiled, her facial expression changing to one of surprise.

"No, not in *that* way. *No,* definitely not." She considered for a moment. "I have no attraction to him. I'm just surprised that he's not the tyrant many in this brigade think he is."

Anna had serious concerns and doubts about the colonel. She'd experienced male predatory behavior before, and she'd heard about other women in the Russian Army becoming "field wives." Anna recognized some of the colonel's behaviors and feared that once her friend relaxed in his neatly woven web, the colonel would pounce.

"Or maybe he just treats you differently than anybody else in this brigade? Hmm?" Orlova cautioned. "You need to be careful, Margarita."

Margarita considered her friend's remarks but decided Anna was overreacting.

The colonel has been good to me, she thought. *He's never tried anything. There have been some off-color remarks, but that's not* unusual *in the army.* She remembered the way he had made the hair at her nape stand on end at first, then brushed it off. *You were just on edge about leaving the boys, and the rumors influenced your distracted mind.*

Out loud, Margarita complied, "OK, will do."

***

As she approached the Russian commander's tent with a cup of coffee, Margarita felt guilty that she had enjoyed accepting a shot of vodka from the colonel on those nights when he was back at the command post. Despite her father being an alcoholic, Margarita, who considered herself more like her mother, knew she could control her alcohol consumption. She rarely consumed more than one shot of vodka for any occasion.

"Sir, I have the coffee you sent for," said Margarita as she stood outside the colonel's tent.

"Bring it in," came the reply.

Margarita entered and closed the tent's entry flap behind her. She saw the colonel sitting on his cot, near the opposite wall of the tent. He was wearing his Russian Army physical training gear: an olive-green T-shirt, black gym shorts, and plastic shower slippers. His ballistic (bulletproof) vest and helmet were

122

neatly stored on the ground, under the head of his cot. He'd purchased the best ballistic vest he could buy because he knew the body armor vests issued to Russian soldiers were near worthless.

It was June, and the weather was heating up. It was not unusual for the colonel to be lightly dressed inside his private space. Besides, the women in Margarita's tent had been hanging around their tent and sleeping that way for the past two weeks, as the daily June temperatures reached into the high eighties.

The colonel patted the cot just beside his thigh.

"Sit down, Margarita," said the colonel.

She did as she was told. Margarita had decided to trust him.

Taking the cup of coffee from Margarita, he stood, opened the tent flap, and tossed the cup's steamy contents out into the early evening grass.

"Tonight, we *celebrate* my one year commanding this brigade. By next year, I will be a general," said the colonel, impressed with himself.

Margarita was not impressed. While she did not believe the colonel to be a bad person, she was not impressed by the handful of self-serving officers she'd encountered in the brigade; the colonel topped that list. Margarita thought that at the end of the day, while the colonel had treated her well, his reported lack of physical courage, which she'd overheard some senior sergeants talking about, indelibly tarnished the colonel's reputation as a leader.

"But it's clear," she'd heard one of the senior sergeants tell his companion soto-voiced outside the mess tent while they'd had a smoke, "the old man has sponsors among the more senior generals."

The colonel reached directly below his cot and grabbed two heavy ceramic coffee cups. Margarita knew they were the colonel's favorites. What she did not know is that they each contained a triple shot of vodka. He handed a cup to Margarita. She smiled nervously at him, holding the cup with both hands, Anna's admonishment to be careful quietly nagging at her.

"You know what they say about our beloved vodka," said the colonel.

Margarita nodded in acknowledgment, knowing that whatever the colonel was about to say, he had said before.

"It is not to be sipped like some cheap French cognac. As you know from drinking vodka before with me in this tent, any Russian worth his salt knows vodka is to be consumed in one go."

He turned and made eye contact with Margarita.

"*Za Lyubov!* ('let's drink to love')" exclaimed the colonel, using a Russian expression for "cheers," appropriate for most any situation.

The colonel threw his head back as he emptied his cup. Margarita did not know the colonel had already washed down four vodka shots before she arrived. Margarita gave it her best go, almost choking as she had to swallow a second and third time to down the triple shot.

The colonel took Margarita's cup from her and placed his cup and Margarita's cup back on the ground near the cot.

He began reminiscing about some of his military exploits, including how he always finished near the top of his class in military schooling, including during his years as a university-level military school cadet. The colonel droned on for several minutes, at times laughing at his own commentary, and at others smiling at his days of outperforming his peers and impressing his leaders.

As the colonel droned on, Margarita felt the effects of the triple vodka. Sluggishness crept up on her. This was new territory. Her father's alcoholism convinced her that she would never allow herself to go down the path of overconsumption. And now, that small voice from the depths of her soul told her she had to fight the urge to become uber-relaxed, joyous, or worse, uninhibited in the presence of "the old man." The realization hit her as the colonel looked at her with a sloppy, greedy smile.

His wild eyes conveyed anything but joy.

Before Margarita could understand what was happening, the colonel pushed her over on the cot, roughly grabbing her hips. His gym shorts were somehow already around his ankles. His naked manhood pushed against her as he jerked her camouflaged pants and underwear below her knees. His brute strength and speed, combined with the traumatic shock enveloping Margarita, enabled that to happen in seconds.

For Margarita, time slowed, as if seeing it unfold in milliseconds would give her time to *do* something. But instead, she froze, every soul-jarring, traumatic moment embedding itself in her memory.

When she felt his hands trying to separate her thighs, a voice in her soul screamed, snapping the spell of slowed time. He was grunting and cursing in frustration. Somewhere in her mind, she knew his fingers left bruises as she fought to keep her legs closed. His vodka-laden breath landed against her face in rough pants. And somehow, before the fear and trauma could choke off her ability to make a sound again, Margarita managed to force out a "Help! Help me!" as loud as she could. That jarred the rest of her body into action. She tried to push the colonel off her, but Margarita couldn't budge him. The vodka made her sluggish, made her weak.

***

Margarita had no idea that her friend, Sergeant Anna Orlova, had kept an eye on Margarita whenever she was able. Tonight, she was smoking a cigarette about forty yards from the office section of tents, along the route to their shared tent. Due to the temperature caused by cooler ground air and a warming second layer of air above the ground—the sound of Margarita's scream refracted toward the damp ground, enabling it to travel farther. Anna heard the scream. She bolted toward the source of the sound. As she ran, another scream allowed Anna to pinpoint the tent's location.

***

Inside the tent, Margarita managed to create enough space to roll herself off the narrow cot onto the ground. But as soon as she hit, the heavy colonel was on her again. She had landed on her side. As she tried to wiggle out from under him, he forcibly flipped her onto her back. She screamed again, only to have him slam his hand on her windpipe, truncating the sound.

Tears streaming as he grabbed her knee and painfully wrenched her leg to the side, Margarita turned her face away from the colonel. That's when she saw the coffee cup he had placed on the ground. She grabbed the heavy ceramic cup by the handle and slammed it with all her strength against the colonel's temple. It broke on his face, little pieces of ceramic embedded in his cheek.

The colonel, enraged, released her throat. As she gasped for air, he tried to slap her face. Margarita avoided the full blow only because he was drunk and she had quickly turned her face. Margarita's left ear rang from it anyway.

"You bitch!" he yelled, spittle flying. "You *wanted* this, I *know* you *wanted* this!"

In the next instant, the tent's entry flap flew open. Sergeant Orlova entered the tent like the former rugby player that she was. She instantly lowered into a crouch and, with a fury born of rage, slammed her body, shoulder first, into the colonel's. Crouched as he was in the semi-dark, hazy tent, his concentration on trying to pin Margarita's arms, the colonel had no idea what hit him as Orlova's body slam drove him into the cot. The cot went sideways, jamming against the tent wall; the colonel sprawled, dazed, over it. For good measure, she kicked the colonel in the exposed groin.

While the colonel moaned, his hands between his legs, Anna stood Margarita up. She quickly pulled up Margarita's underwear and pants. The colonel grabbed Anna's ankle, but she stomped on it with her opposite boot heel, shattering the colonel's wrist. The colonel screamed in pain. The next second, Anna buckled Margarita's top pants button, grabbed Margarita by the hand, and led her out of the tent and into the darkness toward the ladies' tent.

Two young cooks from the kitchen trailer who had heard the commotion were on their way, walking quickly and deliberately toward the commander's tent. They were oblivious to the two dark figures moving about thirty feet away from them in the opposite direction. Anna continued to hold Margarita's hand, guiding her toward the ladies' tent. Tipsy and in a state of semi-shock, Margarita, barely able to put one foot in front of the other, was pulled forward.

The first cook burst through the tent and found the colonel whimpering on the ground, his shirt on, but his gym shorts around his ankles. Curled around the broken wrist, he was moaning and writhing, his other hand between his upper thighs, trying to protect his groin from a second vicious blow. His shower clogs were strewn about on the ground, and the colonel's "junk" was intermittently on display. The two young soldiers did not know whether to laugh or render aid to their downed commander. After sharing a broad grin, the two cooks decided to help "the old man," just as a third person entered the tent.

CHAPTER 33

IT DID NOT HAPPEN

June 2022

"WHAT IS THAT?" ASKED MARGARITA, lying on the cot, looking up at her friend, who held a container about half the size of a shoe box.

"It's the only rape kit we have in this damn brigade," said Anna.

"And it's my personal one. Do you think the men in this army could give a *shit* about something like this? It should be a standard issue item in our medical supplies. But . . . there is no way that it is or ever will be, because in this army. They say Russian men would never do anything like this. But you and I both know that is utter bullshit. Most men in this unit act as if they are a bunch of scouts who go to church twice on Sunday. But I know better. And now, unfortunately, you know better, Margarita. And the rumors I have been hearing coming from the front about those poor Ukrainian women—and men—who have been captured, would make the hair stand up on the back of your neck."

Margarita looked at her friend. After having downed a cup of black coffee and taken something that Sergeant Orlova had given her, Margarita felt clearer, though not better. Whatever the pill was, it had calmed Margarita down and lowered the hyper anxiety she'd been feeling just twenty minutes before—but it didn't stop the horror reel playing in her mind.

As if to establish some kind of protective circle around their fellow medic and soldier, two other Russian Army female medics stood around Margarita's cot. The four remaining women in the tent kept their distance, as they did "not want to get involved."

"You won't be needing that kit," Margarita told Anna.

"Are you sure, Margarita? Are you *absolutely sure?*" Anna asked gently.

"Yes, thank God. And thank you, Anna, for saving me . . . I . . ." her voice cracked, and she paused to take a steadying breath. "But I am sure. As hard as that bastard tried, he was not successful," said Margarita, a sob breaking through.

She cried for several minutes. Anna held her, shushing her gently, as one might a child. When Margarita regained her composure, she continued.

"I might have gotten too relaxed from the vodka, but I was not so drunk that I couldn't fight. He would have had to kill me before it happened. But I *know* it did *not* happen. And besides, *if* it did, do you think it would matter to anyone in authority around here?"

CHAPTER 34

MILITARY CAMP

Late June 2022

KIRA DID NOT LIKE DIMITRY'S "SUGGESTION" to send eleven-year-old Sergiy to the local *Kaskad,* one of thousands of two-week "military camps" for boys—and boys only—held throughout Russia each summer. But as was the case with every "suggestion" Dimitry made, it would eventually turn into a demand. And if Kira did not comply, their discussion would quickly escalate to an argument before finally ending in threats of divorce from Dimitry.

"It will toughen him up!" said Dimitry emphatically to Kira.

"He's plenty tough already," Kira responded. "And besides, you know that the next steps for him after the Kaskad will be to join the Youth Army, which is nothing more than a cannon fodder pipeline for Puchta's wars."

Dimitry knew that the Youth Army held a half-million members across Russia. But Dimitry believed that the Youth Army was a much-needed military preparatory organization for Russian youth—from ages eight to seventeen—to ensure Russia always had a robust youth contingent ready to transform their military experiences into becoming professional soldiers and leaders.

"How dare you say such an unpatriotic thing!" bellowed Dimitry. "Puchta is a great leader who fights wars . . . for Russia's survival! We *need* the Youth Army!"

Kira had grown accustomed to knowing when to keep arguments from climaxing in a state of rage for Dimitry. When she sensed he was on his way to blowing his top, she pulled back. Before the argument went too far, she always acquiesced.

She chose not to respond further to Dimitry's comments about Russia and its president. Kira was among the minority of Russians who thought Alexei Navalny, who was speaking out and leading a social and political movement against Puchta, was better for Russia than the man who had recently entered his twenty-third year as Russia's strongman.

Although he couldn't articulate why, Sergiy felt mixed emotions when Dimitry had told Sergiy unequivocally that he was attending the two-week "military camp."

My real father would be proud of me, he thought. *Someday, I will see my real father again. For now, I know that I'll have to do what Dimitry says. But I don't like doing anything to respect this horrible man who pretends to be my father. He makes me sick. And I don't want to think about leaving Gleb alone with him.*

If it were not for Kira convincing the young boy that two weeks in a military camp would be good for him, he would have fought to stay home. But because Kira—who Sergiy had some measure of respect for but did not yet love—had said he *must* go, he decided he had no choice.

CHAPTER 35
THE INVESTIGATION
Early July 2022

THE "INVESTIGATION" BY THE ARMY COLONEL WAS, AT BEST, PERFUNCTORY, at the worst, a complete sham.

It was the Russian Army's policy, like in most other militaries, that when a military officer was being investigated for possible misconduct, another officer of equal or higher rank did the initial fact-gathering. It was that investigating officer's duty to make a recommendation to his higher-level commander as to whether an official court-martial (a military court proceeding, with a similar format to civilian court proceedings, but with uniformed officers as prosecutor, defense attorney, judge, and when appropriate, jury or panel) should proceed. Once in receipt of the investigating officer's report, it was the higher commander's decision whether to continue with a court-martial, personally adjudicate the case against the accused, or close the case altogether.

"OK, comrade Ivan, this is what I will report. What you described makes sense," began the Russian Army colonel. He had been sent down from the 3rd Russian Army Group headquarters to investigate the incident at the 9th Armored Brigade.

"After several nights of sharing a vodka with you, the soldier in question came onto you. She made seductive gestures toward you, and she decided to play rough with you. You thought she was enjoying it, until she wasn't anymore. And then she was in such a drunken state that she hit you in the head with a blunt instrument. And then she screamed after you reflexively slapped her in self-defense. Then someone barged in and *also* assaulted you. It seems quite clear that you were set up, Colonel. Do I have this correct? It's also quite clear to me that you are innocent. And that's what I will report."

"Yes, comrade colonel. That is precisely correct. After she struck me in the head, she was lucky I did not kill her."

The investigating colonel gave an empathetic nod of acknowledgment to his fellow officer.

CHAPTER 36
A TOUGH LITTLE GUY
Early July 2022

KIRA NOVIKOVA'S HEART SWELLED at the words of the retired Russian Army sergeant, a counselor with the local Rostov-on-Don Kaskad military training camp. The camp was not something Kira wanted for Sergiy. But the Kremlin demanded that Ukrainian kids ages ten to seventeen, orphaned and "adopted" from the war with Ukraine, attend the camp. Non-compliance by parents meant the removal of the hefty stipend they received in compensation for taking care of the kids.

Dimitry insisted that eleven-year-old Sergiy attend in any case, "stipend or not." Kira was at the two-week summer training camp with Gleb to pick Sergiy up and take him home.

"He's a tough little guy," said the sergeant. "With 6 A.M. wakeups, challenging training, discipline, and long days, most kids his age become homesick and cry about wanting to leave within the first three days of the camp. But Sergiy never complained, and as far as I could tell, never even thought about quitting. It's as if he has some kind of military DNA. Did you coach him beforehand?" asked the retired, pot-bellied Russian sergeant.

"Not at all," responded Kira. "But yes, I think he's pretty resilient, too. How did he do with his understanding of military terms and concepts?"

"Very well," said the sergeant. "That's a question I usually don't get. Are you hoping that he might someday be a professional soldier? Because he definitely has the aptitude for it."

"Maybe. I do think about it occasionally."

As soon as she said it, Kira knew it was a lie. Becoming cannon fodder for Vasily Puchta's military ventures was the last thing she hoped for Sergiy. Although Sergiy had made good progress in learning Russian at school and at home, his full facility with the Russian language was the one shortcoming she feared might dampen his two-week training camp experience. Language challenges would have made it even more difficult for him to complete the training.

But complete it, he did, thought Kira as she led Sergiy and Gleb back to her car.

CHAPTER 37

GUILTY

August 2022

MARGARITA ROMANOVA STOOD AT ATTENTION AND FACED THE GENERAL. She could feel herself perspiring and, try as she might to steady them, her knees shook. Being back in Rostov-on-Don, where she'd been only a few months prior—tending to kids who were about to be "adopted"—was positively surreal. Except then, she was living with the kids in an old, but clearly renovated, dormitory-style building. Now, she was standing in the middle of a spacious, high-ceilinged office, facing the Deputy Commanding General of the Russian Army's Southern Military District Headquarters.

This was not a military "trial." It was a sentencing by a Russian Army two-star general. There was no jury, no presentation of evidence, no cross-examination, and no serious consideration of facts beyond those presented by the investigating officer in his report. A three-star general had decided that an official court-martial per the Russian military system, with its civilian lawyers and judges, was too risky, especially in potentially exposing the case to the public. So, the commanding general decided to keep the military legal proceedings "non-judicial" and within the auspices of his own authority and command. This was a sentencing, a meting out of punishment, in which Russian Army Private Margarita Romanova would hear her fate.

Standing beside her was a Russian Army captain. He was the commander of the Medical Company Margarita Romanova had been assigned to, in support of the 9th Armored Brigade. The captain had coached Romanova on what to say and when to say it in response to the general's questions. Also standing in the room were three other Russian Army officers, a lieutenant colonel and two majors. They were bearing official witness to the proceedings.

"Private Romanova, under the authority of the Commanding General of the Southern Military District, I'm going to make this as fair as possible, and present you with two options," began the general.

"Option One. You will be sent to the IK-2 prison colony of Pokrov, Petushinsky District of Vladimir Oblast, for a period of six months. For assaulting a senior officer, I'm sure you understand that six months is a very light sentence. And I'm sure your captain has told you that the IK-2 prison is not exactly Club Med."

Margarita's captain nodded to Margarita.

"Yes, sir, he has told me that."

"Option Two. You will resign and depart from the Russian Army, effective today. Within a few hours, you will be completely free to live your life as you wish. However, no matter which option you choose, you will never breathe a word of the incident between you and your brigade commander again. We have serious confidentiality and privacy regulations within this army, and the consequences for violating them are also serious, very serious. If you do violate them, you will be subject to facing a full court-martial, with penalties much harsher than the ones I just mentioned. Is that clear?"

The captain nodded to Margarita again.

"Yes, general, it is clear," responded Margarita.

"Which option do you choose, Private Romanova?"

Margarita quickly glanced at the captain, and the captain gave his final nod.

"I choose option number two," Margarita responded.

"It is done and shall be so recorded," replied the general. "Sign the documents in the presence of the major standing to my right. You will thereafter be released from the Russian Army, no later than midnight tonight."

CHAPTER 38
HE DID IT AGAIN
September 2022

THE SLIGHT CHATTER, BARELY ABOVE A WHISPER, WAS TOO MUCH for Dimitry Novikova to tolerate.

"Dammit!" he yelled.

"What's wrong?" asked Kira from the nearby master bathroom.

"I told those boys to be quiet and go to sleep!" responded Dimitry angrily.

Kira knew it had been another night of too much vodka for Dimitry. Given his drastic mood swings during the previous six months or so, Kira began to think that her husband was also bipolar. At least, that's what her dearest friend had recently convinced her of.

Dimitry grabbed his leather belt from the top of his chest of drawers.

"Stay here!" he shouted to Kira. "Don't you dare come to try and stop me!"

He headed for the boys' bedroom, but Kira refused to panic yet again.

"Dear God, this is the fourth time in three months. Please help me stop him."

Dimitry burst through the boys' bedroom door and headed straight for Gleb's single bed, located on the opposite wall from Sergiy's. Sergiy could instantly see the terror in Gleb's eyes and the pain-inflicting instrument in Dimitry's hand.

That bastard, thought Sergiy, using a word he had learned at the *Kaskad* military summer camp. *He always picks on Gleb first.*

Little Gleb raised his left arm in a fruitless attempt to protect himself from the painful blows Dimitry was about to deliver. That only angered Dimitry, resulting in him grabbing the six-year-old by his left wrist and whipping the leather belt as hard as he could across the boy's back, buttocks, and upper thighs. Gleb fought hard not to cry out after the first blows, but the third strike forced out a scream that Gleb could not hold back.

Kira heard a scream and bolted out of the master bedroom and down the hallway.

Sergiy, enraged and thinking of nothing but his promise to his mother to "take care of Gleb"—while thinking nothing of himself—launched his body from a standing position on the bed. As if to tackle Dimitry, Sergiy threw his right shoulder into the drunken lunatic's left hip. He did this, hoping to distract Dimitry from Gleb and onto himself. But to Sergiy's surprise, he hit Dimitry just right, causing him to fall forward across Gleb's bed and hit his head on the concrete wall.

Before Sergiy's tackle, Gleb's left leg had been bent up at the knee, in a reflexive effort to protect himself from blows to his front side. When Dimity fell, Gleb's knee caught Dimitry in the gut, causing Gleb's leg to collapse perfectly on the bed without injury.

Kira bolted through the door and grabbed a gasping Dimitry by one arm. She managed to pull him off Gleb's bed and onto the beige area rug separating the two beds.

Sergiy, resolute but shaking, stood in front of Gleb's bed and stared at Kira. Kira looked back at him. She marveled at the little man's courage. Gleb continued to whimper on the bed, the damage limited by Sergiy's courageous and unflinching response. Dimitry kept gasping.

"Let's get you up," said Kira to Dimitry.

Some way, somehow, Dimitry was able to stagger to a standing position, his head hanging. He was happy to again be breathing normally. In his drunken state, he had no idea what had hit him.

Kira led the aging man down the hallway to their bedroom and got him into bed.

CHAPTER 39
AN URGING
Late September 2022

MARGARITA COULDN'T STAND IT ANYMORE. She had to check on Sergiy and Gleb. It was an urge that rekindled within a week of walking out of the Russian Army Southern Military District Headquarters, a free, but emotionally scarred woman. After getting help from Alexandr, who had many family members and friends in the Rostov-on-Don area, she'd found a cashier's job at a local supermarket.

The job was enough to put a 250-square-foot roof over her head in the form of a studio apartment. It also allowed her to feed and dress herself. A cell phone, even a used one, was a luxury, but one she was able to eke out of her earnings. A car would have to wait. But thankfully, buses and trains were easy to travel on in twenty-first-century Russia.

Again, thanks to Alexandr, Margarita was able to get Kira Novikova's phone number. Terrified that Kira Novikova would reject her, it took Margarita several tries to press the green icon on her phone, but she finally managed.

"Hello," Kira answered.

"Hello, Kira, this is Margarita Romanova. Perhaps you remember me? I brought the boys . . ."

"Yes, I remember you," replied Kira. "How are you?"

"I'm fine, thank you, and I hope you are as well."

"I'm well, thank you, Margarita. How can I help you?"

Margarita felt Kira's response to be unenthusiastic and was unsure how the rest of the conversation would go.

"Well, I got injured while in the army, but I'm out now. I thought I'd stop in and see the boys, just to say hi. Perhaps I could take the boys into the village for some ice cream, or to the playground . . . for a little time together. It would only be for an hour or two."

Margarita had already formulated a good "how I got injured" story for everyone to hear. Nobody could ever know the truth about what happened on that terrible night when the Russian colonel assaulted her. The general had made that very clear.

Fearing that Margarita might discover something about Dimitry, Kira hesitated. She had gone back and forth between despondency and resignation that Dimitry would not change on the one hand, and a glimmer of hope that the old Dimitry, the one she had fallen in love with before the alcohol became his master—would once again emerge, on the other. But Kira remembered how sadly the boys had said goodbye to Margarita. She felt deeply that it would be good for the boys to see her again and would also be good for her.

It would only be for a short time, thought Kira. *What could it hurt?*

CHAPTER 40

THE VISIT
October 2022

MARGARITA ROMANOVA'S HEART STIRRED WITH ANTICIPATION. The train had pulled out of the Rostov-on-Don main train station just over two hours earlier. Within ten minutes, it would be pulling into Konstantinovsk, a town of 18,000 inhabitants just over two hours east by car from Rostov-on-Don, Russia's eleventh largest city. Using Russia's most economical and popular form of intra-city, long-distance transportation, the train trip cost her 350 rubles (about $3.70).

As the train approached the town, it slowed, and Margarita found her thoughts were centered on Sergiy and Gleb. She'd unexpectedly fallen in love with the two young boys during their journey from their bombed-out home in Mariupol, through Rostov-on-Don's child "processing center," and onto the custody of their new adopting parents in Konstantinovsk.

I can't wait to see them and hug them, she thought. *I wonder how much they've changed in six months.*

The forty-ruble cab ride (roughly $0.45) from the Konstantinovsk train station to the Novikova home took twelve minutes. Her heart slamming in her chest, she exited the cab and approached the house where she and Alexsandr had handed over the kids to Kira and Dimitry Novikova.

Kira said that Margarita could visit between 4 P.M. and 5:30 P.M., a safe ninety minutes to two hours before Dimitry would come home. Kira had no idea how Dimitry would respond to

Margarita's visit, nor what shape he would be in when he came home. Like many who struggled with alcoholism, Dimitry tried mightily not to let his alcohol habit affect his source of income.

He needed the money to support his alcohol habit. This meant rarely taking a drink before 7 P.M., when he closed the shop and came home. After that, anything in the shop or at home was possible.

Margarita knocked three times. Within seconds, the door swung open. Concerned about the reception she might get from Kira, Margarita was relieved when Kira greeted her with a warm "Hi! How good to see you!"

"Likewise!" said Margarita. "It's so nice to be here."

Turning her head toward her left shoulder to announce Margarita's arrival, Kira cried out, "Boys!"

The boys had their door shut.

"You can go back and knock on their door."

"Thank you!" replied Margarita.

As she approached the door, she could hear the boys playing a game on the floor. It was an old metal replica of an ice hockey rink, with metal levers so the boys could maneuver the players. The two boys were absorbed in it.

Margarita lightly tapped the door and then slowly opened it.

"Miss Margarita!" yelled Sergiy!

Margarita knelt to get on the boys' level. Both boys leapt almost simultaneously into her outstretched arms. As she hugged them, she was surprised and delighted when each boy gave her a kiss on the cheek.

"We have been waiting for you!" said Gleb.

"I've been waiting to see you, too!" she replied.

Margarita stood up. She pulled two bags of Russian tea cookies out of a shopping bag from the store where she worked.

"And these are for you!" she said to the boys.

"Thank you, Miss Margarita!" exclaimed Sergiy first, with Gleb quickly following suit.

"Are you boys ready to go for some ice cream?" she asked.

"Yay!" replied Sergiy, as Gleb nodded his head vigorously.

"I'll see you in the living room?" she asked.

"We'll be right there," replied Sergiy.

Margarita walked out to the living room.

"I would invite you to stay for some tea," said Kira. "But I know you did not come to see me, and I don't want to take up more of your precious time. So, why don't you three go on your way as soon as the boys get their shoes and jackets on?"

"Thank you," replied Margarita. "I'd love to spend some time with you, too, Kira."

It was then that Margarita noticed. Perhaps the light was not quite right before, but now, the blotch of excess makeup applied to Kira's left cheek was apparent. It *almost* covered the bluish-tinted bruise—about the size of a two-euro coin or US quarter—underneath it. Margarita's mind flashed to her mother. She'd seen that attempt at hiding a facial bruise before.

"But I know our time is short," continued Margarita. "I am deeply grateful to you for allowing me a generous hour to take the boys out for some ice cream. I'll have them back no later than 5:20. My train returns to Rostov-on-Don at 5:45 P.M."

"You are welcome," said Kira. "When I told the boys you were coming, they were excited."

Kira knew that "excited" was understated. She *knew* that, truth be told, the boys were *beyond* excited when they heard about Margarita's visit. In fact, the boys hadn't shown that much enthusiasm for *anything* or *anybody* since they had been in her and Dimitry's care. It was a hard reality for Kira to accept. But she could understand why.

For the past month, Kira had been having serious doubts about her initiative to bring the boys into her home. She wanted her reality to be different, but she knew Dimitry was a serious problem without a near-term solution. And by adopting the boys, she had made her and Dimitry's lives more complicated and messier, not better. And the boys—especially Gleb—were paying the price.

Kira had fallen in love enough with the boys to know that she deeply cared for them and their futures, even more so than her own marriage. And she was increasingly skeptical that she could deliver a bright future for the boys, let alone one for her and Dimitry.

Dimitry's reflexive and shocking slap to Kira's left cheek, delivered over a silly argument only a few days prior, had changed her entire outlook on their marriage. And now, privately, she was thinking, *If Margarita or anyone else takes the boys away to a better life, I wouldn't mind it a bit.*

But that was a thought she vowed never to share, not even with her closest friend.

***

Inside the ice cream shop, on a mild autumn day and after a ten-minute walk from the Novikova home, Margarita felt good about visiting the boys. And they'd had a nice chat along the way to the ice cream shop. But Margarita felt like she was having to lead the conversation, even more so than when she'd first met the boys at the converted sports facility just outside of Mariupol, right after their life-changing trauma.

When Gleb went to the ice cream shop's bathroom, Sergiy spoke up.

"Mr. Novikova is mean," Sergiy blurted out.

"Mean? How so?" asked Margarita.

"He hits us really hard when he is angry. Especially Gleb. And he also hit Kira," Sergiy said, refusing to refer to either adult as "my mother" or "my father."

Trying to look caring but not dramatic, Margarita kept licking her ice cream cone after Sergiy said it. But the words pierced her heart.

"He *hits* you?" asked Margarita.

"Yes, he hits us. Sometimes with his hands, sometimes with his leather belt . . . when he's really mad, and especially when he's been drinking. Sometimes, Gleb really screams from the pain and fear."

Margarita paused, thinking of what to ask next.

"I'm so sorry to hear that, Sergiy." Margarita paused, then asked, "How often does that happen? Does it happen often . . . like every day?"

"No, not every day. But it seems like almost every week or so now."

"And is that the same with Kira? Dimitry hurts her every week or so?"

"No, he just started hitting her. Like . . . a few days ago. She was crying more than I'd ever heard her cry. Miss Margarita, do you think my real father will ever come get us?" asked Sergiy.

The question gave Margarita pause.

"I'm sure he will come get you," said Margarita. "Someday, he *will*."

Margarita briefly glanced out the shop's window. She had no idea if what she said was true. She'd remembered that Sergiy had told her that their father was a soldier.

"Do you have other family members . . . any other . . . favorite ones?" asked Kira.

Sergiy smiled a big smile.

"Yes, I do. I have my Aunt Mila and my uncle Hennadiy."

"What was their last name again?" asked Margarita.

"Kovalenko," replied Sergiy.

"Where do they live?" asked Margarita.

"They live in Kyiv. Every summer, we got to see them at a family reunion. And every Christmas, they gave us gifts. They are both so nice."

CHAPTER 41
I MUST DO SOMETHING
October 2022

IT HAD BEEN A LONG NIGHT OF TOSSING AND TURNING. At morning's first light, Margarita understood she had to act.

I must do something, she thought. *No, I* will *do something. To do nothing would be wrong.*

The week since her visit to the boys had been a long one. Every day and night, her mind went to the boys' plight, trapped in a home with an abusive adoptive father and a mother incapable of or unwilling to protect the boys from him.

I've seen this movie before, she thought.

Again, Margarita corrected herself.

No, I've lived it. But my little brother didn't live through it. And I can't let something so terrible as that happen again.

As her mind grappled with thoughts of what to do, she arrived at one clear choice.

I must somehow find their father, she thought. *And perhaps their aunt and uncle, who Sergiy said lived in Kyiv.*

CHAPTER 42
THE ITALIAN
December 2022

MARCO CONTI COULDN'T TAKE HIS EYES OFF THE auburn-haired, blue-eyed, fair-skinned woman. It was the second time in an hour—and the third time in three days—that the thirty-three-year-old Italian was in Margarita's supermarket checkout line. Conti was in the store doing his semi-annual checkup on the company's wine, prosecco, and grappa displays and sales. During his stops, he would sometimes buy a few items from the stores he was evaluating.

During his first run through the checkout line, he managed to see the woman's name on her plastic nametag. Their eyes briefly met when she'd asked him, "Would you like a bag for these items, sir?"

Her empathetic eyes immediately drew him in, but he quickly averted them so as not to seem too forward, or worse, creepy. Now, being the fourth person in line, he could afford to take a longer look at Margarita Romanova as she focused on ringing up the purchases by a weekly neighborhood Russian shopper. Marco was stunned by the twenty-four-year-old's unique beauty. She was the most beautiful woman he'd seen in his three years and six trips visiting Russia on business.

Conti was on the fourth day of a one-week stop in Rostov-on-Don. Conti's father was the majority shareholder and CEO of a major wine and spirits consortium in Siena, Italy. Annually, the company captured about five percent of the $181 million wine and spirits trade Italy did with Russia in 2022.

As a European Union trading partner with Russia, Italy ranked second in the EU (and fifth in the world) behind Germany in overall trade with Russia. Also in 2022, Italy imported over $25 billion in goods from Russia, with almost half of that comprising petroleum gas. Russia, on the other hand, imported $6 billion in a wide variety of goods from Italy, with wine and spirits ranking third on the list.

Margarita pretended not to notice the intriguing man whom she'd remembered seeing less than an hour before. Her personal security systems were flashing yellow . . . but not red. Dark-complected with smooth as silk skin, dark eyes, and curly black hair, the six-foot, one-inch-tall man stood out. He looked far more handsome and refined than Margarita's average customer. Given his pedestrian clothes, though, it was apparent that he was trying not to stand out.

Since the sexual assault and being booted out of the Russian Army, Magarita had not only honed her predator profiling skills, but she was also paranoid about being monitored by the FSB.

Well, he sure as hell doesn't look like your average muscle-brained FSB goon, she thought, before again thinking this was the guy's second time through her checkout line within the afternoon.

Marco Conti, whose father insisted the younger Conti get his "feet and hands dirty" in learning the company's business from the bottom up, was anything but your average customer. Before the week was over, Marco would touch base with eleven of Rostov-on-Don's biggest supermarkets. Knowing that his wine and spirits distribution company had built good ties with Russian wine-selling enterprises beginning in the mid-1990s, Conti's father had insisted his son learn Russian as part of his business management curriculum at *Alma Mater Studiorum—Università di Bologna.* With its roots reaching back to the year 1088, the University of Bologna was considered by most to be the oldest university in the world.

Conti's father had also insisted to Marco's mother that Marco not be raised with a silver spoon in his mouth. It was important to his parents that Marco learned to respect everyone, from the supermarket janitor to the CEO—or highest-ranking person—in the business. So here he was, going through Margarita's checkout line again, a little intrigued and a little captivated by her eyes.

As the man put a simple bottle of water on the checkout counter, Margarita replied, "Will this be all, sir?"

"Well, yes, that is all, *signorina,*" replied Conti, surprised at just how tongue-tied he was. "Except . . . do you ever get to take a break around here? It would be my pleasure to invite you to the coffee shop right across the street."

Marco tilted his head toward the supermarket's large glass windows and the coffee shop across the street. He knew it was a feeble attempt to break the ice with the woman, *but at least I tried,* he thought.

Margarita was knocked back on her heels by the man's question. She could not believe this handsome man was asking her out on a date. As it had been almost six months since her horrifying ordeal with the colonel, she was still not exactly in the market to meet a man. And while this man with some kind of accent gracing his Russian words seemed to be very kind, she had no idea who he was. At the same time, a coffee just across the street seemed innocent enough.

"Well, they do give us breaks, sir," she chuckled, "but I've already taken my breaks for the day."

"So, signorina, you'll be joining me after work, then?" asked Conti.

"Well, I get off pretty late," said Margarita. "But perhaps another time."

That's all Marco needed to hear. He realized that he had a chance to someday—perhaps soon—spend a few minutes with this fascinating woman who had sent his heart racing.

CHAPTER 43
SECOND CHANCE
December 2022

MARGARITA TOLD OLENA, HER CLOSEST FRIEND IN THE CITY, what the man had said to her in the checkout line earlier that day. Katya had left the Rostov-on-Don child processing center in May and deployed to the combat zone in Ukraine. But the "bun lady" had requested that Katya be returned to the Center "to help out" with the increasing numbers of kids flowing through it, and that request was approved.

"Wait? What? Tell me again what he called you," said Katya.

"*Signorina,*" said Margarita. "Or something very close to that. I didn't fully catch it, or I just don't clearly remember it."

"Signorina . . . hmmm," said Katya ponderously on the phone. "Look, I'm not a foreign language expert, but that sounds to me like Spanish or maybe Italian. So, what you're saying is the gorgeous guy invited you for a coffee right across the street, and you told him to check back another time? Are you crazy?"

Margarita went silent on the phone.

Katya remembered what had happened to the dear friend she was talking to.

Quietly, Margarita started, "Well, the last time I was offered a drink . . ."

Katya interjected.

"I'm sorry, Margarita. That was very stupid and thoughtless of me to say to you. I do know what happened the last time you accepted a drink from someone. I'm so sorry."

"No, no," responded Margarita. "It's OK. I know you didn't mean anything bad by it. And it's about time I pulled my head out of the depressive sand it's been in for much of the past year. I should always remember it could have ended up much worse were it not for Anna. And besides, I couldn't believe it, but I was seriously attracted to this guy." She paused, considering. "He seemed . . . well . . . he seemed different than the yahoos I've met in this city. Aleksandr is a really good guy, but I can't say that I've ever thought of him as anything more than a friend. Besides, he's about ten years older than me, and he seems to be already taken."

"Well, OK. But I'm still sorry. What are you going to do if this guy comes back?" asked Katya.

"What would you do, Katya?" asked Margarita.

"No matter what, I'd play it *safe* and play it *slow.* Have a coffee with the guy, sure. But do it across the street. And I wouldn't get in a car with him or anything like that, no matter how attracted you might be to him."

"OK, my friend," I will keep you posted.

"Thank you, my dear. Seriously, I hope he's your prince. You surely deserve one."

CHAPTER 44

COFFEE TIME

December 2022

IT HAD BEEN TWO DAYS SINCE THE MYSTERY MAN had asked Margarita to join him for a cup of coffee. But since then, she'd not seen him. Just when she was beginning to think that another visit was not meant to be, *there* he was. Only this time, Margarita had seen him enter the store. But she'd pretended not to notice or care.

It had been a slow afternoon. Her heart was pounding as she pretended not to watch while hoping to catch a glance of him out of the corner of her eye.

Before she knew it, the mystery man was the second person in line at her cash register. Finally, he stepped up to put a bottle of water on the register's conveyor belt. His smile was so dazzling that Margarita's lips curved in response.

"You must really like the water here," she quipped.

"And you must have a heck of a good memory," he replied, chuckling.

"It's not that hard when a customer only buys a single item," she answered.

Conti smiled.

"Well, your water is pretty good here," he replied.

Margarita grinned.

"I just might miss it when I leave Rostov tomorrow," said Marco.

Margarita did not respond.

"Speaking of returning tomorrow," continued Marco. "I'll be returning home late tomorrow night. But I'd still like to have a coffee with you when you have time. Maybe when I come back in a few months . . . or if you're available, when you get off work, perhaps tonight, or tomorrow morning for breakfast?"

Margarita *wanted* to say, *How about in ten minutes*?

But she didn't want to sound too eager. She decided to play it cool.

"Well, if you don't mind coming back in about an hour and ten minutes or so, I'll take you up on that coffee."

Conti felt like doing a backflip.

"That will be wonderful," he stammered. "When you get off work, just come on over to the café, and I'll have a table ready for us. Or I can meet you here in the store and walk you over. Whatever you prefer."

"I'll see you at the café at 6:10 P.M.," replied Margarita.

"*Va bene* (OK)," replied Conti. "*Grazie* (thanks)."

***

At 5:40 P.M., Marco Conti asked the concierge of the Radisson Blu Hotel in Rostov-on-Don to call him a taxi for the eight-minute ride along the Don River, toward the city's eastern half. He preferred the Radisson because of its excellent views of the Don River, its decent restaurant, cozy bar, and cleanliness.

Conti always took a fifth-floor suite at the Radisson. The most expensive hotel in the city, rooms started at $120 per night. It was safe, spacious, and the fifth floor was still reachable by the ladders of a local fire truck. It was also an excellent place for entertaining the city's top supermarket managers.

Within minutes, a taxi arrived to take him to the café opposite Margarita's supermarket. Upon his arrival, his excellent Russian language skills and "Western business casual" dress got him a good table in the spacious café. Within minutes, he saw the attractive and physically fit, auburn-haired Margarita crossing the street.

Right after punching out of work, Margarita removed her supermarket smock and slipped into the ladies' bathroom to freshen up. Her tightly-fitting, long-sleeved blue shirt amplified the blue in Margarita's eyes and showed every curve of her five-foot-seven-inch, medium-build frame.

As Margarita approached Jake's table, Jake stood up. As he had learned to only reach out and shake a lady's hand if she offered hers, he remained reserved when Margarita did not offer her hand. He did, however, pull out her chair to seat the Russian beauty. That was a first for Margarita, something no man had ever done for her before.

"Thank you," Margarita smiled, a little surprised.

After exchanging pleasantries of the "so, how has your day been?" variety, Magarita ordered a cappuccino, Marco an espresso. Then Margarita asked a more direct question.

"So, I take it you're not around from around here, are you? While your Russian is excellent, I detected a slight accent."

"Well, that's because Russian is not my mother tongue . . . it's Italian," responded Conti.

Katya nailed it, she thought.

"I mean, I know the water that we sell in our store is good, but you came all the way from Italy to buy two bottles of water in our Russian supermarket?" asked Margarita, smiling.

"Apparently so!" exclaimed Conti, chuckling. "You do have excellent water in your store."

The light banter continued . . . for almost two hours. Along the way, Margarita tried more than one pastry.

Her favorite was a twelve-layer, custard-filled Napoleon Cake, named after the famous French general whose military exploits into Russia met with devastating losses sixty miles outside of Moscow, at a place called Borodino. There, in the battle of the same name, Napoleon Bonaparte's army suffered 28,000 to 35,000 casualties in a single day at the hands of Tsar Alexander I's Russian forces. The battle was so costly to Napoleon's Grand Armée that it was unable to recover.

Despite Napoleon's six-month military campaign into Russia, culminating in the harsh winter of December 1812, he was unable to achieve his strategic goal of subduing Russia. His failures on this front were the first major signs of his demise. It eventually earned him his first trip in exile to the then-French (now-Italian) island of Elba.

Just prior to saying goodbye for the evening, the two—to Conti's delight—exchanged telephone and email information. Conti offered to walk Margarita home, but when she declined, he ordered her a cab. Before it departed, he paid the driver. Marco's gesture was another first for Margarita.

"*Buona sera* (good evening)," said Conti just before the cab departed.

Mimicking Conti's farewell as best she could, Margarita gave the greeting back to him, "Buona sera."

On her ride home, Margarita pondered if the Italian man was for real, and if he really was just a wine salesman. He never asked for or suggested anything. He just seemed to want to get to know Margarita a little better and, when possible, laugh a little, too.

CHAPTER 45

IT'S BETTER THAN WATER

December 2022

MARGARITA'S MANAGER WALKED INTO THE EMPLOYEES' BREAKROOM. It was eight minutes before she was to begin her 9 A.M. to 6 P.M. shift at her cash register.

"How do you know Marco Conti?" asked the manager.

"Why do you ask?" replied Margarita.

"Well, about forty-five minutes ago, Conti walked in with this three-bottle box of prosecco and asked that I give it to you. The only person in this store he's ever gifted prosecco or wine to is me. And it was always just one bottle."

Margarita tried to gauge whether her boss was jealous, simply curious, or perhaps somewhere in the middle. But it was clear that her boss knew Marco Conti, too.

"Well, I did have a cup of coffee with him last night . . . right across the street," she said.

"A cup of coffee? That's it?" asked her boss, now smirking. "And he gave you this?"

Margarita felt the conversation moving into uncomfortable territory. She decided not to be coy.

"Yes, that's *it,*" said Margarita firmly, a frown forming on her face.

"No, wait," she continued. "That's not the whole story, actually."

She paused.

"I knew it," replied her boss in a low voice.

"*Excuse* me? Knew *what?*" asked Margarita.

Another female employee was having a cup of coffee at the same breakroom table where Margarita was seated. She, too, was about to begin her shift. She did her best to keep a poker face, anxious about the next words to be spoken and by whom.

Margarita's boss stopped cold. He quickly realized that if he said what he was thinking, he might not only offend Margarita, but his best—and one of the supermarket chain's best—suppliers as well.

"Ah, nothing," replied the store manager, quickly retreating.

"Because the rest of the story—to be more precise—is that I actually had three cups of delicious cappuccino and two large pieces of delicious cake with Mr. Conti as well. We spent almost two hours talking . . . and drinking coffee and eating cake."

"Well, here you go," replied her forty-something boss, gingerly placing the box on the table. "Sorry, I didn't mean to imply anything."

Margarita slowly nodded her head in response.

The three bottles would have cost her almost a full day's wages. The box came with a little red ribbon on the top and a small card in a sealed envelope, taped to the box's side. Each bottle's label could be seen through cutouts in the standard Conti Vineyards company gift box.

With three minutes to go before her shift began, Margarita took the sealed card off the box and put it in the pocket of her smock. She walked out of the breakroom. Seeing that her boss was not behind her, upon arriving at the cash register, she pulled the envelope out of her smock and opened it.

Inside the envelope was a white, heavy stock card containing a handwritten message.

"Cara (dear) Margarita,

Thank you for an amazing evening. The coffee was almost as good as your store's water. ☺ And the conversation was even better. I hope we stay in touch.

Tanti auguri (many greetings),

Marco"

During her lunch break, Margarita discreetly took out the card twice, each time reading it slowly. Conti's words cycled through her thoughts all day long. She looked forward to sharing them with Katya later that evening.

Margarita's boss vowed to himself never to mention the discussion with her or Marco Conti again.

I don't want to piss off Conti, he thought, *and I don't want to lose my best employee, either.*

CHAPTER 46
HAPPY EASTER
April 2023

FROM THE MOMENT SHE'D RECEIVED WORD from her closest Russian Army friend, Anna Orlova, that Anna would spend a couple of days of her one-week leave in Rostov-on-Don, Margarita was thrilled. Anna had not only become Margarita's "best army buddy" but she'd also saved Margarita from being raped.

If Anna hadn't knocked that asshole off me on that terrible night, Margarita had often thought, *I might not even be alive.*

Just a few days before the Russian Orthodox church celebration of Easter (based on the Julian Calendar, not the Western Christian world's Gregorian calendar), Anna was released for one week of leave from the Russia-Ukraine front.

In the preceding six months, Margarita had dabbled in trying to locate Ukrainian Sergeant Roman Levedeva, Sergiy and Gleb's father. She was discreet about her internet searches, using the name "Lebedeva"—the Russian version of Levedeva—to do her searches. But each time, she came up empty-handed. So, she decided to change her approach.

Finding Sergiy's uncle should be easier, she thought. *His last name is not only Ukrainian but also Belorussian, which will provide me some cover. Nonetheless, I must remain careful.*

Margarita uncorked a celebratory bottle of Italian Prosecco to share with her friend.

"This was gifted to me by my new acquaintance, Marco Conti," she told Anna.

The first sips tasted wonderful. Margarita knew it would be a big ask, but she thought her reunion with her friend Anna might present an opportunity to ask a question. Before the sexual assault, she had told Anna about Sergiy and Gleb, and her deep love for both. She updated Anna with the dire, unjust, and sometimes violent situation Sergiy and Gleb now found themselves in. Anna responded to Margarita's story with a tear streaming down one cheek.

Margarita pushed a piece of scrap paper across the kitchen table toward Anna.

"Anna, could you please help me locate this person?" asked Margarita. "Before I left Konstantinovsk, I found out from Sergiy that his uncle was a Ukrainian military officer. Sergiy said this man and his wife, Mila, live in Kyiv. Even a general duty location would be very helpful, and a physical address would be fantastic."

The question gave Anna pause. She was aware that in Vasily Puchta's Russia, individual liberties were being rolled back to the Soviet era restrictions often talked about by Anna's parents and grandparents.

My parents and grandparents seemed to have grown comfortably accustomed to them, though, Anna often thought.

But doing searches on the internet about a Ukrainian military officer could raise eyebrows.

Then again, thought Anna, *I'm a very small fish in a huge pond, and I've proven my dedication to Russia by volunteering to serve on the front lines. And it's possible—although not certain—that the FSB has Margarita on some kind of watch list, given her horrible incident with the Russian colonel. So, for Margarita to be searching for a Ukrainian colonel could be dangerous and prompt a lot of questions.*

Anna took a sip of her prosecco. She thought of several social media platforms that might lead her to Kovalenko. And then the rage from her rape and Margarita's sexual assault and almost-rape by a Russian Army officer rose in her.

Tamping down those thoughts before they cast a darkness over her mood, "OK, my dear friend," responded Anna. "I will do it for you. I will have a look."

"Thank you, Anna," responded Margarita, raising her glass to make a toast with Anna. "And Happy Easter!"

"Happy Easter, my friend!"

***

It had only been eighteen hours since Anna left Margarita's small studio apartment when Anna knocked on Margarita's door. Anna had called Margarita to say she was again stopping by, without giving further details. Some degree of paranoia that somebody might be monitoring your phone calls was healthy in heavily monitored Russia.

But again, Anna reassured herself, *the chances of someone expecting this frontline medical sergeant to do anything that the Russian state might frown upon are very low.*

As soon as Margarita opened her apartment door and let Anna in, Anna cut to the quick.

"Well, *that* didn't take long," said Anna, marching up to the old kitchenette table for two and putting a piece of scrap paper down on it.

Margarita picked it up, read it, and nodded. It contained the city—Kyiv—and the Ukrainian government ministry where the Ukrainian colonel worked.

"Thank you," she replied. "I very much appreciate it."

Immediately, Margarita began to think about how best to contact the Ukrainian military officer and uncle to Sergiy and Gleb.

CHAPTER 47
THE CAFÉ
May 2023

I CAN'T BELIEVE I'LL SOON BE BACK IN ROSTOV-ON-DON, two months before I'd planned to be, thought Marco Conti, smiling broadly, as his connecting flight from Moscow touched down in Krasnodar International Airport, a three-hour drive to Rostov-on-Don. *I can't wait to see Margarita again.*

Marco Conti's heart was beating like it had when he'd first fallen seriously in love, some eight years earlier. That love affair did not last more than a year, however, as it soon became apparent that the local Italian girl, who knew of the Conti family's wealth, was interested in that wealth more than Marco's heart and soul. Her eventual flaunting of her association with Marco was more than Marco and his family could bear. It resulted in a tough life lesson that his mother had often tried to teach him: people who try to crawl into your good graces are seeking only transactional and profitable results.

In the intervening months, the distant communications between Marco and Margarita began with weekly, keep-it-cool emails. After a month, the emails became twice weekly, and then after a couple more weeks, almost every other day. And then a phone call, or two, or three, from Marco. Expectations were kept low. Just simple talk as each conversation inched toward greater understanding of the other person. As time passed, they both knew they increasingly wanted to *be* with each other.

After two months of distant communication, Marco decided to ask the question.

"So, are you seeing anyone else?"

"Only friends, nothing close to serious," replied Margarita. "And they are all—how might you say it in Italy—fully in the friend zone."

Marco laughed.

At hearing these words, Marco *wanted* to ask, "So, what is a beautiful woman like you doing without a serious suitor?"

But he knew that if he asked that question, he'd be going farther than he should at this stage of their distant dance. However, Margarita had a question of her own.

"How about you, Marco?" began Margarita, "Are you seeing anybody?"

"Haha," responded Marco, "no, not even semi-seriously. Right now, I'm far too busy with my job. Although when I become seriously interested in someone, I seriously *make time* for them. For whatever reason, though, there hasn't been anyone for whom that has been the case in the past few years. But you never know, that could change."

Both smiled at their chatty dance and its little gems of revelation.

After concluding with their most recent talk, Marco decided to move up his semi-annual visit to the city's major supermarkets, each of which was a significant buyer from his father's Italian wine and spirits company. While Marco's next visit to Rostov was originally scheduled for July, *I'm moving it up to May,* he decided.

***

Marco was seated at the same café, same table, and at the same time as his first extended encounter with Margarita. Not wanting to overdress, he wore his newest tight-fitting jeans, brown loafers, and light-blue, long-sleeved, button-down collar shirt. His sleeves were rolled halfway up to the elbow. A thinly profiled *Patek Philippe* Swiss watch, with a gold face and black leather strap, was on his left wrist. It was a gift from Marco's father, presented upon Marco's completing his University of Bologna Master of Business Studies.

As the aluminum and glass front door to the café swung open, Marco's eyes lit up, and his heart rate picked up. Margarita's auburn hair lay gently on her shoulders and a silk open-collar, long-sleeve shirt. She wore tight-fitting black pants with a large, black strap and gold buckle belt. She'd splurged for the best ladies' Italian black leather, open-toe sandals she could find. Margarita had taken the afternoon off so she could get "the best pedicure ever." Her bold red nail polish matched the red lipstick of her otherwise modest makeup. It had been the final touch, and she felt better than she had in a long time.

Margarita approached the table confidently, smiling. Marco stood and stepped toward her. He gently put his hands on Margarita's arms just below her shoulders and exchanged two air kisses with Margarita, one on each cheek, their skin brushing slightly. Their modestly applied colognes and perfumes added to the blossoming chemistry.

After Marco seated Margarita, she began with small talk.

"So, is coffee and cake your usual evening meal choice? Because if it is, I could get used to it," she quipped, grinning.

Marco laughed.

"Well, not exactly. But . . . I didn't want to change our trend!" replied Marco.

They laughed together.

"But, if you'd like to have an actual dinner, say tomorrow night, I'd be delighted to invite you. And we can save the coffee and cake for after the dinner, if you'd like," suggested Marco.

"Well . . ." began Margarita hesitatingly, not wanting to convey that a dinner was something she was hoping for.

"Well, that settles it," interjected Marco before Margarita could complete her sentence. "I always hire the same driver while I'm in town. He's been the same one for the past three years. I trust him. He goes by Georgiy. I'll have him come by and pick you up at your place, if that's OK, and bring you to the restaurant. After dinner, he'll take you home."

Margarita smiled.

"Well, I don't want you to get the wrong impression . . ."

"*What* wrong impression?" interjected Marco. "A full meal will be fun! Don't worry, Margarita," continued Marco warmly. "You haven't given me the wrong impression at all. I completely get it. Us Italians are the kings and queens of long meals!"

Margarita's boisterous laugh drifted through the restaurant, drawing inquisitive looks and smiles from a couple of nearby tables.

"OK. Then yes! I'd love to have dinner with you tomorrow night," she replied, the laughter still in her eyes.

For Margarita and Marco, the next three hours of chatting, joking, and laughing came easily.

CHAPTER 48
THE DINNER
May 2023

MARGARITA DESCENDED THE THREE FLOORS OF HER APARTMENT BUILDING. Reaching the bottom floor, she walked through the building's exit doors. Marco's driver, the thirty-something Georgiy, waited curbside in the driver's seat of a silver 2023 *Lada Largus.* The Largus was an SUV-type vehicle sold in Russia under the French Renault brand. The smaller, sub-compact *Lada Granta* was the most popular car in Russia. Marco Conti preferred the larger Largus for its ability to blend in with other Russian car brands and for its added safety features.

Margarita walked through the building's double-door exit. Upon seeing her, Georgiy exited the Lada and opened the rear curbside door for Margarita.

Before getting in the car, Margarita had a question for the driver. Although Marco had mentioned the driver's name the night before, the question was for courtesy and security reasons.

"What is your name, sir?" asked Margarita.

"Georgiy," he responded.

"Pleased to meet you, Georgiy," she replied, nodding. "Marco has told me all about you."

"I hope most of it was good.

"It was," replied Margarita, smiling.

"And your name, Madame?" he asked.

"Margarita."

"Pleased to meet you, Madame," he replied.

Margarita got in the back seat. Georgiy shut her door and got back in the driver's seat. Within a minute of pulling away from the curb, Margarita asked Georgiy another question.

"Which restaurant are we going to, Georgiy"? asked Margarita.

"The very nice one in the Radisson Blu Hotel," replied Georgiy. "I've forgotten its name." *And I can't afford it,* he added to himself.

***

Georgiy maneuvered the car near the hotel's main entry door. Margarita spotted Marco near the hotel's entry doors before Georgiy did. It was a cool day in mid-May, so Marco opted for a black cashmere sweater with a zip-up collar. Underneath the sweater, he wore a white button-down shirt. Casual and slim-fitting black slacks and black leather lace-up shoes completed his casually elegant, understated ensemble.

Margarita was glad she'd grabbed her black leather jacket before leaving the apartment. Covering her upscale denim shirt, the jacket would do well in fending off the cool evening spring air. Black pants, black ankle-high leather boots, and her mother's turquoise earrings and necklace completed her outfit.

After Georgiy stopped the car, Marco stepped up and opened Margarita's door.

"Good evening, Madame. I understand you are here to meet some crazy Italian guy for dinner tonight?" he began.

"As a matter of fact, I am," replied Margarita as she exited the back seat. "His name is Marco. You wouldn't happen to know him, *would you?*"

"Never heard of him. But I hope I'll serve as a decent stand-in," said Marco, offering Margarita his left arm.

"I'm sure you'll do just fine," replied Margarita with a broad smile, putting her arm through Marco's. She enjoyed that they could lightheartedly tease one another.

Marco walked Margarita into the dining room and to a back corner table he had already reserved with the hostess. Margarita was impressed by the room's refined features, including white tablecloths and fresh flowers at each table.

Well, this is a first, she thought to herself, thinking that this was the first time she'd been taken to a fancy restaurant for what might end up being a long meal.

Once at the table, Marco pulled out Margarita's chair to seat her.

For the next two and a half hours, they worked their way slowly through an Italian four-course menu, with some of the best Italian wine available in Rostov-on-Don. Each bottle was produced by the Conti Vineyards back in Italy. Marco could have given Margarita a full-blown wine tasting course on each bottle and the wine it contained. But that was the farthest thought from his mind. He didn't let—nor want—Margarita to know that each bottle was a Conti Vineyards-produced wine.

Perhaps she might notice, he thought, *but if she doesn't, I really don't care.*

Before he'd gone out of the hotel to meet Margarita, he'd told the restaurant's sommelier how he wanted the evening to progress.

"We won't be needing a Wine List tonight," he said. "We'll only serve Conti Vineyards' wines."

"*Si, dottore,*" replied the sommelier, using the word "doctor" as an Italian sign of respect to anybody, whether they were a certified doctor or not. The Italian- and French-trained sommelier knew all about the Conti Vineyards and who he was talking to.

"Once my guest determines what she wants to eat, I'll inform you of which of the Conti wines we'll have. I'll never say 'Conti,' though. I will simply mention the grape or blend."

"*Si, signor,*" replied the sommelier.

With each glass of wine perfectly paired to each of Margarita's entrée choices, Margarita only took three or four drinks of each wine, always leaving the glass half full. And following Marco's example, she drank at least a like amount of water between wine glasses.

After Margarita had tasted each wine, Marco asked, "Do you like it?"

For the five different glasses of red wine, containing Barbera, Cabernet Sauvignon, Merlot, and Sangiovese grapes—and one glass with blends thereof—Margarita twice responded, "I really like it," twice responded, "I love it," and once responded, "it's amazing." Marco smiled and mentally filed away each response.

Their dinner was lighthearted and filled with laughter. The time flew by. In her soon-to-be twenty-five years, she'd never met a man like Marco. *I've never felt so comfortable around any man in my life,* she thought. *Can this guy be for real?*

Before asking for the bill, Marco asked Margarita if she wanted a "*digestivo.*"

"What's a *digestivo?*" asked Margarita.

"It's something in Italy that we have after a meal to help settle our stomachs . . . or so we say, haha. Maybe it's just a good excuse to drink something a bit stronger than normal. Like a *grappa,* or something like a vodka, maybe."

At the word "vodka," Margarita's mind flashed back to that terribly traumatic night. She couldn't believe it had been nearly a year since the ugly occurrence. She tried to shake off the dark thoughts, but a touch of sadness crept onto her face and into her posture. Margarita's shoulders curved forward protectively, her hands clenching. Her eyes unfocused as her mind replayed one of the more brutal moments. She went very still.

Noticing the change in Margarita's demeanor, concern bloomed in Marco's face.

"Margarita. *Margarita,*" he called softly. Margarita's eyes refocused. "Are you OK? Was it something I *said?* I'm sorry if it was."

"No, no," rubbing her hands, "it's OK, Marco. My mind just drifted for a moment." A deep, centering breath, "I'm the one who is sorry for letting my mind wander." She tried for a smile.

"It's OK, Margarita. It happens to me all the time. But are you *OK?*" His empathetic smile pierced Margarita's heart.

"I'm fine," she replied, mentally shoving the paralyzing thoughts away. "This has been such a wonderful meal, Marco! I totally loved it."

"Well, so did I, *cara mia* (my dear), so did I," replied Marco.

Margarita's face lit up. "But I *will* take a cup of coffee," she said. "I don't want to break our trend!"

"No, we shall *not* break our trend," said Marco emphatically. "We are world champions at drinking coffee!"

Marco and Margarita both laughed. He was glad to hear it. She'd been so quiet and still for a moment.

As Margarita drank a cappuccino and Marco an espresso (no self-respecting Italian would ever drink a cappuccino after about 10:30 A.M.), Margarita wondered where the night might lead. She could feel herself increasingly falling for Marco. But she hadn't been with a man since a few months before that horrible evening in Ukrainian territory, the previous June. And she was not yet sure she was ready to be with a man again, not *even* a man as kind, gracious, and handsome as Marco Conti. At least not yet.

Margarita didn't have to wait long to find out what would come next.

The waiter brought the check, and Marco took it straightaway. He placed his credit card on top of the check in the silver tray.

"Once I take care of this, Margarita," said Marco, "I have Georgiy standing by outside. He'll take you home . . . or wherever else you might want to go. It truly has been a fun evening!"

Margarita was delighted, and a little relieved.

"It really has been," said Margarita. "You were a wonderful stand-in for whoever that Italian guy was! I didn't miss him a bit!"

Their laughter wove through the restaurant, a bright thread tinged with sparkles of love.

Marco paid the bill and, arm-in-arm, escorted Margarita to the waiting car. When Georgiy—seated in the SUV's driver seat—saw the couple approaching, he made eye contact with Marco and opened his door.

Marco quickly waved him off, telling Georgiy, "It's OK, I got it."

Georgiy shut the door and waited.

Before Marco could open the car door for Margarita, she leaned into Marco's shoulder, her lips merely inches from his ear.

"Thank you again, Marco," she said softly, hoping for a goodbye kiss. "It was an amazing dinner."

Marco Conti read the clue, and he did not intend to disappoint. He turned and fully, gently embraced Margarita. Then he lightly brushed the tip of her nose with his lips. When her lips parted in a little gasp, he kissed her. Carefully, softly at first.

Emboldened by his gentleness, Margarita put her arms around Marco's neck, lifted to her toes, and deepened the kiss. Margarita's knees trembled as the embrace and the kiss filled with passion. Marco's heart slammed in his chest. Marco broke away, ending the kiss. But the sensuality of their shared kiss left both breathless.

"See you soon?" asked Marco as he opened the door for Margarita.

Margarita grinned, got in her seat, and slowly fastened her seatbelt without answering. Marco shut the car door. He wondered if Margarita had heard the question or simply chose to ignore it.

Margarita rolled down her window. She leaned forward, close to the window's opening. She wanted to give Marco one last hint of her perfume and one last look into her glistening eyes.

"*Si, presto* (yes, soon)," replied Margarita with a big smile and speaking two of the hundreds of Italian words she'd learned in the preceding four months.

CHAPTER 49
THE OPERA
May 2023

TEARS FORMED IN MARGARITA'S EYES. She willed herself not to resist a single tear. Out of pure joy and a revelation filled with love and light, she *wanted* to let the tears flow. Although the second-level private opera box she and Marco were seated in was dark, the light emanating from the stage below revealed the tears in Margarita's eyes and on her cheeks. Out of the corner of his eye, Marco Conti caught a glimpse of them. He reached for Margarita's hand, and she squeezed it tightly. They shared a smile.

He was thankful he had extended his one-week stay in Rostov-on-Don by several days. He and Margarita had a wonderful time seeing each other at least once—and sometimes twice—every day. What they *did* together didn't matter as much as *being* together. A walk in the park, a visit to the zoo, a movie, or a visit to a café, they were each fun and magical in their own way.

But now, seated in the opulent Rostov State Musical Theater and watching Act III of the Italian opera *Turandot,* Margarita's heart and soul were pierced . . . forever. Although she could understand little of the language, she'd read the plot for Act III in the opera's program. The emotion brought forth by Giacamo Puccini's words and the *Nessun Dorma* (Nobody Shall Sleep) aria sung by the Italian Russian tenor on the stage stirred something deep in Margarita's soul.

Margarita had heard the aria—which ended in the powerfully emotive words "*All'alba, Vincerò! Vincerò! Vincerò!* (At dawn, I will win! I will win! I will win!)"—before. It was during one of her mother's video recordings of the great Italian opera singer Luciano Pavarotti. At the time, she couldn't grasp the words' meaning or context.

But now, for Margarita, it did not matter. There was no going back. She knew she was deeply in love with Marco Conti. And not knowing if she'd ever reach this point in her life, she was deeply grateful for it. And Marco Conti was deeply thankful that he was in love with Margarita Romanova.

CHAPTER 50
LUNCH
Late May 2023

THE LATE MAY SUN CARESSED MARGARITA ROMANOVA'S CHEEKS. She'd been seated at the outdoor café with Marco Conti for over an hour. The single glass of white wine and grilled fish platter from the Sea of Azov had put her in a very comfortable place. But the anxiety creeping up inside her was undeniable. Marco was leaving the next day. Margarita decided, after days of holding back, to tell Marco about the two other loves of her life.

"I have to tell you, Marco, that I am in love with two other young men," she began.

Marco's eyebrows rose as his heart skipped a beat.

Not wanting to make this more than a moment of anticipatory torture for Marco, Margarita wasted no time in telling Marco her unexpected story.

"I'm not even sure I can legally talk to you about this, Marco," she said. "But my heart is telling me you should know."

She briefly paused. Marco nodded and braced himself, wondering where Margarita's next words would lead.

Margarita told Marco the story about Sergiy and Gleb.

When she was finished, Marco briefly put his head down in sorrow. When he raised it and looked into Margarita's eyes, unshed tears were in his eyes. Marco had heard brief references in the news during the previous year about Ukrainian children being abducted to Russia. But while he had shaken his head at the potentially horrible consequences, he'd given them no further thought. But Margarita had just made it real and personal.

"I am so sorry to hear that, Margarita," he said. "That is a story that causes anguish in my soul. I cannot imagine that something like that could happen in the twenty-first century, in Europe."

Margarita nodded in agreement.

"Neither could I," she responded, "Nor can I believe I was part of something like that."

"It wasn't your fault, Margarita. You were a soldier, and you did your duty. Is there anything I can do to help?" asked Marco.

Margarita again nodded.

"Yes, actually there is, Marco," she answered. "I hesitate to ask you this, but I don't think there is any other way I can approach it."

"Tell me, ask me . . . anything," replied Marco. "How can I help?"

Margarita began to tell Marco about not being able to locate the boys' father, Roman Levedeva, a Ukrainian soldier.

"But I do know who their uncle is and where he supposedly works," she replied.

She proceeded to tell Marco about the boys' loving reference to their aunt and uncle, and what her friend had discovered about the Ukrainian colonel.

"After you get back to Italy, if you could contact Colonel Kovalenko from there and tell him everything about the boys, I'd deeply appreciate it," she added. "I'm sure he will be delighted to hear it. There is too much danger for me to try and do that from Russia, and perhaps for you, too."

"I will promise you that when I get back to Italy, I will contact him," replied Marco.

Margarita reached across the table and put her hands on Marco's.

"Thank you, my dear," she said, more tears welling in her eyes.

Margarita and Marco's lunch date was creeping into anxious territory for them. Marco was leaving the next day, and neither one wanted their enchanting time in Rostov to end. They'd each consumed everything one could have in a full lunch, including ending it with a *limoncello,* a delightful Italian after-dinner drink made from lemons and originally from Italy's idyllic island of Capri.

"Well, I do have an early flight tomorrow, *cara mia* (my dear)," said Marco. "Georgiy can swing you by your place first and then take me to the hotel, if that's OK with you?"

Margarita felt sad about soon parting ways with Marco. She cared deeply for him and was not sure when she would see him again. Marco had the same worry.

"Actually, Marco," she said, reaching across the table to again hold Marco's hands as her heart slammed in her chest. "I had another thought. How about you and I go to your hotel and have a last drink at that beautiful hotel bar of yours? One for the road, so to speak. And *then,* Georgiy can take me home."

"I think that's a splendid idea," Marco replied as his heart raced in his chest.

***

Sharing a drink at the hotel's bar, nerves from the building anticipation between them caused Margarita and Marco to chatter aimlessly. There was no doubt in either one's mind that before they said goodbye, they wanted to *be* with each other like they'd each been dreaming about. During the ride in the back of the SUV, with Georgiy at the wheel, they held and caressed each other's hands almost the entire trip. Each was trying to convey, subtly or not, that "it was time."

Margarita decided to throw caution to the wind. At almost the same moment, Marco came to the same conclusion.

"Well, Marco, you've been extremely courteous the entire time we've been together," she said, "and you've taken me to some fun places. But there was one place I didn't get to see."

"What place was that?" asked Marco, his mind switching gears from what he'd been about to say and searching for the place she might be referring to.

Margarita pondered whether to string Marco out a bit longer. Instead, she decided to just *say it*.

"Your hotel room. Is it a nice one?" asked Margarita, smiling, doubting herself, and questioning whether Marco would perceive her as going too far.

"It's more than nice," Marco replied. His voice husky, he continued, "It's *beautiful* and it has a great view. I think you'll like it."

Just to be sure, Marco asked a question of his own.

"Would you like another drink?"

"No *grazie,*" she replied.

"I'm finished with this one, too," she added, touching her cocktail glass.

"*Va bene* (OK)," replied Marco.

Not interested in lingering, he looked at the bartender, who was standing about ten feet away. Since it was 3 P.M., Marco and Margarita were the only ones at the bar.

"Igor, could you please put these drinks on my tab?"

Igor appreciated the generous tips Marco had left him over the preceding four years and always enjoyed it when Mr. Conti stayed in the hotel. And so did the rest of the hotel's staff who encountered him. Marco had always treated Igor—and the rest of the hotel staff—with dignity and respect.

"No, boss, I will *not,*" shot back Igor emphatically with a big smile. "Those two drinks for you and your lovely lady are on me."

Marco responded with a smile of his own.

"*Grazie, amico mio* (my friend)."

Margarita grabbed her leather clutch from the bar, eager to leave with Marco.

"Let me lead the way," said Marco, guiding Margarita out of the bar and into the hallway where the two elevators were located. After the elevator doors slid shut, they reached for each other, passionately kissing as their hearts trembled.

The doors slid open on the fifth floor, as they, half-laughing, half-kissing pulled each other less than forty feet down the hall to Marco's suite. The green light above the door handle flashed as Marco's key card unlocked the door. Margarita and Marco all but fell through the door when Marco swung it open. Marco shut and locked the door behind them.

For the next two hours, they saw little of "the view" Marco had mentioned. Their intimacy, passion, surrender, and heights

of exhilaration far exceeded their dreams . . . time and time
again.

CHAPTER 51

FIRE!

Early June 2023

THE UKRAINIAN ARMY SERGEANT MANEUVERED THE BEAST of a military tracked vehicle out of the thick wood line and away from the three-person crew's hide area. Located about 100 yards on either side of him, his two fellow sergeants were doing the same thing, driving their Multiple Launch Rocket System (MLRS) vehicles ("Self-Propelled Loader/Launcher," or "SPLL," pronounced *spill* in military acronym jargon) to their predesignated firing positions.

Each 26-ton launcher carried two pods of six rockets each, for a total of twelve deadly rockets on each vehicle. Inside the twelve rockets were a combined total of roughly 8,000 "incendiary munitions" (explosive shrapnel-spreading firebombs, about half the size of a baseball or cricket ball).

Firing their twelve rockets each, upon air detonation or ground impact, the bomblets would turn a sixty-acre (twenty-four hectares) area into a saturated flaming hell on earth of molten shrapnel and shards of iron. The hot shrapnel was capable of penetrating "soft" military targets such as "thin-skinned" vehicles, tires, tents, and human flesh.

The Ukrainian lieutenant awaited the final orders from his captain, located at the battalion headquarters some four miles away. The nearby Ukrainian front-line infantry soldiers were excited with anticipation to witness—for the first time—the MLRS rockets launch.

The Ukrainian infantry soldiers had been catching hell from a combined Russian armored and infantry unit that had pulled back to only three miles from their front, and the Ukrainians had lost several of their buddies over the previous days. They were eager for mortal revenge against the Russians.

The "clear to fire" word came down from the captain. Over the radio, the lieutenant double-checked with his three launcher teams to ensure they were ready to simultaneously fire on their designated target: the field headquarters of a 2000-man Russian armored brigade task force. Each of the three ranking sergeants, located in the cab of each launcher, had trained on the MLRS rocket launchers in the United Kingdom. Each sergeant responded with a "Roger."

The launcher crew chiefs were now *ready* to flip the single switch, electronic firing mechanism. Twenty seconds after that, the lieutenant issued a "stand by" over the radio, and ten seconds after that, he issued the order: "Fire!" The crew sergeants immediately flipped their firing switches to "FIRE" mode.

Flashes of brilliant white light, smoke trails, and the "swoosh" sound of each supersonic rocket penetrated the pre-dawn darkness as each launcher ejected its twelve death- and destruction-dealing rockets. The rockets' top speed quickly reached Mach 2 (approximately 1,500 miles per hour). All thirty-six rockets from the three vehicles were fired in under sixty seconds.

The nearby infantry soldiers cheered with shouts of "fuck yeah!" and "get some!" a phrase one of them had heard from his US Army trainer. To avoid being targeted by the Russians, the Ukrainian artillery sergeants had been trained to "shoot and scoot,"—quickly moving their launcher after the last rocket was fired at least 1 mile (about 1.6 km) away—to avoid possible Russian counter-artillery fire.

After about forty seconds of flight time, the rockets disgorged their lethal payloads over the target area. The effect was as if 24,000 hand grenades, some exploding in the air and others on the ground, had been launched at the brigade task force headquarters by Satan himself.

Of the 136 soldiers and officers in the camp that night, the MLRS rocket attack killed thirty-seven of the Russian soldiers and wounded another forty-eight. The rest, because of where they were sleeping (like inside the cab of a vehicle that was lucky to have only its tires punctured or inside a tank), by the Grace of God, survived physically unscathed or with only minor injuries.

CHAPTER 52
THREE DAYS LATER: HE'S DEAD
Early June 2023

RUSSIAN ARMY SERGEANT ANNA ORLOVA HELD HER CELL PHONE under her bed sheet. She couldn't wait for the civilian hospital nurse to leave her room. She had been transported to the hospital east of Rostov with seven other soldiers after their headquarters had been attacked by Ukrainian artillery early in the morning. Most of the soldiers were sleeping when it happened.

That was much worse than any nightmare I've ever had, she thought, *but by the Grace of the Almighty, I survived, and the doctor said I would be fine.*

The Russian brigade's veteran survivors all said the attack was likely conducted by a Ukrainian multiple launch rocket unit.

Anna couldn't care less about who, or what, was the source of the attack. She felt lucky to be alive, having only taken some small shrapnel in her upper thigh and shoulder. While certainly wounded and in intermittent pain, the doctor told her that he had easily removed the half-inch piece of shrapnel from her leg and another smaller piece from her shoulder.

"You were lucky that neither piece of shrapnel hit a major organ or artery. Your wounds will fully heal in three weeks or so," said the doctor. "And I expect you'll be able to leave this hospital in a few days or so."

Anna couldn't wait to tell her friend Margarita some good news. The attending nurse and Anna's hospital roommate and fellow soldier had just left the room. It was a rare chance to make a private phone call.

Anna pressed the green call button on her cellphone. But a voice message immediately came on the line, directing Anna to Margarita's voicemail. Anna decided that if she was not explicit and did not name names, it would be safe to leave Margarita a message.

"My dear Margarita, it's Anna. I'm in the hospital. But I'll be OK. The shrapnel might leave a sexy scar next to the tattoo on my leg, but my wounds are nothing serious. I could be playing rugby again in a few weeks. I just wanted to let you know that fucking *pig* of an officer is dead, killed by artillery. Yes, you know the one I'm talking about. I love you, my friend, and hope to see you soon."

CHAPTER 53

A GENTLEMAN ON THE LINE
July 2023

COLONEL HENNADIY KOVALENKO SAW THE LIGHT FLASHING ON his desktop telephone. He picked up the receiver.

"Yes?" he responded.

"Sir, it's the MOD ("M-Oh-Dee," for Ministry of Defense) switchboard. I have a gentleman on the line who said he is an Italian winemaker, and that he recently returned to Italy from Russia."

"Yes, go on," replied Kovalenko, thinking the "gentleman on the line" might have some information of military intelligence value for Ukraine or perhaps someone he had met at a diplomatic reception in Rome.

"He said it was *really important* to tell you, I quote, 'I know where Sergiy and Gleb are.' Should I patch him through?" asked the operator.

Kovalenko sat back in his chair, his heart beating a rapid tattoo inside his chest. As if to acknowledge the presence of God, he looked up at his high office ceiling. He prayed silently, *Dear Lord, let this be good news.*

"Sir," said the operator again. "Are you there?"

"Yes," He nearly shouted, "Yes, I am here. And yes, please put him on."

The operator did as the colonel instructed. Hennadiy heard a "click," and the person came on the line.

"Colonel Kovalenko?" asked the man.

"Hi, yes, this is Hennadiy Kovalenko. *Lei e Italiano, giusto* (You are Italian, correct)?" asked Kovalenko, immediately testing whether the man was indeed Italian.

Marco Conti was surprised that Hennadiy Kovalenko said a few words in perfect Italian. Conti had no idea that Hennadiy Kovalenko had served as the Ukrainian Defense Attaché to Italy at the Ukrainian Embassy in Rome.

"Well, yes . . . *si, sono Italiano* (yes, I am Italian)" responded Marco Conti. "My name is Marco Conti. Would you prefer to speak in Italian or English, sir?"

"For now, let's keep it in English. Mr. Conti, did I hear the operator correctly? That you know where my nephews are?"

Hennadiy Kovalenko took a deep breath and slowly exhaled, anticipating Mr. Conti's response.

"Yes, you heard correctly," replied Conti. "Here is what I know about Sergiy and Gleb . . ."

Conti told Kovalenko everything about the boys that Margarita had told him, without mentioning his source's name, location, or even gender. He simply referred to his source— Margarita—as "a person." He did not want to unnecessarily reveal Margarita's identity, at least not yet. In his description of the events and facts, he included the exact name of the boys' town as well as the address where they were located and the names of their adopting parents.

Hennadiy Kovalenko's heart soared. Someone was providing what seemed to be very legitimate and specific information about the boys' location. And most of all, the fact that the boys were alive was encouraging. But he became very concerned after hearing that the boys had an abusive adoptive father and a mother who was incapable of doing much about the abuse.

To drive home his appreciation and gratitude for the person on the other end of the phone connection, Kovalenko decided to switch to Italian.

"Sir, I'm deeply appreciative that you gave me this information. Someday, when I have a chance to step away from this horrible and unjust war, I'd like to meet you. I'm not sure if you know, but I once served as a military attaché to your beautiful country, in our Ukrainian Embassy, in Rome. I have many wonderful Italian friends in Italy. I hope to make another one."

"Ahhh, *now* I understand why your Italian is so good!" replied Conti. "The feeling is mutual. I would love to meet you, too, sir. And I pray for your country, too."

"But Mr. Conti, please tell me this: why did you take the time and effort to find me and relay this information to me?" added Kovalenko. "You have never met me before."

"It's because I care *a lot* about the person who asked me to relay this information to you. And that person cares deeply about the boys. She wants them to be treated well and to have a good future. Perhaps it might help your understanding to know that she, too, was the victim of an abusive father. Furthermore, the boys' story touched my soul as well."

At this point, Conti realized he'd revealed his source's gender.

"But sir, if you wouldn't mind, please do not share what I just told you about my source with anybody," added Conti. "She fears for her life if the Russians discover that she has asked me to pass this information to you."

"I completely understand," replied Kovalenko. "And of course, I will not share it."

And then it occurred to Marco Conti that he, too, had another question for the Ukrainian colonel.

"Colonel, one more thing. My source told me that the boys had a father, a Ukrainian soldier. She tried to look him up, as I did, with no success. Since he could not be found, she decided to contact you. The boys mentioned you and your wife, Mila, to my contact. I thought you should know this."

"You did the right thing, Mr. Conti." Then Hennadiy gave him the information about Roman's death, hoping it would reach the boys. "The boys' father died a heroic death fighting the enemy in the opening days of the war. I want to thank you again for having the courage and decency to reach out to me. Is it OK if I contact you in the future? I will only do so if absolutely necessary."

"Yes, without a doubt, Colonel. You may. If there is any way I can help, please let me know."

CHAPTER 54

THE ITALIAN CONSULATE, MOSCOW
October 2023

"I'D LOVE FOR YOU TO COME TO ITALY."

As Margarita Romanova approached Moscow's Italian Visa Center located at *Malyi Tomashevskiy lane, 6 boulevard 1,* those were the words that she remembered for the umpteenth time. Marco Conti had spoken the heart-warming words to Margarita some two months prior over the telephone. And here she was, about to meet with an Italian consular officer and present her final documents for her visa authorizing her visit to Italy and the Schengen Zone. The Italian visa also granted her access to the twenty-eight other European countries in the Zone.

What Margarita could not have known is that Marco Conti's father, the legendary Italian winemaker who brought the Conti Vineyards to its much-heralded international status, had contacted a friend and senior diplomat in Italy's Ministry of Foreign Affairs. The elder Conti's request was simple: "Please expedite the issue of an Italian visa for Margarita Romanova, a Russian citizen, to visit Italy for one year."

As an Italian visa—the legal authority given by the Italian government to visit Italy for a prescribed period, typically ninety days to six months—the request and endorsement were not uncommon, although a one-year requested length of stay was.

"I give my full endorsement to Margarita Romanova," the seventy-something senior Conti had told his well-placed diplomatic friend.

When he'd said it, Signor Conti understood that he'd be fully responsible for anything illegal that Romanova might do while in Italy. But with tears in his eyes, his son Marco had prevailed upon his father: "Papa, she is not just some one-night or temporary fling. I love her more than I can say."

The elder Conti believed his son was truly in love with the Russian woman, and he decided to stake his personal, hard-earned reputation on his son's heart and request.

***

Sitting in front of the dapper, thirty-something Italian consular officer, Margarita felt an ominous turn in her interview with the officer. The officer had been briefed that the Russian female visa applicant was coming into the Italian consular offices that morning with a strong endorsement from Italy's Ministry of Foreign Affairs. An endorsement of that nature was something that only happened a few times per year. It was also from the same ministry that issued the officer's monthly paycheck.

Still, it would be the officer's recommendation to the Consular Attaché, the senior consular officer in the embassy, that would weigh heavily as to whether the beautiful Russian's application would be approved for a temporary—albeit extended—visit to Italy. Anything beyond one year would have to be reapplied for or granted based on a change of status, such as marriage to an Italian.

"I see that you were a soldier in the Russian Army," the officer said to Margarita. "But you served for less than a year. Why?"

The thought of whether she should mention her terrible ordeal with the Russian Army colonel flashed through Margarita's mind. The military commander and judge she'd stood before during her last hours in the Russian Army had told Margarita to never breathe a word of the incident to *anyone*.

But then she remembered the words of Marco Conti. "Just be honest during the interview. Be yourself," Marco had told her.

What Margarita did not know is that the consular officer knew a lot about Romanova before she'd stepped into the small room designated for consular interviews, and that the officer was trained to detect a lie in a New York minute.

Margarita decided to follow the words of the man she loved and needed more than anybody in the world.

"I was sexually assaulted by a Russian Army colonel," Margarita said.

She then provided the Italian consular officer with the broad outline of her sexual assault and "non-judicial punishment" that she'd received at the hands of a Russian general.

Her brutally honest account was an account unlike any other the Italian consular officer had ever heard. It touched his soul. And he knew Margarita was telling the truth.

"Come back tomorrow morning at 9 A.M., and your one-year visa—effective tomorrow—will be ready," the officer said.

Margarita Romanova left the office and the consulate, her spirit in the clouds.

CHAPTER 55
THE VINEYARDS
November 2023

THE VIEW TOOK MARGARITA ROMANOVA'S BREATH AWAY. From her third-floor window, for as far as her eye could see, there was nothing but vineyards covering the hillside below her. A cobalt blue sky served as the vineyards' backdrop. The vineyards' *terroir*—the soil, sun-kissed topography, and local microclimate—was optimal for producing some of the best Cabernet Sauvignon, Merlot, and Sangiovese grapes from Italy and the world.

Anna will never believe this, she thought. *How did I end up here?*

How Margarita "ended up" in the sixteenth century, three-story stone castle with eight modern and well-appointed apartments, each offering a magnificent view, was not without drama. While Marco Conti's mother and father supported their son in his love of this beautiful Russian woman he had spent time with during the preceding year, some of his friends, family members, and acquaintances had serious doubts about this auburn-haired Russian beauty.

While some who were in the wine or olive oil businesses knew of the important trade market that Russia represented for Italy, many had condemned Russia's brutal invasion of Ukraine in 2022. Others were torn between enmity for the Russian dictator and neutrality in condemning the Russian people, while others believed the Russian people were blindly following a dictator to the gates of hell.

"You know, the Russians take years to plant spies," a friend had warned.

An uncle had simply said, "Be careful, Marco."

But to each warning, he always provided the same answer.

"I found her working in a grocery store. She didn't find *me*. There is no way the Russians were targeting me—a wine salesman—to be spied upon. And she has a heart of gold."

CHAPTER 56
VAL GARDENA
January 2024

JAKE FORTINA COULD NOT BELIEVE HIS GOOD FORTUNE. He was skiing with his beautiful Italian wife, Sara Simonetti-Fortina, and their handsome son Giacomo in Val Gardena, an idyllic valley in Italy's equally idyllic Dolomite mountains. The red-hued mesa visible off in the distance, the cobalt blue sky, the stunning vistas, and crisp winter air reminded Jake of Utah's Wasatch mountains.

Located south of the Alps, and therefore receiving more than its fair share of alpine sun, Val Gardena and its surrounding majestic mountains and idyllic villages were Jake and Sara's favorite places to play in the winter.

Occasionally looking down the white slope, Sara kept her cellphone's camera focused on Giacomo.

"That's it, Giacomo, you are doing great!' encouraged Sara. "Isn't this fun?"

Giacomo, skiing without poles, raised his arm to signal that he had heard his mother and that he was having a ball.

Skiing eight to ten feet behind Giacomo was Jake, connected to Giacomo by a ski learning harness with a strap. Only a few months after his second birthday, Giacomo was wearing his über cute ski jacket, helmet, and goggles.

Jake's heart warmed as Giacomo fearlessly descended the long, gradually declining, snow-covered slope on his tiny skis. Jake gave the harness connecting him and Giacomo just enough slack for Giacomo to think he was doing the work entirely by himself, but Jake also kept enough tension in the strap to make sure he could quickly control Giacomo in the event the little guy got into trouble.

Behind the two of them, Sara Simonetti-Fortino was skiing and videotaping the whole father-son adventure.

"*Vai* (go), Giacomo!" she encouraged between giggles, "you are doing *fantastico!*"

***

Little Giacomo slept soundly, sprawled out on the restaurant's corner bench beside Sara. The bench provided seating for two sides of their corner dinner table. The top of Giacomo's head barely touched Sara's outer thigh. Sara, in blue jeans and a white ski sweater, occasionally looked down at her precious son. Five hours in the cold mountain air, skiing like he was born to do it, had worn the little man out. Now, in the Hotel Edda's cozy restaurant, with its warm air and food in his tummy, Giacomo had been lulled to a deep sleep.

"He passed out before he'd even finished his French fries," said Jake, smiling.

Jake and Sara raised their wine glasses for a toast.

"To us and our beautiful boy," toasted Sara.

"To our beautiful family," replied Jake.

Locking eyes, they clinked their crystal wine glasses. They each took a sip of their favorite Lugana white wine. The Lugana grapes were grown southwest of Verona, just two hours to the south of Val Gardena. The microclimate at the southern end of

Lake Garda, combined with the fertile soil deposited at the south end of the lake by a receding glacier, made for excellent wine.

"How did we end up here, like this?" asked Sara, her heart glowing.

"I asked myself that every day," replied Jake with a smile.

Jake and Sara paused to relish the moment, and Jake poured more wine into Sara's glass.

It was miraculous in more ways than one that the two military officers had met in Garmisch-Partenkirchen, Germany, and had reunited in Verona, Italy, some four years later. After Verona, in the pursuit of two Iranian terrorists, they survived life-threatening moments not once, but twice. At least, those were the ones they were aware of. Along the way, they had fallen in love, both grateful for second chances.

"I can't describe it any other way than by Divine intervention," added Jake.

"I agree, *caro mio,*" replied Sara. "That and . . ."

A teasing smile played across her lips, "Your good looks might have had something to do with it."

Jake laughed loudly, causing a few of the customers to turn their heads in Jake's direction.

"Only good looks?" Jake's broad grin was contagious. "That's all I get?"

Sara grinned.

"Because you are like Richter Scale beautiful," added Jake.

"Richter scale? Where on that scale?" teased Sara.

Jake chuckled.

"Like Mount Etna, full of enormous energy and exceptional beauty, towering above the rest."

Sara giggled. Jake smiled with love in his eyes, hoping his comparison wasn't too corny.

"Thank you, darling," replied Sara.

After a brief pause, Sara continued.

"Jake, listen. How *are* you? It's been almost two years since you've been supporting me as a stay-at-home dad while I continue my Carabinieri career in Verona," said Sara. "Your support has been wonderful—and I deeply appreciate it—but I fear that your corporate consulting job has not been very fulfilling."

Jake looked down at his wine glass for a few seconds. He thought about his two-year gig as a defense consultant to a large US-European defense company.

"Well, it has not been as fulfilling as wearing a US Army uniform, that's for sure. But here's the thing, *cara mia:* I don't know that anything ever will be as fulfilling as leading the dedicated and selfless men and women with whom I volunteered to serve my country. And many of my retired military friends say much the same thing."

"Well, I'm sure there is some truth to that," replied Sara. "But I also believe that some of our very best years are still to come. And I know that we will always keep family first, but that does not mean that we can't do other things that will fulfill us, meaning *you* and *me.*"

"I agree," responded Jake. "One hundred percent. My problem is that I'm not quite certain what—besides living a wonderful life with you and Giacomo—those other things are yet. I have some ideas, but none that fire up my passions like service to a greater cause and service to others."

"I do believe, Jake, that you'll figure it out very soon," said Sara. "It's not just a hunch. I feel it in my bones."

Sara was not quite sure why she'd said it so convincingly, but she did believe, for some reason, that Jake was about to turn a new page.

CHAPTER 57
THE UKRAINIAN GENERAL STAFF
Late January 2024

IT WAS ALMOST TWO YEARS PAST WHAT WOULD NORMALLY HAVE BEEN Colonel Hennadiy Kovalenko's mandatory thirty-year retirement date from the Ukrainian Armed Forces. But given the war with Russia, Ukraine's Ministry of Defense had asked him to stay on active duty for an additional two years to serve on Ukraine's General Staff. Ukraine was fighting for its life against the Russians, and Colonel Kovalenko didn't hesitate to comply with the General Staff's request. But those two years were about to end in five weeks, and Hennadiy felt that he'd arrived at a decision point.

As for Mila Kovalenko, the two years had gone by rather quickly. The war with Russia was about to enter its third year. And Mila, given that her husband, Hennadiy, at age fifty-six, was experiencing issues with high blood pressure, decided to prevail upon her husband to change his life's direction.

"Hennadiy, I feel like you've done more than enough in the service of our country," said Mila over a Sunday afternoon coffee with her husband. "You gave our country and the Ukrainian people two more years beyond what should have been your mandatory retirement date. I know I've mentioned this before. But I do believe it is finally time for you to retire . . . isn't it? If you seriously want to continue to serve, perhaps you could stay as a civilian in the Ministry of Defense for two or three more years. I know that you were offered that opportunity a while back."

Hennadiy felt like many soldiers, sailors, marines, airmen, coast guard, and other members of other services often do when faced with the question of taking off their military uniform for the last time. It's a momentous occasion. For some, it's borderline traumatic. Hennadiy considered Mila's comments.

"You know, Mila, you are right. I think we know my health could be better. And that civilian duty position—if the Ministry will still take me—could work out well. But I'm not ready for that yet."

"Well, then you could just fully retire," said Mila.

"Yes, I could," said Hennadiy. "But I feel like I have one more mission—a *vital* one—that I must accomplish."

"What's that?" asked Mila.

"We've both been increasingly concerned about Sergiy and Gleb. It's been two years since they were taken. And we now have that wonderful Italian man who contacted us last summer, and who said he knows where they are. To this point in time, every single attempt by Ukrainian citizens to recover their children from the hands of the heartless Russians has been met with denial by the Kremlin. The Russians deny that the kids have been abducted, let alone where they might be. But I now know I *must* do something to bring those two beautiful boys back to Ukraine, even if I die trying. I've exhausted all the official channels. And this voice in my head keeps telling me to contact Marco Conti, that wonderful man who called me a few months ago."

CHAPTER 58

CAN WE MEET?

Early March 2024

COLONEL HENNADIY KOVALENKO FELT PENSIVE as he eyed his cellphone. It had been several months since the momentous phone call from Marco Conti. After providing details about where Hennadiy Kovalenko's nephews had been abducted to, there had been no help from the Russian government in getting the boys back to Ukraine. But Marco Conti's last words to Hennadiy Kovalenko were, "If there is any way I can help, please let me know."

Hennadiy pressed the green call button.

"*Pronto,*" replied the person on the other end, speaking the common Italian "hello" (which also means "ready").

In perfect Italian, Hennadiy responded.

"Hello, Mr. Conti, it's Hennadiy Kovalenko. I hope this call finds you well. I could very much use your help."

"Hi Hennadiy, all is well, and I hope the same is true with you. Please tell me, sir, what it is you need, as I stand ready to help," replied Conti.

"Thank you, sir. It's about my two nephews. My wife, Mila, and I desperately want to bring them home to Ukraine. I am now retired from the Ukrainian military and will not rest until I bring them home. I've tried all of the official channels. I'd like to come to Italy to talk to you about the boys, face to face."

"Well, it's interesting that you mention that," replied Marco. "My source, whom I told you about before and who asked that I pass information about the boys to you, is here now, in Italy. She is extremely concerned about the boys, too. She wrote them a letter for Christmas, but has not heard back. As I mentioned to you before, one of the boys reported that their adopted father was quite abusive. That said, I will gladly welcome you here, at our vineyards, in Italy. When can you come?"

"I can be there as early as next month, if it's OK," replied Hennadiy.

"In the middle of next month will be perfect. The vines will be producing their leaves then, and the spring flowers will be blooming. Tuscany will be beautiful. It will be my pleasure to host you!"

"Thank you, *signore,*" replied Hennadiy.

The two set exact dates for the visit and amicably ended their phone call.

Hennadiy looked up a contact on his cellphone and again pressed the call button. The person replied.

"Pronto."

"*Jake?* This is Hennadiy. How are you, my friend?"

"Hennadiy . . . how are *you?* I have been thinking a lot about you lately! How is Mila?"

"She is fine and I'm fine. The Ukrainian Air Force has finally put me out to pasture."

"As in a retirement pasture?" asked Jake.

"Yes, militarily retired, haha. But Jake . . . I need your counsel. I have a personal and *vital* mission I deeply want to accomplish. It's the most important mission of my life. And I'd also like to *celebrate* my retirement with you. Just like old times, sharing some good Italian wine and grappa. And, so . . . how about we meet for a weekend in Tuscany? And if you'd like, bring Manny Alvarez, too. I'd love to see him again after our adventure in Calabria. And Sara, if she'd like to join us."

"Will Mila be coming?" asked Jake.

"Not this time," replied Hennadiy. "We will be making later trips to Italy, that is for sure."

"Well, I hope one of those trips will be to visit us in Verona. Sara and I will have a bottle or two or three of *Amerone* waiting for you," responded Jake, referring to the robust, top-shelf red wine from the Veneto region of Italy.

"You can count on it, my friend," replied Hennadiy.

"Well, you can count on me coming to Tuscany, that's for sure!"

CHAPTER 59
YOU MUST GO
Early March 2024

SARA SIMONETTI ARRIVED HOME AFTER A TOUGH DAY at the Carabinieri headquarters. She took a shower, put on some tight jeans and a long-sleeved, V-neck, white, button-up linen shirt. On her way to the living room, she stopped by the fridge and poured herself a glass of chilled white Lugana wine.

As she entered the living room, Jake wasn't sure, but he felt a positive energy emanating from Sara that suggested it could be a fun evening.

"Hi, *cara mia* (my dear)," began Jake from his place on the couch. "How was *your* day?"

"Good, but like you Americans say, it was nothing to write home about," replied Sara, chuckling. "And yours, *caro* (dear)?" she asked.

"It's been pretty good. Guess who called me today?"

"Let me guess, *guapo* (handsome)," she replied, tossing in one of about 100 words in Spanish she knew. "The company you are consulting for. They said they're giving you a huge bonus, and we can travel the world together now. Sound about right?"

Sara smiled and stepped toward Jake. She put her wine glass down on the coffee table. Jake stood up from the couch to meet Sara, and Sara gave him a sensuous kiss and a big hug, which he warmly reciprocated.

"No, not a bonus." Jake chuckled, smiling broadly. "But some day we will surely do that world trip, bonus or no bonus."

Sara nodded in affirmation.

"I know we will take that trip, *caro mio,*" she said.

"This call was not about a world trip, but it was pretty good," said Jake. "The call was from Hennadiy Kovalenko."

"Oh? What did Hennadiy have to say?" asked Sara, interjecting. "How is he? How is Mila?"

"He recently retired, Sara. And Mila is doing well. Hennadiy wants me—and you, if you'd like—to meet him for a weekend . . . in Tuscany. Said he wants to raise a glass or two of wine with me to celebrate his retirement."

Jake grinned and then added, "What do you think?"

Sara looked in Jake's eyes, smiling and pausing briefly before answering.

"Well, as much as I'd like to see him and Mila, I think I will sit this one out and stay here with Giacomo. But you, Jake . . . you *must* go. He's been such a good friend to you, and I would say vice versa. Yes, you must go!"

"I thought that's what you might say. But I just wanted to check with you to be sure."

"And I say we celebrate your trip to Tuscany *now* . . . with a shot of Ukrainian vodka."

Sara was not actually asking. Jake was hoping his thoughts about this being a fun evening were on the mark.

"Vodka? Hmmm, let me think about that, Sara," replied Jake, scratching his chin and feigning indecision.

"I'll be right back," responded Jake, his heart rate picking up.

Jake walked swiftly—but not so swiftly as to look like he was in a rush—to the kitchen. He grabbed a frosted Ukrainian vodka bottle and his two favorite shot glasses out of the freezer. They had "US Embassy Rome" stenciled on the sides. The shot glasses were a couple of keepsakes from his two-year stint in Italy as Assistant Army Attaché at the US Embassy.

When he came back with the liquid goods, Sara was lying on the couch, her long legs extended. Her blouse, strategically unbuttoned, was open to nearly her navel. Sara's *olivastra* skin shimmered against her beautiful white blouse and his favorite of her lacy underthings. She had, as Jake and Sara occasionally joked about, that *come-hither* look.

Jake walked over to where she reclined on the couch, set the glasses and bottle on the table, and gazed at his stunning wife, the mother of his child, as soul-deep satisfaction filled him. He did not sit, but leaned over her, running his fingers across her collarbones, up the graceful column of her neck, and then her sumptuous bottom lip.

"You," he whispered, "are what undoes me and puts me back together again. My *bellissima cara mia.*"

He growled the last syllables next to her mouth, one hand tracing the curves the open shirt revealed.

Sara arched into his hand, his mouth, and poured every ounce of her passion into a kiss.

Jake supported her neck with one hand as he pulled her to his chest, wrapping the other around her waist.

Sara ran her hands over Jake's well-muscled chest and arms, drowning in the wonder of him. Breaking the kiss, panting, "You wear too many clothes, husband."

Smiling, he played with her, rubbing his nose to hers, kissing each of her eyelids, teasing, "Do you think so?"

"Mmmhmm, I do, *caro mio.*" Sara's voice was husky with desire.

"What should we do about it . . ." a kiss to her chin, a brush of lips, a gentle bite on her neck, "do you think?"

Reaching to kiss him as he pulled back to see her flushed cheeks, read the hunger in her half-closed eyes, she grunted in frustration. "Perhaps, we could adjourn to the bedroom?"

He gently kissed her forehead, his eyes closing. "Yes, I think that sounds like a wonderful idea."

They stood together and began retreating to the bedroom, the vodka forgotten. Between their impassioned kisses as they walked down the hallway, articles of clothing began to litter the floor. There was her shirt. There was his. A bra wound up slung over a sconce in the hallway. A pair of slacks was forgotten, half inside-out, kicked into the bathroom doorway.

By the time they reached the bed, they were gasping and moaning.

When they joined, Sara cried out in ecstasy, again arching into Jake, who whispered private words to her in between the caresses of his roaming tongue.

When they shattered together, they drank the pleasure from each other's lips. Again, and again.

CHAPTER 60
RESPECT
March 2024

THE SEVENTY-SOMETHING ITALIAN MAN SMILED AT MARGARITA ROMANOVA. Margarita smiled back at him.

"You know, madame, I respect you," said the man who had worked in the Conti Vineyards, located ten miles north of Siena, since he was fifteen.

"Why *is* that?" asked Margarita.

"Because you are the first woman I've witnessed since the 1960s pick up a *pennato* (a curved knife for vine pruning) and stand out here among these vineyards for weeks, come rain or shine. And I must admit, I have trouble keeping up with you. You are a *donna* (lady) who deserves a lot of respect. Why do you do this when you could be shopping in Florence, or having an Aperol spritz at some nice café in Siena?"

"Quite simply, because it interests me, *signore* (sir)," she replied. "I want to learn everything I can about winemaking. I don't just want to read about it in a book. I want to do it, feel it, smell the aromas. Besides, it's a beautiful place to have an office, isn't it?"

And, Margarita thought, *it sure as heck beats standing at a cash register all day.*

The old man knew exactly what Margarita was speaking about. He was very grateful to the Conti family for giving him his first job. The job had been enough to sustain him and his wife after they married at age nineteen. Since then, for decades, the man's wife had worked in one of Siena's tourist shops. Meanwhile, the *signore* had risen from being a simple vineyard *contadino* (farmer) to the *responsabile del vigneto* (vineyard manager). He'd performed every manual job in the vineyards, from vine pruner and vat cleaner to tractor driver and wine bottle storage chief. And whenever he came across a worker who was taking shortcuts, he let them know without hesitation.

He and his wife lived in a modest, one-bedroom stone home with a fireplace that was no more than 1,200 square feet. But the hillside Tuscan vista that came with it was priceless, as were the magnificent sunsets on most evenings, with a glass of Conti wine at their sides. And the older couple got to drink some of the best wine in the world, not only for special occasions, but as table wine.

Conti wine normally sold for $24–30 per bottle in local Italian wine shops and $95–120 per bottle at restaurant tables in Florence, Rome, and Siena. The old couple was allowed three bottles per week at $6 each. The Conti family was indeed generous.

The Conti's US East Coast Italian American distributor in New Jersey was happy to pay $32 for a Conti red wine, reselling it for about $40-$42 in a US wine shop. The best Conti vintages would go for about $120 per bottle in a US restaurant, sometimes even $150 per bottle in Manhattan, Washington, D.C., or Miami.

The old man smiled at Margarita and responded.

"You are partially right, madame. This is the *most* beautiful place to have an office. And you, signorina, have changed my impression of Russian people, at least *some* Russian people."

"What impression did you have?" she asked.

"Please do not take offense, madame. But I've long thought Russians to be brutish, crude, and devoid of any sense of humanity. What they have done in Ukraine has been horrible and continues to be so. I was born five years after World War II ended. Once they'd consumed a bottle of wine or several shots of *grappa* to soothe their pain, I remember Italian Army veterans—even fifteen years after the war ended—talking about their horrific experiences and treatment as war prisoners of the Russians. And my father told me those were the *lucky* prisoners. *They* got to come back home to Italy. But m*any* did not come home, dying in captivity."

Margarita's thoughts turned to the Russian Army colonel who had brutally assaulted and almost raped her. She swallowed hard.

Margarita stopped her vine pruning and turned her head toward the man.

"I can see how you feel that way," she said.

A minute of awkward silence passed before the man also stopped pruning and looked back at Margarita.

"But *you, signorina,* you seem to be different. All the other workers here respect you. And to *that,* I tip my hat."

While they hadn't fully expressed it yet, Marco's parents were developing similar feelings for the Russian woman. She was not only beautiful but had also plunged into learning the Italian language. And she had character, too.

CHAPTER 61

"I'M IN!"
April 2024

HENNADIY KOVALENKO ENSURED HE WAS THE FIRST TO ARRIVE AT THE WINERY and the converted fifteenth-century Tuscan *castello.* One of the castle's beautifully appointed one-bedroom apartments would serve as his lodging for the next three days. Hennadiy wanted to arrive early enough so he and Jake could have a talk about the plight of his two cherished nephews, Sergiy and Gleb.

Thoughts of the two young boys' lives under their oppressive, violent, and alcoholic surrogate Russian father had made Hennadiy sick to his stomach . . . and soul. Ending the boys' nightmare was now the top priority in Hennadiy's life. Hennadiy still needed to tell Jake Fortina, however. It was Hennadiy's hope that Jake and maybe their friend Manny would help him, as he'd once helped them.

Gravel crunched beneath his feet as Hennadiy walked through the castle's massive wooden front doors and out to one of the eight, four-top round tables. The tables served as gathering spots for outdoor wine tasting events and small dinner parties for the castle's overnight guests, many of whom booked romantic stays at the castle. In every direction, green, vine-covered hills were silhouetted against a bright blue sky. Every view boasted soul-stirring vistas.

I wish I had taken more time to visit this beautiful country, thought Hennadiy, recalling his time as a military attaché at the Ukrainian embassy in Rome.

Kovalenko had little time to further reminisce as Jake walked out through the castle's doors. A big smile formed on his face as Hennadiy stood at his old friend's approach. Embracing, eyes misty, the now-retired colonels were surprised, each in their own way, at how their emotions stirred at the sight of each other.

Some three years earlier in Rome, Ukrainian Air Force Colonel Hennadiy Kovalenko had sheltered Jake. Concerned that he was under threatening surveillance and his life was in danger, Hennadiy and Mila had offered Jake a room in their apartment. The accepted offer lowered Jake's public profile and kept him out of sight of his enemies. Jake's enemies included Iranian government officials, Russian transnational criminals, and the Italian 'Ndrangheta mafia, among others.

But Hennadiy Kovalenko had done much more than open his home to the hunted and newly retired US Army lieutenant colonel. When Jake's beloved wife, Italian Carabinieri Lieutenant Colonel Sara Simonetti, disappeared, Hennadiy had risked his life to help Jake find her. And so had US Army Sergeant First Class Manuel "Manny" Alvarez.

"My dear friend, I've missed you," Jake began. "I'm sure you've been under a lot of pressure during this terribly unjust war. But I pray that the Ukrainian people will come out of this nightmare whole and free, with your country and nation intact."

"We will, Jake, we will. As long as we still have friends in the West, we will," said Hennadiy.

After asking about each other's wives, Hennadiy asked one more question before getting down to business.

"Is Manny Alvarez coming?" he asked.

"He sure is," replied Jake. "He should be here within the hour. He's driving up from Rome. He's still assigned to the embassy."

"Fantastic," replied Hennadiy. "I can't wait to see him."

"Me neither, my friend," replied Jake. "It's been too long for me, too."

Hennadiy sighed and decided it was time to put his cards on the table.

"Jake, I suspect you are aware of the thousands of Ukrainian kids that have been abducted by the Russians from our cities and towns," said Hennadiy.

"I am," said Jake. "It reminded me of those heinous kidnappings by other terrorists—you might remember Boko Haram—of teenage girls from their boarding school in Nigeria some ten years ago. It's utterly despicable, evil."

Jake shook his head, recalling the terror that beset Nigeria over multiple years that would result in over 1,700 teenage girls being abducted. They were taken after the April 2014 terrorism attack on the Chibok school in the Borno state of Nigeria.

Hennadiy nodded his head solemnly as he recalled the brutality the parents and family members had to deal with, not knowing the fate of their teenage daughters.

"It is such a pathetic irony that Vasily Puchta told his people he was going to topple the Ukrainian government to 'rid it of Nazis,' when the Russians in the Kremlin are behaving no better than the Nazis," said Jake. "But most of the world could give a rat's ass about Russia's criminal behavior. All that matters to many is that gas stays under three dollars a gallon."

Jake looked toward the rolling hills and vineyards. Then he looked back at Hennadiy. The two men had learned to allow each other a moment for reflection.

"Sorry for that diversion, my friend," said Jake.

"That's absolutely nothing to be sorry about, Jake," replied Hennadiy. He shook the dark thoughts away before continuing.

"Jake, those Russian abductions hit home with Mila and me," began Hennadiy.

"*How so?* As in *close* to home?" asked Jake, knowing Hennadiy and Mila didn't have children . . . or perhaps they did, but never spoke of them.

Hennadiy proceeded to tell Jake the saga of the boys' mother dying in a Russian artillery attack while in her home in Mariupol, and how the boys' father died a Ukrainian war hero during the initial days of the violent Russian onslaught. And he told Jake that the people he'd just talked about were his and Mila's closest family members. And that meant the two abducted boys were now their closest *surviving* family members. He also told Jake how he'd already tried all the official channels without success, as Russia wasn't even acknowledging the abductions.

"Next to Mila, I love them more than anybody on the planet," said Hennadiy. "And that's saying *a lot* because . . . and this is going to sound corny as hell . . . I love you and Sara, Jake . . . and that little crumb-snatcher of yours."

Grief tinged Hennadiy's wan smile.

"Likewise, my friend." Jake returned the smile. "We love you and Mila, too. Whatever you need, Hennadiy, *I'm in.* I'm *all in.*"

"Thank you, Jake," replied. "I deeply appreciate it."

Hennadiy looked out across the vineyards. But he saw only the boys. He knew this was going to be a big ask from Jake. He wanted Jake to fully understand the risks. After all, Jake was now a father, too, with a beautiful and vibrant young son.

"Listen, Jake . . . ," began Hennadiy.

"The answer is yes, Hennadiy," said Jake forcefully.

"I didn't even ask the question yet!" laughed Hennadiy, grateful.

"You don't have to, my friend," responded Jake. "I know how much those boys mean to you."

Now it was Hennadiy who forcefully interjected.

"And I know how much that young boy means to you, Jake."

"He does mean more than I can describe," replied Jake. "But like I said, I'm all in. So yes, I will do whatever it takes to bring the boys back, including going with you into Russia to bring them safely home."

Hennadiy's throat swelled as he fought back tears. Unable to speak, he simply nodded to his friend, and his friend nodded back.

CHAPTER 62

THE DINNER
April 2024

JAKE FORTINA AND HENNADIY KOVALENKO WATCHED THE CAR COMING INTO VIEW. After finally cresting the hill, it turned into the castle's parking lot. Jake smiled, nodding. He and Hennadiy recognized the Italian diplomatic license plates on the blue, five-year-old Volkswagen Jetta. US Army Sergeant First Class Manny Alvarez and his wife had purchased the VW because it was "economical and could be fixed pretty much anywhere in Europe."

"*There* he is," remarked Jake.

Manny Alvarez parked the car, got out, and briskly walked to the table where Jake and Hennadiy were seated. As he approached, Jake and Hennadiy stood. All three men had big smiles on their faces. The last time they had seen each other was more than two years earlier in Vicenza, Italy, where Jake and Sara's son Giacomo was baptized in the same church where Jake and Sara were married.

Jake Fortina and Manny Alvarez shared a long history of service in the army and had known each other for almost fifteen years. Their relationship began when then-Captain Jake Fortina commanded a US Army Special Forces (aka, "Green Berets") Operational Detachment, Alpha ("A-Team") in Afghanistan. Then-Sergeant Alvarez served as one of the A-Teams' two assigned combat medics. Their crucible of combat against a

Taliban force, which was roughly six times the size of their team, had bonded the two warriors.

Years later, Lieutenant Colonel Fortina presided over Alvarez's promotion to Sergeant First Class. Not long after that, the two men teamed up to serve together at the US Embassy in Rome.

Alvarez had also teamed up with Kovalenko to support Fortina's search for Fortina's wife, Italian Carabinieri Lieutenant Colonel Sara Simonetti, making their bonds lifelong if not eternal.

"*Now* we can get this party started!" said Jake as Manny approached.

Jake's enthusiastic and lighthearted comment was soon followed by a serious tone as Hennadiy Kovalenko explained what he needed: *help* in the rescue of his two nephews from Russia.

***

Marco Conti looked around the annex to the villa. He felt a sense of pride. He had recommended the annex's construction to his father some twelve years earlier. The addition of the modern, one-story, 1,800-square-foot stone building with its big floor-to-ceiling tinted windows, magnificent views, modern kitchen, and top-shelf wine cellar had been excellent for hosting parties, wine tastings, and wedding receptions.

Marco reserved the building for the entire evening. The reservation was limited to himself and four guests: Marco's fiancée, Margarita Romanova; Hennadiy Kovalenko; Manny Alvarez; and Jake Fortina. Their feast would include plates of wild boar and polenta with porcini mushrooms, or Tuscan risotto with wild mushrooms, grilled bell peppers, and tiramisu or fresh fruit. Every morsel would be paired with the finest Conti wines, some dating back to the very best twenty-first-century Tuscan vintage years, including 2013 and 2015.

Marco began the meal with a Prosecco-fueled toast welcoming Alvarez, Kovalenko, and Fortina to the Conti Vineyards, and "to a just and swift end to the war in Ukraine."

Since she'd been living in Italy for six months, Margarita had come to know the full truth about the brazen and violent Russian military attacks on Ukraine, its cities, and Ukrainian civilian men, women, and children. She now fully understood that the Russian attacks to "topple the Nazi regime in Ukraine" and to "save the Ukrainian people from the Nazis" in 2022 were a pure sham intended to fuel the ego and maniacal political goals of the man in charge at the Kremlin.

Having served in the Russian Army as a medic, Margarita felt a confluence of naivete, guilt, and gratitude. Naivete for her initial willingness to lap up Kremlin propaganda; guilt for being part of the Russian organization that abducted children from Ukraine's streets, in many cases after their parents died at the hands of the Russian armed forces; and gratitude for the man she was now in love with, and where she now found herself.

Jake and Manny did not know the degree to which this very cordial dinner would be a business meeting. Its premise was clear but complicated, and its topic was fraught with danger: how to physically rescue the two boys from their adoptive home in Russia and get them safely back into Ukraine.

After the toast, it was Hennadiy Kovalenko who spoke first.

"Mr. Marco Conti, *mille grazie,* sir, for contacting me several months ago, for agreeing to meet with me, for your exceptional generosity, for sharing this splendid place, and for allowing me to invite two of my dearest friends here this weekend."

"The pleasure is all mine," responded Marco.

"And Margarita, I can't thank you enough for watching over my two dear nephews, Sergiy and Gleb, and perhaps just as importantly, for reaching out to me through Marco. Your initiatives took courage, and I hope and pray that they will be life-changing for the boys."

"Thank you, Hennadiy," replied Margarita, "but I only wish I could have done more. And I stand by to help."

"And to my two American buddies," continued Hennadiy, "thanks from the depths of my soul for coming here to join me."

Both Americans nodded in acknowledgment.

"It's the least I could do," responded Jake.

"As long as we don't get stopped on the *autostrada* (Italian highway) by an Italian customs official—holding a machine gun—I'm good with it," replied Manny with a big smile, in reference to their last adventure in Calabria.

Everybody laughed.

"All I can promise you is that the customs official won't be Italian," replied Hennadiy, "Russian, maybe. But definitely *not* Italian."

Hennadiy described the incident of him and Manny getting stopped near Naples, en route to Calabria, and the entire table erupted again in laughter.

Then the conversation refocused on how to get the boys out of Russia and back to Ukraine. But it also became a lively exchange between all five dinner attendees. A host of options for getting in and out of Russia were considered, as were the risks. Jake and Hennadiy had several questions for Margarita, including what the layout of the boys' home was like, what their routines were, and what the routines of their adoptive parents were.

Everyone at the dinner wanted the boys' nightmare to end.

CHAPTER 63
OPTIONS
April 2024

JAKE FORTINA, MANNY ALVAREZ, AND HENNADIY KOVALENKO WERE LASER FOCUSED on a single mission: how to get Sergiy and Gleb—and themselves—safely out of Russia. But first, the men had to figure out how to get into Russia, and what to do once they got there.

At a quick espresso break after the meal and before the serious analysis got started, Jake pulled Manny aside. Jake told Manny what he did not want to hear. But Manny knew Jake and Hennadiy Kovalenko, who sided with Jake, were right.

"Manny, there is no way on God's green earth you can go on this mission. You still have four months of active duty left. If you get captured inside of Russia, it will be a completely different deal than if you were captured during our Calabria mission," said Jake.

"After you helped Sara and me in Calabria, the Italian government gave you a medal, which you richly merited. The best you can hope for if the Russian government snatches you inside their borders is the frozen hell of a gulag inside the Arctic Circle. And that's probably after they torture you, assuming they don't kill you. Besides," added Jake, "if something were to happen to you, your bride would never forgive me, nor would mine, nor would I forgive myself!"

"And what about you, Jake?" asked Manny. "You know you're risking capture, too, right . . . sir?"

"Yeah, I do, Manny. But that's not gonna happen. And *if* it were to—and again, it won't—I'm retired. Hell, there's probably a senator or two in DC who probably thinks I *deserve* capture by the Russians. You, on the other hand, by still being active duty military, would cause a major diplomatic incident. Not to mention that Hennadiy and I would feel compelled to come bail your ass out."

Jake smiled broadly, and so did Manny.

Manny Alvarez didn't like it, but he knew his former boss and now friend was right. It was decided, at least for now, that Jake and Hennadiy would be the two going into Russia to get the boys.

Hennadiy shared with the group that much like one-third of his fellow Ukrainians, he spoke "excellent Russian." That would help the pair tremendously.

***

Marco Conti shook his head. It wasn't a negative headshake, but rather, one that conveyed a certain, "I can't believe how analytical and thorough these military guys are" attitude.

"These guys"—Jake, Hennadiy, and Manny—were applying their own recollections of the military planning process (with a variation also known as the Military Decision-Making Process) as they openly discussed how to get into Russia and then *how to get the boys safely out.*

For now, they were focusing on the first three parts of the rather simplified planning process, much of it written on napkins and eventually some extra paper they retrieved from the two cooks cleaning up the kitchen. 1. Analyze the *mission,* including consideration of the operational environment. 2. Develop courses of action for achieving the mission, and 3. Analyze those courses of action by comparing different options and (eventually) selecting the best one. Step 4 would include the development of the final plan.

A range of options for entering Russia were discussed. Should they try to get false passports and go through somewhere like Belarus first, before crossing the border into Russia? When going from Belarus into Russia, or from any other bordering state, should they cross "conventionally" (i.e., going through a passport control station, albeit with false passports, at the border) or try to infiltrate into Russia at night, over a remote, difficult to guard border area, such as with Finland or Mongolia or Kazakhstan, or anywhere else along Russia's roughly 13,000 miles of borders and eleven time zones?

Once they got into Russia, how would they move to Konstantinovsk, where the boys were located? Should they fly into Moscow and be met by their own diplomatic personnel at the airport? That might work for Jake, but not at all for Hennadiy. As of February 24, 2022, Ukraine no longer had diplomatic relations with Russia. Or perhaps they would stow away— between merchandise, to limit x-ray effectiveness—on a commercial truck entering Russia from Ukraine, or again, any other neighboring state?

Every option was fraught with some degree of risk, including death. The challenge was to pick the one with the best chance of success and least risk to the safety and well-being of the boys, as well as Jake and Hennadiy.

CHAPTER 64
"ARE YOU SURE?"
April 2024

JAKE FORTINA AND HENNADIY KOVALENKO WERE THE LAST TO LEAVE THE DINNER. They sat beside each other at the round table for six, each drinking what was supposed to be *"only one shot of limoncello,"* until it wasn't.

Jake, with a somewhat serious air, looked at his friend.

"Are you sure, Hennadiy? Are you really *sure?* Do you feel it in your soul?"

"Sure about what?" asked Hennadiy, half-expecting he knew what Jake would say.

"Are you sure about this mission, my friend? You know that if the Russians get hold of you inside their borders, they will concoct every pro-Russia story imaginable and squeeze—and likely torture—every drop of knowledge and anti-Ukraine propaganda out of you that they can. And if you are lucky, after spending your retirement years in a frosty, God-forsaken Russian gulag, they will trade you for ten or twenty or a hundred Russian prisoners held by Ukraine. That's if they don't first torture you until your last breath."

"To me, it's one hundred percent worth the risk to get those boys out," replied Hennadiy. "Look, Jake, they are *my* sons now. Mila and I also happen to be their Godparents. They are the children Mila and I never had, and we love them both dearly. As you well know, Jake, some things are worth dying for, and I can't—I won't—go to my grave without rescuing them from that evil son-of-a-bitch . . . or die trying. These boys have their entire lives ahead of them. That is, if that sick Russian bastard doesn't destroy those precious boys first, mentally, emotionally, or physically. To your question, yes, I feel deep in my soul that this is something I cannot put off. I feel guilty for waiting too long as it is. My hands have been so tied by my position before now. Of course, we must be very thorough in planning for this, but I have no doubt I want to go through with it."

All Jake needed to do was think of his young son, Giacomo.

"I get it, Hennadiy. I get it," said Jake.

"But what about *you,* Jake? Are you *sure?* You have as much to lose as I do. Not only would the Kremlin love to hoist your head on a pike, but the Wolf, Stepanov, and many of their private army henchmen, some of whom are likely still operating in Russia, would love to do the same thing."

Hennadiy chuckled and then continued.

"You and I have made a hell of a lot of enemies, Jake. Seems we both need to go back to charm school," said Kovalenko, chuckling.

"I'm right there with you, Hennadiy. I can never thank you— nor *repay* you—enough for helping me when Sara got in trouble."

"Wait a minute. *Can never repay me?* Trust me, I never expected that you should nor would, my friend. *Never.* But let's just say if—no, *when*—we pull this off, we'll call it even. And then let's take an amazing vacation with our ladies and our three boys. Maybe to Disneyland. What do ya' say?"

"I'm in, my brother. I'm all in," replied Jake. "Disney Paris or Disney Florida?"

CHAPTER 65
IT'S DECIDED
April 2024

THE SUMPTUOUS BREAKFAST LASTED LONGER THAN USUAL FOR JAKE.

Normally, Jake started his day with an espresso and about fifteen minutes or so of reading *Jesus Calling* and the Scriptures. In an effort not to overeat, Jake normally wouldn't touch a morsel of food until mid-morning. But *this* breakfast, which had gone on for almost ninety minutes, had been more than a morning meal and social gathering with Hennadiy and Manny. It was part business meeting and part military planning and troubleshooting session.

"Ok, it's decided, then," said Jake as he put down his espresso cup and looked at his Ukrainian friend for affirmation.

"Yes, it is," replied Hennadiy. "The best option is to go in covertly, right under their noses, in a legal border crossing. All the other options require far too much logistical support and have too many moving parts, presenting too many variables that could go wrong and cause the mission to fail."

"Well, I do prefer simplicity," replied Jake. "Now, the question is, *amico mio,* how do we get the right *paperwork,* and *who* do we go in as?"

US Army Sergeant First Class Manny Alvarez was ready to chime in. Barely able to sleep, he'd been ruminating on an idea all night. In the process, he'd also developed a few corollary options for how best to accomplish the mission. He'd learned a lot from his former Special Forces A-Team Commander, then-Captain Jake Fortina, as well as his senior A-Team sergeants. Those lessons would stay with him for a lifetime.

"Gentlemen, did I understand correctly that Mr. Marco Conti has legitimate wine sales interests in Russia, and makes a couple of trips into Russia each year?" asked Manny.

"That's correct," replied Hennadiy.

"And when he described last night how he met Margarita, didn't he say that city—what was it called, Rostov—was not that far from the boys?"

"He did," said Hennadiy. "It's located about two hours by car from Konstantinovsk."

"Well, I have an idea. OK, *some* ideas," said Manny Alvarez. "But I need to do a little more homework."

CHAPTER 66
SOME DAY, IT WILL STOP
April 2024

SERGIY TUCKED HIS LITTLE BROTHER INTO BED and stroked his brother's hair.

"Someday, it will stop, Gleb," said Sergiy. "Someday, it will *all stop.* And we'll be back on the beach, on the Sea of Azov, having fun with Papa. And you'll be playing with that big green crocodile again."

Sergiy's heart warmed as Gleb smiled.

"Promise?" asked Gleb.

"I promise," replied Sergiy, holding up the two fingers of his right hand to show Gleb that they weren't crossed.

"How much longer do you think it will be before we see Papa again?" asked Gleb.

"I don't know exactly, but I don't think it will take a long time," replied Sergiy. "We will both be with him again, someday."

Gleb wholeheartedly believed his brother. Sergiy was one of the few human beings on the planet whom Gleb still believed in and looked up to. Sergiy and a kind, twenty-something schoolteacher. He believed in her, too. And he still believed in Margarita, although it had been a long time since he'd seen her. And then there was Spider-Man. Gleb believed in Spider-Man.

Sergiy crawled into his bed, faced the wall away from Gleb, and repeated the words his mother told him to say before she took her last breath. He said them loud enough to be audible, but

"

barely above a whisper. This time, as he had for the past several months, his prayer included Gleb.

"Help us, Jesus."

The prayer always calmed Sergiy because he felt like his mother was there with him in those private moments with Jesus, so he didn't want Gleb to hear it. But Gleb could hear him.

Within a few weeks before his thirteenth birthday, it was all Sergiy could do to dream about when and how he and eight-year-old Gleb would escape the house of random and unpredictable pain and ever-present mistrust. Sergiy had dreamt up several plans, some of which involved retaliation against the old man, and all of which involved Sergiy and Gleb going home to Ukraine.

Maybe, he sometimes thought, *we will go back to Ukraine with Margarita, if she ever comes back.*

The brutal old man was growing weaker by the month as the alcoholism slowly ravaged him. But he still periodically erupted with physical attacks on the boys while his distraught wife occasionally, but less frequently these days, did her best to limit the damage.

Sergiy would often take the brunt of the old man's blows. The increasingly athletic Sergiy thought the day wasn't far off when he'd be able to handle the old man himself.

CHAPTER 67
WHAT IF?
April 2024

WHAT IF? IT WAS A SIMPLE BUT POWERFUL QUESTION. Depending on how it was answered, it could go a long way in making the child rescue mission a success. And Manny Alvarez knew that rather than dumping the question into the mental "impossible" or "never-to-be considered again" bins, he had to ask it.

It was midday with a bright ball of spring sunshine overhead as the three men walked through the glorious Conti Vineyards. Lunch would be at 1 P.M., again with Margarita and Marco.

"What if, gentlemen," Manny said to the two retired military officers, "what if we get you into Russia as salesmen for the Conti Vineyards?"

Jake Fortina suddenly had a huge grin on his face.

My brilliant sergeant, my brilliant frickin' sergeant, he thought.

Jake and Hennadiy turned their heads to look at each other, but Jake let Hennadiy do the responding.

"Whoa, that sounds like a stretch, Manny," responded Hennadiy.

Hennadiy thought that Manny's idea had merit, but it would require—at the very minimum—the full support of Marco Conti, if not Marco's father, too.

"The whole dang damn mission is a stretch," replied Jake. "But we *will* get this done, Hennadiy."

"You're right, it is a stretch," replied Hennadiy. "And I knew that from the day I committed to it. But what about identity papers, like passports? Visas? Driver's licenses? How do we handle the ID and Russia entry and exit requirements?"

"*Which* driver's licenses? You were a military attaché here a few years back, Hennadiy. Don't you still have your Italian driver's license?" asked Jake.

Hennadiy, half-encouraged and half-embarrassed for not thinking about it, responded.

"Actually, I *do* still have it," he answered, with a big smile on his face.

He pulled out his wallet, and there it was.

"And it's still good for fifteen more months!" said Hennadiy, chuckling.

"And of course, I still live and drive in this country, so I have mine, too," replied Jake. "Hell, I even pay Italian taxes now with this consulting gig I have. I even have the *codice fiscale* ("fiscal code," a special Italian code which enables people, including non-Italian citizens, to bank, conduct financial transactions, and pay taxes in Italy). Of course, my driver's license does have my *actual* name on it," said Jake, "so I'm not sure that will work."

"That will depend," replied Manny. "If you use it for everything, that's probably not the best use of it. But it does have an Italian last name on it. I'm not telling you anything you don't already know, sir, but of course, if you overexpose it, it will introduce too much risk in tracking you. Plus, who knows how many people on this planet would like to rub you out."

Jake nodded his head.

"OK, in a pinch," added Jake, "in the middle of nowhere, having a spare Italian driver's license might help. Many countries accept US driver's licenses, although I don't know that Russia does. That said, not getting caught with a license at all would be the secure thing to do. What do you think, Hennadiy?"

"You're right," said Hennadiy. "Your Italian last name might work, but maybe only *once,* at best. But as for me, I prefer a 'G' in front of my first name. Hennadiy with an 'H' is Ukrainian, but 'Gennadiy' is Russian. The last name 'Kovalenko' is prevalent in Russia, so that's no problem. Us Ukrainians used to inter-marry Russians and vice versa, much less so now since that asshole took over Russia. But when we're knockin' around inside Russia, I need to be a Gennadiy."

"And what about the visa thing?" asked Jake.

"You'll be happy to know—and I was surprised to learn of it—that the Russians allow a sixteen-day *electronic* visa for Italian citizens," answered Manny. "For an American to get a visa, however, it's a lot more onerous, and there is no electronic option for Americans. But, if the Russians issue an American a visa, it's usually good for at least ninety days."

"Well," responded Jake, "having been a military attaché at two US embassies in Europe, I have no doubt that my name—and Hennadiy's name, because he was a military attaché, too—has populated every intelligence database the Russians have. So, in the end, we're going to have to go in with different, or at least modified, names. And as to the sixteen-day visa, that will be enough time to get the boys out. If it's not, then we've become slow and sloppy in our advanced ages!" chuckled Jake, thinking of when he'd first heard "slow and sloppy" from a former US

Army Ranger instructor who was screaming at Jake as he navigated the "Darby Queen," a Ranger training obstacle course at then-Fort Benning, Georgia.

Jake shuddered and smiled at the thought of breaking the course's thin layer of ice as he'd entered the water. Tiny ice crystals clung to him as his elbow and knee joints numbed instantaneously, before he began crawling through the course's water-filled trenches on a sub-freezing January morning.

At hearing "advanced ages," Manny Alvarez decided not to let the comment pass.

"Hey! Speak for yourselves on that advanced age thing!"

All three aging warriors laughed raucously.

CHAPTER 68
THE PITCH
April 2024

THE TUSCAN SUN WAS HIGH IN THE PARTLY CLOUDY, BRILLIANT BLUE SKY.

Marco Conti made a command decision: "For lunch today, we will dine outside!"

"*Si, signore,*" responded the head chef. "It's a perfect day for it."

With the outdoor tables suited for four guests, the chef directed two *camerière* (waiters) to go inside the villa annex and set up one of the tables for six. With the flair of a Spanish matador, one of the two waiters draped a white linen tablecloth over the table. He walked around the back of the charming, massive villa and picked some nearby spring flowers, returning to place them in his favorite vase in the center of the table.

As only four of the castle's eight rooms were occupied, the chef knew his team's sole focus was on the five guests: one Russian lady, two American men, one Ukrainian man, and Signor Conti, the son of the man who owned it all. And while he wanted to make his colorful guests feel welcome and well-cared for, the chef knew his primary audience was Marco Conti.

"We are going to shine today like that bright, beautiful sun," the chef told his four-person team.

***

The lunch was glorious. They dined on delicious plates of seafood caught in the nearby Tyrrhenian Sea—only sixty-five miles away as the crow flies. The local *Vernàccia* white wine, with its fruity, floral aromas, was a good match for the fresh fish hauled in before dawn by local Italian fishermen.

Jake Fortina asked Marco Conti to talk about the Conti family winery's history. Conti did not disappoint, regaling everybody with Tuscany's wine history, too.

"Our winery is one of the younger ones in Tuscany," said Marco. "Our history only dates back roughly 250 years, so about the time the United States became a country. The *Ricasoli* wine estate, however, at Brolio Castle, dates to 1141. It's the oldest winery in Tuscany. We are, nonetheless, very proud of what we have accomplished on this magnificent terrain. It has excellent drainage and exposure to the sun."

With a fresh fruit dessert complete, Marco Conti became serious.

"So, please, Hennadiy, tell me how you think you'll be able to bring the two boys back home to Ukraine," said Marco.

Hennadiy took the opportunity to pitch the highlights of the plan he, Jake, and Manny had been discussing. Hennadiy was sure to include what Margarita had told the trio about the boys' home, its surrounding area, their daily habits, and whatever else she'd gleaned from the boys during her visit to the ice cream shop with the boys.

Marco Conti made deliberate eye contact with Hennadiy, then Jake, and, finally, with Manny, nodding his head several times.

"OK. It sounds like you've seriously thought this through. I would expect nothing less from professional military men. Now, tell me what you *need*. How can I help?" said Marco.

Hennadiy, knowing that a door of opportunity had just been swung wide open, looked at Jake for permission to answer the question. Jake looked at Marco, then at Manny, and then back at Marco.

"Thank you for your very kind and generous offer, *signore,*" replied Jake. "Let's let the man who hatched the idea tell you what we need. Manny, please go ahead."

"What Hennadiy and Jake need more than anything else, *signore,* is to go into Russia with a highly legitimate cover," said Manny.

"Such as?" asked Marco.

"Such as employees of the Conti Vineyards."

Marco's eyes lit up, grinning broadly, "Go on," he said.

"It would be optimal if both men could go into Russia with you, perhaps on one of your next trips," said Manny. "We know this is going to take some time to set up, perhaps as long as six months or so. Our biggest challenge will be getting the right identification papers for both men. We know it's a huge ask, and maybe next to impossible, but if Jake and Hennadiy could somehow procure Italian identity documents, like passports, that would also give them a shot at getting electronic approvals for sixteen-day Russian visas."

Marco nodded his head quickly. His grin turned into a big smile.

"We also know that it could be risky for you and for the Conti Vineyards business in Russia," added Jake.

"Wow, you guys don't mess around, do you? And here I thought you were just sitting out here and walking through our vineyards enjoying a bit of vacation time."

Everybody around the table laughed.

Margarita Romanova's heart swelled at the surreal moment. She was deeply grateful that four caring adults were mapping out a way for the two boys to get rescued from the wholly undeserved darkness in their lives.

"Well, I can tell you this: the Conti family never lets the word 'impossible' stand in its way. What I have not yet told you is that my father, Vittorio Conti, has asked to help in any way he can. Did you know that during the many centuries of our Venetian Republic, which lasted 1,100 years, from 697 to 1797, child abuse, especially child molestation, was punishable by death?"

The heinous acts and, just as importantly, the progressive and profound nature of that kind of law, which said much about the Venetian people, silenced the table.

"So, yes. I will speak with my father."

Trying to lighten the mood, Marco smiled and added, "He has more connections than the pope. And in this country, that is saying something."

"*Mille grazie,*" replied Hennadiy, gratefully.

Jake, Manny, and even Margarita added their own heartfelt versions of "thank you."

CHAPTER 69
BLAKE CONNERS?
April 2024

MANNY ALVAREZ HESITATED. NEVER AFRAID OF TAKING A RISK, this time he hesitated.

What the hell am I afraid of? he asked himself. *I'm either gonna hit the jackpot or I'm gonna waste a few minutes on a phone call. The guy did his time, and he's out now. He was never a threat to me or Jake.*

"The guy" Manny was thinking about was Blake Conners, the retired US Army Special Forces sergeant first class and former member of Russian oligarch Anatoly Volkov's (aka, the Wolf) private army. Conners was a key member of the Wolf's operational leadership team. But when the Wolf threatened massive death and destruction in Italy and Europe writ large, Conners bailed out and checked into the US embassy in Rome.

There, he first encountered Manny Alvarez and his boss, then-Lieutenant Colonel Jake Fortina. The treatment Conners received from both US Army professionals was far better than he'd expected. Conners was thankful and never forgot it. Conners later spent time in the Fort Bragg brig before finally being released without any long-term judicial consequences or jail time.

Manny rechecked his watch. With Italy's time zone being six hours ahead of the East Coast, that puts the time at 5:30 P.M. on the US's eastern seaboard. He looked out the window at the vineyards.

Aw, to hell with it, Manny thought to himself. *Here goes.*

He pressed the green call button on his phone.

Sitting in his North Carolina home's living room, Blake Conners saw the cell phone ringing on the coffee table in front of him. The "39" country code told the former US Army noncommissioned officer that the call originated from Italy, or at least that it was an Italy-registered phone number. Not knowing if the call was from friend or foe—as he'd left both in Italy but mainly the latter—he decided to let it ring through and go to voicemail.

Manny decided to leave a message:

"Blake, it's Manny Alvarez. Hope the hell you're doing well. I could use your help. Please call me when you get a minute. *De oppresso liber* (pronounced day-op-presso-leeber)."

Manny Alvarez's sign-off was the Latin motto—"To Free the Oppressed"—for the US Army Special Forces. It instantly put a smile on Blake Conners' face. It took him back to his *good years* of US Army service, before he was rejected for service in the US Army's elite of the elite "Task Force."

Blake Conners immediately called Manny Alvarez back.

CHAPTER 70
FAMILY MEETING
April 2024

MARCO CONTI ENTERED HIS PARENTS' IDYLLICALLY SITUATED villa. Beautifully arranged but not ostentatious, it was a five-bedroom, 3,200-square-foot, stone and marble home. Heading to the spacious living room with its large stone fireplace and big bay window overlooking the vineyards, Marco passed by a few family photos. He felt proud of his parents, especially his father.

As he always did for big family talks—unless the daily outside temperatures were over seventy-five degrees Fahrenheit—the seventy-something paternal icon of the Conti family would have their fireplace going and a bottle of his better vintage, fifteen- to twenty-year-old Sangiovese red wine at the ready. For family meetings like these, which happened once or twice per year—this one requested by Marco—the elder Conti often preferred an older wine vintage. Locally produced cheeses, wild boar salami, and fresh sourdough bread were always available to accompany the red vino.

Marco knew his father had several influential Italian government connections. The senior Conti earned them over decades of an almost cosmic combination of treating his workers well, participating in local Siena civic activities and charities, producing world-class wine, paying his taxes, and staying true to his faith, his family, and his word.

In Siena, Florence, Rome, and beyond, Vittorio Conti had become more than a respected *signore:* for the past twenty years or so he'd been referred to as *dottore* (doctor), a high honorific title given to a man who may or may not have a doctorate degree and who may or may not be a medical doctor.

Il Dottore possessed no formal education beyond his secondary education years. But he had a half-dozen honorary academic degrees and was a constant learner. *Dottore*—honorary degrees or not—was an earned, honorific title that conveyed a single word above all: *respect.* From the vineyard workers to the halls of Italy's parliament in Rome, Vittorio Conti was *Il Dottore.*

For this family meeting, Marco's younger sister would not be present as she was living in Milan, doing her best to make her way in the international fashion industry.

When Marco asked his father about supporting the two Americans' and the Ukrainian's plan—with a grateful and heartfelt endorsement from Margarita—Marco believed that what his father said would ring through eternity.

"Marco, listen," said Vittorio Conti. "And look around you. We have been blessed beyond our family's wildest dreams. We have a healthy and beautiful family. We grow some of the best vines and grapes, and drink some of the world's best wine, a drink that Jesus miraculously made from water in his first recorded miracle. Our winery even survived Nazi occupation. We do not want for *anything* material in this world. What matters most, my son, is our faith in God, our family, and how we treat others. Almighty God has commanded that these be the most important values to us as we make our way in this earthly world."

Vittorio looked into the fireplace and then at his wife of forty-three years, Claudia. He glanced back at his son. Marco knew his father well enough to know that there was a time to respond and a time to listen, and he felt this was still the time for listening.

"I—we, your mother and me—want to do whatever we can to help those boys get out of their nightmare. No child deserves that. And if it means I prevail upon some high-placed friends to bend the bureaucratic rules a bit, so be it."

"But Papa, aren't you at all worried about our Conti wine business crashing down in Russia, if we are caught or connected to helping them?" asked Marco, testing his father's resolve.

"Not at all, my son. What matters most is getting those boys out of the country and to a much safer and more nurturing place. Besides, you know as well as I do that the Russian economy is crashing and that anything except the cheapest rot-gut vodka is becoming too expensive for the Russians. But more importantly, I'm growing sick of doing business with a country that is run by that evil reincarnation of the worst leaders in Russia's history. Tens of thousands of Russian young men and women—not to mention Ukrainians and their families—have died because of that *stronzo* (piece of fecal matter)."

"Vittorio!" replied Claudia, in a mild retribution to her husband and best friend over his in-the-gutter choice of words.

Marco was also surprised. He'd rarely heard his father use such accusatory, biting, and salty language.

Vittorio looked at Claudia in respectful acknowledgment.

"Sorry, *cara mia.*"

Turning back to Marco, Vittorio continued.

"But what I am most worried about is you, *caro mio* (the masculine for "my dear," common in Italian). "You are our only son. Your sister said she wants nothing to do with the wine business. While disappointed by that, I respect her and her right to make her own way in life. And who knows, maybe someday she will change her mind and help you with our family business, Marco. Your mother and I do pray, however, that this will all be yours someday."

There were a few hints and references over the preceding years about Marco taking over the Conti Vineyards and wine business. But Marco had never heard words this strident spoken by his father about Marco's future in the family wine business.

"*Grazie Papa, e grazie Mama,*" replied Marco, looking at his father, and then his mother.

"Marco, we *do* want to help those boys, but please promise me, my dear, that you will do nothing risky in Russia," his mother implored.

Marco slowly nodded his head.

"I promise, Mama," replied Marco. "I promise."

"Marco, I will be more specific than your mother: once you get those two men safely inside the country, I want you to get back out of Russia and come home as soon as you can. I fully support their mission, but I expect them to accomplish it on our terms, not theirs. You, and our business, will be taking huge risks, and we must mitigate those risks where possible and still help get the job done. *Capisci* (Understand)?"

"Yes, sir. I understand."

Marco Conti did not like being hemmed in, but he also understood where his parents—and business partners—were coming from.

***

Marco Conti walked out of his parents' house and onto their adjacent driveway. He inhaled slowly, exhaling faster. His parents' view of the vineyards, with several Sill Italian Cypress trees lining the driveway all the way to the main road below, never failed to stir his soul.

He sent a group chat (labeled "The Four Amici") text message to the other three men.

"*Cari amici* (Dear Friends), I would be a terrible host if I didn't take you to Siena for a coffee. I will pick you up in one hour. *Ci vediamo* (lit., We'll see each other)."

CHAPTER 71
THE VINIFICATION PROCESS
April 2024

MARCO POINTED HIGH INTO THE CATHEDRAL'S DOME. His three guests listened intently. Marco whispered just loud enough for his new friends to hear, but not so loud as to disturb the other three dozen tourists or so visiting the world-famous Tuscan and Italian landmark. In the form of a Latin cross, *Il Duomo di Siena* (Siena Cathedral) was conceived and created between 1215 and 1263.

"You see the gold gilded lantern up inside the cupola?" asked Marco.

All three men nodded.

"Bernini completed and added it in the 1600s. It is meant to depict sunlight flowing into the cathedral. Ever heard of Bernini?"

Manny and Hennadiy both thought they had heard vague references to Bernini, but they had no idea that he was perhaps the best—and certainly one of the best—Italian artists to have lived.

Jake, on the other hand, was like a kid in grade school who knew the answer and could not wait to tell his teacher. He smiled broadly as he nodded his head enthusiastically, recalling the magnificent Bernini fountain unveiled in Rome on June 12, 1651. The fountain depicted four rivers that flowed on as many continents: the Danube, the Ganges, the Nile, and the Plate.

If Michelangelo is considered the dominant Italian artist (painter and sculptor) of the sixteenth century, then Bernini succeeded Michelangelo atop the pantheon of the greatest Italian artists of the seventeenth century.

Noticing the enthusiasm on Jake's face, Marco had to ask.

"Jake, you got an answer?" asked Marco.

"Ya, I have heard of Bernini. He was an Italian sculptor who also designed the Four Rivers fountain in *Piazza Navona,* in Rome. That is my favorite fountain on the planet, and it sits in my favorite piazza (plaza) not only in Rome, but in Italy."

Marco was impressed by the American's knowledge of the iconic Italian sculptor. He smiled broadly and nodded his head before turning and leading the trio to the Piccolomini Altarpiece, located in the left nave as one faces the front of the Cathedral.

"This nave and altar were made between 1481 and 1485 from solid Carrara marble," said Marco. "But those four niche sculptures are what make the nave—and are among the things that make this cathedral—exceptional. Michelangelo sculpted the statues between 1501 and 1504."

Marco nodded toward the sides of the altar's large arched entryway.

"OK, I've heard of *him,*" said Manny, grinning. "I've heard of Michelangelo."

Jake and Hennadiy smiled.

"The sculptures set in the four niches are of Saints Peter and Paul, and Pope Gregory and Pope Pius. Back then, apparently, you had to please the Popes to land the big art contracts. A little or a lot, haha—how do you say it in English—currying of favor might get you the biggest contract."

"Some things never change," quipped Manny.

The trio chuckled right along with Marco.

"Like the Sistine Chapel?" asked Jake lightheartedly, referring to Michelangelo's otherworldly masterpiece covering the Vatican chapel's entire ceiling. "That was a big art deal, wasn't it?"

"No doubt it was," replied Marco. "That 'deal' stands at the pinnacle of the big art contracts, haha. But that ceiling is magnificent, don't you think?" asked Marco. "Can you imagine a guy lying on a scaffold with about a half meter (about 20 inches) perspective, painting an entire, 500-meter-square (5,381-square-foot) ceiling that looks perfectly proportional from the floor, some 20 meters (66 feet) below?"

"It's beyond magnificent," replied Jake. "I'm not sure there are words to describe it."

"*Sono d'accordo* (I agree)," responded Marco. "Now, let's go get some coffee."

***

It was about a five-minute walk, Marco leading the way, to the *Caffe Fiorella* (Flower; the caffe is also referred to as the *Torrefazione* (roasting) *Fiorella*).

"Wait here," said Marco before walking into the cafe's bar area.

Marco went in to confirm his group of four could take one of the two outside tables. He made eye contact with the lady behind the bar.

"*Si,* Marco, the one on the left is for you," said the lady. "By the way, how is your family? I haven't seen you in a while."

The stunning Sienna-born lady, in her mid-thirties with a natural mix of thick blonde and brown hair flowing down to her shoulders, piercing green eyes, and *olivastra* skin, knew Marco Conti's story. At least the part of his story that mattered to her. She knew Conti had broken off a relationship with a woman who thought a trip to the altar with Marco was assured. The Conti family turned against her after Marco and his family learned that she referred to the Conti family's wealth as if it were her own. But in the past few months, the rumor was that Marco Conti had fallen for a Russian woman. That disappointed the woman behind the bar and about a half-dozen other suitors in Siena, and beyond.

"I've been crazy busy with the winery and my boring work travels," replied Marco. "And my family is fine, thank you for asking. And yours?"

"*Stiamo bene* (we're good)," she responded. "*Grazie.*"

The quartet seated themselves at their outside table. A twenty-something waitress from Argentina came within minutes to take their orders. Everybody went for varying versions of espresso: *macchiato* ("stained" or "marked," with a splash of milk); *in vetro* (in glass); *ristretto* (lit. "restricted," a single shot) and *doppio* (double). (An order of *un caffè*—a coffee—in Italy, is a single shot espresso, typically with a pack of sugar on the side.)

Hennadiy Kovalenko ordered the double shot and added a shot of a different kind.

"*Un amaro, per piacere.*" (A bitter, please. An amaro is an Italian alcoholic drink made of several, and sometimes many more than several, herbs.)

Unlike cafes in the United States, in Italy, the terms "bar" and "caffè" are practically interchangeable. Both serve coffee and alcoholic drinks. In the early morning hours, local workers—blue- and white-collar—walk in for a stand-up cappuccino or espresso, sometimes with a croissant, before starting their day. In the late afternoon or early evening, they might stop by for a single small beer or glass of wine before heading home.

Marco looked at Jake across the table.

"So, Jake, what do you know about the vinification (wine making) process?" asked Marco.

"I know just enough to be dangerous," joked Jake.

"Well, you're going to have to learn much more than that if you and Hennadiy want to go to Russia with me as employees of Conti Vineyards."

Hennadiy, who had been admiring a stylish Italian woman as she strolled into the café, snapped his head toward Marco.

"So . . . it's *on?*" asked Hennadiy, about to jump out of his chair.

"*Si,* it's on," responded Marco, looking at Hennadiy, then Jake.

"*Mille grazie signore* (a thousand thanks, sir)!" said Hennadiy.

"You both should learn everything about the vinification process, our winery, our past vintages, and what we produce. You both already know *a lot* about my country, and speak exceptionally good Italian, so that is good. And Hennadiy, I know that your Russian is very good," said Marco. "So, you will have no problem."

Hennadiy nodded in acknowledgment.

"But you, Jake, I know you speak excellent Italian, and I understand you once studied Farsi, correct?"

"I did," replied Jake.

"That's good," replied Marco. "Because learning some Russian will be easier. Farsi is extremely challenging for people of Western tongues to learn. You don't have to be an expert in the Russian language, but you will need to be at least conversant. OK?"

"Roger that," replied Jake, relishing the challenge of learning a new language. "How much time do I have?"

"You should have ample time to get ready. I will be going back to Rostov-on-Don in four months, and my intent is to take you both with me. In the meantime, my father will work on the paperwork. If it takes longer than four months, I will wait until everything is ready before I go back, with you two along with me. You have my father's—and my mother's—full support, as of course, you have mine."

CHAPTER 72
I WANT TO HELP
Late April 2024

MANNY ALVAREZ WAS DELIGHTED that he had reached out to Blake Conners. Conners immediately expressed his desire to help Manny and Jake.

"After all, if it wasn't for you two guys," Conners had said to Manny, "I would have either done something that I would have had nightmares about the rest of my life, or I would be dead. Let's just say neither option was a good one for me."

Conners had walked into the US embassy in Rome and had confessed to them about his having joined the private Army of Anatoly Volkov (aka, the Wolf). Conners left the Wolf Pack before things went "to hell in a hand basket," and before he incriminated himself by being involved in the use of a weapon of mass destruction. That weapon would have killed thousands of American sailors, and its collateral damage would have killed thousands of Italian citizens, not to mention terrorizing Europe, the United States, and much of the world.

Manny had lacked firm details during the phone call with Conners two weeks prior. But now Manny knew the full plan. Getting into Russia, snatching the two kids, and getting them back out of Russia would not be easy to do. In fact, it would be monumentally challenging, just like some missions Jake and Manny had gone on in Afghanistan, and just like their mission to find the love of Jake's life, the Carabinieri officer, Sara

Simonetti. And it would require excellent logistical support, tailored to their mission.

That was where Conners came in. In making his requests for logistical support, Manny was operationally savvy enough to know that he could not reveal any part of the trio's plan to Conners. Conners could only know *what* they needed, where *it* was needed, and when it was needed.

All three military men—Fortina, Kovalenko, and Alvarez— knew that everything the team did to save the kids would come at a cost, financial or otherwise. Conners thought he owed something to Jake Fortina and Manny Alvarez because the two engineered his rescue from the clutches of the Wolf and members of the Wolf's Wolfpack. Manny vowed to himself to do his best in leveraging the debt Conners owed them both. But he also knew it would come at a financial price. Somebody, or several people, in Russia would likely need to be paid to get the job done.

"What's my budget?" Manny asked Hennadiy Kovalenko, who was footing the entire operation's bill.

"For now, $50,000," Hennadiy had said. "If you think you'll bust it, let me know, and maybe I'll up it."

"Actually, that should be enough, but just barely," said Manny.

Thinking of the two boys, Hennadiy immediately adjusted the figure to $75,000.

"That should be more than sufficient," Manny told him.

Manny knew that Connors, in acting as liaison to some former Pack friends in Russia, was not asking for a dime.

"But inside operators in Russia will be asking for payoff money," Connors had told Manny.

These days, that much money will go a hell of a long way with a former Pack member, now living in Russia, who is barely surviving off small-time extortion and drug-selling operations, concluded Manny.

CHAPTER 73
THE WARNING
June 2024

"DO NOT FOLLOW ME INTO THEIR BEDROOM, OR YOU WILL GET IT WORSE THAN THEM."

When Dimitry said it, Kira believed him, chills racing up her spine.

In the past few weeks, while she'd believed in God but never felt very faithful or religious, she found herself praying more frequently. And with Dimitry having left the master bedroom for the boys' bedroom again, she was praying fervently that the boys would not be badly hurt.

Dimitry had grown increasingly despondent over the past months. Due to the war with Ukraine and international sanctions against Russia, the Russian economy was suffering. Multinational companies had stopped investing in Russia; some had pulled out of Russia altogether.

While some countries—like Brazil, Mexico, and Serbia—did not participate in the international sanctions against Russia, Russia's economy was declining, as was Russia's employment rate and the buying power of the ruble. With the average Russian adult earning under $700/month in 2023, times were hard. And when times get hard, the average Russian buys less meat and potatoes, but more cabbage, beets, bread, and vodka, always vodka.

As a result, the monthly profits from Dimitry's butcher shop had declined by forty percent over the preceding year. And he was mad at the world about it. That meant more beatings for Gleb and Sergiy. But in the previous months, Dimitry often beat Sergiy before picking on little Gleb. The twelve-year-old Sergiy always fought back, but was eventually subdued.

Given that the boys' teachers were talking about the boys' condition when they came to the school after a beating, Dimitry was careful not to beat them in the face or lower arms, where their bruises would be more visible. But now that the school year was over, he didn't have to worry about that anymore.

And beat them he did. Kira remained in her bed, frozen in fear.

CHAPTER 74

FRANZ JOSEF STRAUSS INTERNATIONAL AIRPORT

September 2024

"I LOVE THIS AIRPORT," SAID HENNADIY KOVALENKO.

"I do, too," responded Jake Fortina, referring to Munich's Franz Josef Strauss International Airport, named after the post-World War II, down-to-earth Bavarian politician from the 1950s through the 1980s.

"Why do *you* love it, Hennadiy?" asked Jake as he led the trio through the glass doors and into the international terminal.

"I flew in and out of here more than once from Kyiv, traveling on behalf of the Marshall Center," said Hennadiy, referring to the George C. Marshall European Center for Security Studies, a German-American government partnership for combating terrorism, transnational organized crime, and cyber and other national security threats.

"As you know, Jake, the Center's only about eighty minutes or so by car, due south of us."

Jake, who had met Hennadiy at the international Marshall Center located in Garmisch-Partenkirchen, Germany, nodded in acknowledgment.

"I never had a late flight from here," continued Kovalenko, "they never screwed up my bags, and I always could count on an excellent last German beer before I departed Germany for Ukraine."

"I get it," replied Jake. "This airport is often rated by customers as among the top ten on the planet."

"That does not surprise me," responded Hennadiy. "By the way, what do you say if we grab a beer or other beverage after we get through security?"

"I like my wine," responded Marco, "but today I'll try one of these Bavarian beers you two guys keep squawking about."

It had taken five months to get things lined up, but the international trio, now fast friends, were ready to go on their mission. They had rehearsed and briefed each other on the plan and its contingencies a couple of dozen times. It was Marco's job to escort them into the country and to provide Jake and Hennadiy with some legitimate cover for being there. After that, Jake and Hennadiy were to be on their own, and Marco would head home.

Back in Tuscany, some five months earlier, Marco turned the two men over to a friend and top-shelf men's store owner in Siena and told him, "Make these two guys look Italian, and befitting representatives of one of Italy's great wineries."

It was Marco's "gift" to his new friends. The intervening five months allowed time for the men to wear the clothes and feel comfortable with their new personas as Italian citizens. They also took the time to sharpen their Italian language skills and accents. Jake also learned some Russian.

Marco's sincere concern for the two boys he had never met deepened Margarita's love for him, and she increasingly yearned to have a child with him. Their nights had become heart-pounding and steamy engagements, with each knowing they had found their soulmates.

For this mission, Hennadiy, the five-foot-nine-inch retired Ukrainian colonel, had lost twenty pounds. The weight loss made him look at least ten years younger. Hennadiy now sported colored contact lenses, changing his eye color from a light blue to hazel. His hair, what little he had left, went from white to a "sandy blonde."

Jake had grown his hair to a length to match Marco's. It was a quasi-70s' look, not worn by Jake since he had left high school in the mid-90s. The original dark, flowing hair, curling in places, had been shaved off when he'd entered West Point.

The stakes for the mission were high. The lives of two innocent children hung in the balance. Jake and Hennadiy risked being caught trying to get the kids out of Russia and eventually, back to Hennadiy's home in Kyiv. Or wherever he and Mila decided to settle with them.

There were a hundred things that could go wrong and many that needed to go right. And truth be told, Jake and Hennadiy could end up in a frigid gulag, or worse, if they were caught. But all three men were passionately committed to doing what few people on the planet would even consider: risk it all to provide two young, war-orphaned boys—and the closest surviving relatives of Hennadiy and Mila Kovalenko—a safe and better life.

Heading for passport control so they could exit Germany, Jake thought, *this first stop will validate if our passports are viable.*

The Munich Airport, like many airports in Europe, including Rome, had automatic electronic passport checks. Much like the electronic scanners for boarding passes, one simply placed their passports face down flat on a glass scanner, looked into the adjacent camera, and had their mugshot automatically taken. If everything matched up, a green light would flash and, viola, the electronically controlled gate would open.

Jake prayed silently. He placed his passport face down on the scanner. He looked into the camera, and it flashed.

"Bingo," he said to himself as the light turned green and the gate opened.

Hennadiy and Marco got the same results.

As the men left the passport control area behind and worked their way to their departure gate, grins split their faces.

"We owe you—and your father—a drink," said Hennadiy, turning his head toward Marco.

"We owe him a hell of a lot more than that," said Jake.

"Right you are, my friend," said Hennadiy, nodding his head enthusiastically.

"Speaking of drinks," said Marco. "Let's stop for this supposedly world-famous Bavarian beer you guys keep yapping about."

"The drinks are on me," said Hennadiy.

CHAPTER 75
SHEREMETYEVO INTERNATIONAL AIRPORT
September 2024

THE THREE MEN WALKED OFF THE PLANE'S EXIT RAMP, with Jake and Hennadiy each carrying an upscale, Italian-made backpack.

"We'll need to travel very light," Jake had said back in Tuscany.

Hennadiy fully agreed.

Marco exited the plane with his carry-on, Swiss-made, black leather roller bag, which he'd long preferred.

Marco had made business trips to Russia twice per year over the preceding five years. He understood this would be his last one. If the Conti wine business somehow survived in a new Russia, somebody else would do the company's legwork in the vast country.

Marco led the way through Moscow's Sheremetyevo's International Terminal to the domestic terminal. The domestic terminal connected international and Russian passengers to multiple cities across Russia's eleven time zones. To exit the international terminal and access the Russian domestic terminal, the trio would have to clear the passport control station.

With sketches and maps developed by Manny and with input from Marco and Margarita—who both knew the "terrain" in Russia—the trio had discussed, rehearsed, and troubleshot the plan multiple times. The team knew the plan in their sleep.

Sheremetyevo International Airport was the first Russian airport to implement electronically read, biometric passport control in 2021. The three men passed with flying colors. But after they turned the next corner, they realized they must *also* pass a human-controlled passport checkpoint and receive a human-placed stamp in their passports.

Ahead of them were four lines of about a dozen people each. Marco took the lead, stepping up to one of the lines. This contingency had been discussed during their brief-backs and rehearsals. Before Marco picked a line to get into, he quickly observed who was sitting in the two glass-encased double booths. Each booth contained two side-by-side seats for Russian customs officials.

Marco picked the line with a younger, less experienced officer who looked to be in her twenties. In the booth next to the younger woman was another in her late thirties. The trio didn't know it, but the younger woman had replaced a young man who two months prior had left for Army duty on the Russian front, in Ukraine's Donbas region. The twenty-four-year-old man was already dead.

After waiting patiently, it was Marco's turn to approach the border control booth. Marco looked the border police lady in the eyes and passed his passport through the glass's opening, about chest-high for Marco.

"The two men behind me are traveling with me," said Marco.

The young lady nodded, expressionless.

The lady looked briefly at Marco and placed his passport down on her scanner. Her computer screen changed to a new page. The electronic data on the screen perfectly reflected the personal data that was on Marco's hard copy passport. The lady looked away from the screen and at Marco's passport, slowly thumbing through its pages. She was interested to find ten Russian border entry stamps over the previous five years. Each of them indicated the Russian border crossing point as Sheremetyevo International Airport.

"And you said the two men behind you are traveling with you?" she asked.

"Yes," responded Marco.

"What is your business in Russia?" she asked. "I see you have been here several times."

"I'm a wine salesman from Tuscany . . . in Italy," said Marco with a slight smile. "And the two men behind me will replace me."

The lady showed no emotion as she looked at his passport again. The lady slowly reached for her wooden and metal stamp while continuing to peer into Marco's passport.

"OK," she said, finally stamping his passport with an audible "thump" and giving it back to Marco.

She nodded to Jake and Hennadiy to step forward. She repeated the process first with Jake, this time looking closely at Jake's eyes and then his eye color listed in Jake's passport.

As she did, Hennadiy Kovalenko fought off a twinge of fear. He could not remember if he had removed his colored contact lenses before passing through the previous electronic scan. Then he couldn't remember if he had put them back in after passing the biometric and electronic scan in Munich.

But it didn't sound any alarms when I just passed through the electronic screening, so I must be good, right? He thought.

The lady stamped Jake's passport and handed it back to him. Jake and Marco, a few steps beyond the booth and officially inside the borders of Russia, casually waited for their friend and partner to step up to the passport control booth.

Hopefully, he'll join us in a minute, thought Marco.

The inexperienced lady took more time with Hennadiy. He looked nothing like the previous two Italian men who came through. She turned and whispered something to her elder partner. The more experienced lady looked straight at Hennadiy. Hennadiy stayed calm, trying to appear nonchalant, almost disinterested.

The older lady leaned back toward her partner and said in a low voice, "Yes, there are many Italians with blue eyes and blondish hair."

Hennadiy, staying calm, could not distinguish a word of their conversation.

The lady stamped Hennadiy's passport.

Instantly, Hennadiy felt like a one-hundred-pound weight was lifted off his shoulders.

The lady pushed the passport back to Hennadiy, nodded, and did not say a word.

"*Grazie,*" replied Hennadiy.

The older lady then looked at her younger partner.

"How did the Italian men smell?" she asked with a grin.

"What do you *mean* 'how did they *smell?*" asked the younger lady, perplexed.

"Well, almost all the Italian men I've met or have come through here smell good," replied the older border police official.

The younger one just smiled and motioned the next passenger forward to the window.

Not communicating, the three men continued to what turned out to be yet another corner, and then another set of human lines beyond it. These queues were the Russian version of American TSA screening lines. During the rehearsals, Marco had told them the lines would be next up before completely gaining access to Moscow's domestic airline terminal.

Staying together, Marco again led the way to one of the screening lines.

Standing at the conveyor belt, Jake was very thorough in removing anything with even a speck of metal in it: wallet (metal credit card), watch, ballpoint pen, belt, shoes with metal eyelets. Anything that could possibly have metal in it, he took it off and put it in the plastic bin. He went through the magnetometer with flying colors. And so did Marco.

Hennadiy was instead directed to step into the large, full-body human scanner, rather than the walk-through magnetometer.

The Russian screening official told Hennadiy to step out of the scanner and stand fast.

While gathering their carry-on bags and putting back on their shoes, belts, and watches, Jake and Marco—out of the corners of their eyes—occasionally checked what was going on with their buddy.

The scanner attendant grabbed his hand-held scanner and pointed at Hennadiy's left hip. The man said something in Russian. Rather than speak back to the man in Russia, which he clearly understood, Hennadiy wisely responded to the man in broken English, understanding that most travelers and international airport workers recognize English as the international language.

Pointing to his hip, Hennadiy made what looked like a hammer hitting a nail motion and then said, "New! New!"

The man's eyes lit up, and he smiled. People with titanium hips, shoulders, or knees—particularly among Western travelers—was something the scanner attendant saw at least a half-dozen times a day. And that was especially true when Russia hosted the 2018 FIFA (*Federation Internationale de Football Association*) Soccer World Cup, from mid-June 2018 to mid-July 2018.

"*Khorosho* (OK, fine)," replied the man in Russian, waving Hennadiy on.

Hennadiy gathered his personal items and his backpack.

The three men began to walk out of the screening area and into the domestic terminal area.

They went about ten paces before someone behind yelled, "Sir, sir!"

All three men looked back. A Russian screening agent was running toward them.

The three men felt as if the world was moving in slow motion, as it does when trauma is about to make a visit or has already burst through the door.

A twenty-something woman, poker-faced, finally stopped within arm's reach of the three men. She extended her arm and opened her closed fist. Inside the woman's hand was a metal money clip with euro bills in it.

"You forget this," she said in broken English. "In your bean (bin). You forgot it in your bean."

She handed the money clip—containing three bills of twenty euros each—to Hennadiy.

"*Grazie, grazie,*" said Hennadiy, peeling off a twenty-euro bill and handing it to the woman.

The woman clutched the bill and looked around nervously. The twenty euros (about twenty-one dollars) was roughly what she would earn working five hours at the airport.

"*Tank* you," she replied, a big smile on her face.

The three did not say anything to each other until they got to the seats at their departure gate, with the sign "Rostov-on-Don/Krasnodar Airport" clearly visible. Jake and Marco were trying hard to suppress laughs.

Once seated at their gate, Jake could not resist the urge to say something.

Turning toward Hennadiy, just loud enough for Marco to hear, Jake asked Hennadiy: "Travel much?"

Hennadiy grinned sheepishly.

"Well, I hope that means all the stupid sheet (shit) that *could* happen, happened today," he said in English.

"*Sono d'accordo* (I agree)," said Marco, laughing. "I'm sure it did! I'm sure we got all the stupid shit out of our system today!"

CHAPTER 76

KRASNODAR INTERNATIONAL AIRPORT
September 2024

THE THREE MEN EXITED KRASNODAR INTERNATIONAL AIRPORT. The airport was about a three-hour and twenty-minute car ride from Rostov-on-Don. The Rostov-on-Don Airport was shut down due to airspace security concerns after Russia invaded Ukraine in February 2022. After the war began, Krasnodar Airport became the primary alternative for flying to Rostov-on-Don.

Marco immediately spotted Georgiy standing near his vehicle, curbside. Georgiy waved at his best customer as soon as he saw the group exit the airport.

Before entering the car, Marco introduced the two men to Georgiy.

"These are my new salesmen," said Marco. "Someday—perhaps soon—they will replace me."

Georgiy nodded in acknowledgment.

"Gents, this is Georgiy, the guy I've been telling you about. Best driver in the country."

"Pleased to meet you. Anything you need, gentlemen," Georgiy said, "Just let me know."

Jake and Hennadiy each said, "nice to meet you" and "thanks" in their own ways.

Georgiy took the men's carry-on luggage and stored it in the back of the SUV.

Before he got in the driver's seat, Georgiy thought, *it does not surprise me that two men are needed to replace my dear friend Mr. Conti. I will miss him.*

Since the war with Ukraine started, Georgiy's transport business had declined, but he'd made enough trips to know the three-hour trip to Rostov-on-Don like the back of his hand.

***

"These digs don't look bad," remarked Jake as he spied the modern Radisson Blu hotel to his right front.

Georgiy guided the vehicle to the right toward the temporary parking covered area, just in front of the hotel's double-glass doors.

"This is my hideout and place of solace," said Marco as Georgiy brought the vehicle to a stop. "It's one of the best hotels in the Rostov-on-Don area and, like most places in Russia, it does not break the bank. Plus, it has a pretty good gym and a great bar."

"I like the 'good gym' part," said Jake.

"And I love the 'great bar' part," said Hennadiy. "As long as they have good Ukrainian . . ." He coughed to cover the mistake, "I meant good *Russian* vodka, I'll be a happy camper," said Hennadiy.

Fortunately, when Hennadiy committed his gaffe, Georgiy was outside the vehicle and moving around the back to get the bags. Georgiy did not hear a word of Hennadiy's comment.

As Georgiy grabbed the bags, the doorman quickly approached the three men and asked if they needed help with their bags.

279

All three—to the man—said, "No, thank you" in Russian, including Jake.

The doorman noted that one of the men had a slightly stronger foreign accent than the other two.

CHAPTER 77
DAY 2, ROSTOV-ON-DON
September 2024

MARCO LED HIS TWO "FUTURE REPLACEMENTS" through the grocery store's glass sliding doors. This store was his favorite of the several stores in the Rostov-on-Don area that the Conti Family had established good relationships with. Sure, before the war started, Conti sales were profitable in this and other stores in the southwestern Russian city of roughly one million people.

But good Conti wine sales were not the main reason the store was Marco's favorite: it was because this was where the magic with Margarita had begun. Walking into the store where he met the love of his life had a surreal and, at the same time, joyous feel.

She is never coming back here, and, after this week, neither am I, thought Marco.

Since the war started, wine sales dropped by half and were still falling. And even though the Conti Vineyards had sold their wines in Russia at prices that met middle and upper middle-class Russians' pocketbooks, now only the most well-heeled Russians could afford Conti wine.

Marco led the two men to the area where Conti wines were typically on display. As he approached the wine shelves, he looked at them and nodded his head.

"What do you see *here?*" he asked Jake.

"Well, for one thing," replied Jake, about to take his best guess at what Marco was asking about, "There are not very many . . . actually, let me rephrase that . . . there are very few choices. In a wine store in Italy or the US, you might have, what? Forty, fifty, to 100 or more different labels of red wine, depending on the store's size and location. Here I see about a dozen or so, and only two are from Italy, yours and one other. I see Croatian reds, Georgian reds, even a red from Albania. . . ."

Marco looked at Jake in surprise. *Damn, this guy is pretty observant,* thought Marco.

"What else do you see?" asked Marco, switching to Hennadiy.

"There is no Ukrainian vodka?" quipped Hennadiy, just above a whisper. "What a *tragedy.*"

All three men broke out laughing.

The store manager heard the eruption of laughter through the open door of his office. He headed the trio's way.

"I'll tell you what you see," replied Marco. "The red wine section is too well-stocked."

"Too well-stocked?" asked Hennadiy.

"Yes, too well-stocked. They only carry thirteen labels of red wine, but there are plenty of bottles behind each label. That means they are not selling. Either that, or they just restocked all the red wine last night. But with the wine coming from five different countries, how likely is that? The inventory is not moving."

But I already knew that, at least about the Conti wines, thought Marco.

"Mr. Conti!" said the voice, now about ten steps away.

"Yes, sir, it's indeed me," replied Marco, looking at the store's manager. "We were just about to come and see you. How are you, sir?"

"I've been better," said the manager. "Sales have been down not only with wine, but with pretty much anything but the essentials. Because of the war, many countries have boycotted certain items from being sold to Russia, and that has exacerbated the supply problem. People are practically living on bread, cabbage, and potatoes these days. We have less meat to sell, even when we can get it."

"Well, they sure aren't living on red wine, are they?" said Marco.

"Sadly, that is true, with the exception of the wealthier people," said the manager.

Marco took a minute to introduce Jake and Hennadiy to the store's manager.

"I'll be stepping back from my visits to Russia," said Marco. "And one of these two guys will be taking over the account of your store. However, if things keep going like they are, you will see him only once per year, if that. That said, my family knows that bad economic times don't last forever, and we'll be back in Russia selling Conti wines stronger than ever. So, don't lose hope."

"I hope you are right," said the store manager. "I hope you are right, Mr. Conti," he repeated, "And I hope I am still the manager by then."

CHAPTER 78
DAY 3, THE BAR
September 2024

"SIX STORES IN TWO DAYS," SAID MARCO, referring to the trio's visits to the six major supermarkets where Conti wines were sold.

"Not bad, guys. Five more stores and we'll have this city covered."

Seated at the Radisson Blu's bar, with Marco seated in the middle, the three men clinked their glasses.

"At least the wine is still selling well *here,*" added Marco, chuckling.

Igor, the barman that Marco had come to know during his five years of visiting Rostov-on-Don, eyed his Italian friend. The Russian had a southern Russia-born-and-raised uncle who boldly headed for western Europe after the Berlin Wall came down. He now lived in southern Germany. He also had a cousin from Georgia, the one situated in the Caucasus region. She was one of the courageous protestors against Russia's heavy-handed approach to the colorful country and its people, sandwiched between Russia to the north, Turkey to the south, and the Black Sea as its western border.

And Igor had come to love and respect Marco Conti.

He's not only a generous tipper, but he's a real mensch, thought Igor.

Privately, Igor was no fan of Vasily Puchta. He hated the direction Russia was moving in, as did many Russians. He was sick of hearing about the war with Ukraine. He knew that news coming out of Russian government-owned media outlets, especially television, was pure Kremlin propaganda.

Over the years, Igor developed his own calculus, his own "rule of five," for how to interpret Russian news reports. It's a rule that had no basis in science, but Igor believed it gave him a better understanding of reality. And he knew far too many local people who had buried their young sons, "the heroes of Russia."

Occasionally, his uncle, who lived in Germany, would verify that Igor's "rule and thoughts were not that far off." And often, Radio Free Europe broadcasts, which Igor was capable of picking up on his ham radio, verified that calculus.

If the Kremlin's locally owned Rostov-on-Don television station said X number of Russian soldiers died in a battle, Igor would multiply it by five. If the Kremlin said Russians had killed Y number of Ukrainian "Nazi" soldiers, he would reduce the Y number by a factor of five.

Igor had a moral choice to make. What he had witnessed in the hotel over the preceding three months, but more importantly—the three preceding days—was cause for alarm. Igor was deeply worried about his Italian friend. The time to do something about it was now.

CHAPTER 79
"SOMETHING TO SNACK ON?"
September 2024

IT SHOULD HAVE BEEN SOMETHING IGOR DID NOT HAVE TO WORRY ABOUT. But the barman *did* worry about his beloved Italian customer. Igor knew the doorman "hired" by the hotel a few months back was no more a real doorman than *Ded Moroz* (Grandfather Frost, Russia's rough equivalent to Santa Claus or Saint Nikolas). The thirty-something, square-jawed doorman was right out of FSB (Russia's Federal Security Service, a rough FBI equivalent) central casting.

Russia's FSB was responsible for Russia's domestic (inside Russia's borders) counterintelligence, antiterrorism, surveillance, and "guarding political stability" activities. The fourth part of the FSB's mission was a license to vanquish Vasily Puchta's enemies and critics, including journalists, competing oligarchs, and political opponents. The preferred method of murdering these "enemies of the state" was through "accidents," including "unfortunate falls" from hospital windows and apartment balconies, or tumbles down long stairs or staircases. Sometimes, outright assassination on the streets was "necessary." All the while, Puchta's fingerprints could not be found or traced to any of the murders.

Igor surmised the doorman's main mission was to keep an eye on guests—be they Russian or international—that frequented Rostov-on-Don's best hotel. But he was perplexed as to why the doorman or the FSB might take an interest in his best customer, or the two Italian men with him. After all, Marco Conti had been coming to the hotel for five years, and nothing about him seemed out of the ordinary, other than him being a genuinely decent person who sold Italian wine in Russia.

Watching the doorman take notes and make a phone call after Marco and his new employees came and went, Igor knew the doorman was keeping tabs on the trio. After Marco, Jake, and Hennadiy arrived at the hotel on their first night, the doorman extended his work hours from his regular shift of 8 A.M. to 6 P.M. Now, the doorman worked from 6 A.M. to 9 P.M. There was no night doorman beyond 9 P.M., but little did Igor know that within three days, there would be one, twenty-four hours a day.

As he saw his three Italian customers get to about halfway through their wine glasses, he decided to make his move.

"Care for any snacks with that wine? Peanuts? Chips?" he asked the group.

"Actually, both would be great," replied Marco. "Thank you, Igor."

"Coming right up, Mr. Conti," replied Igor. "Care if I top off those wine glasses, too? It'll be on the house."

"You're too kind," replied Jake.

"I don't know how anybody could pass up free Conti wine!" chuckled Hennadiy.

The three men again toasted.

"To Igor and Conti wine!" said Jake.

Igor turned around from facing the three men at the bar and faced the counter behind him, with the big mirror on the wall and bottles of liquor arrayed along the bottom of the mirror.

Glancing into the mirror, out of the corner of his eye, Igor could survey most of the bar area and down the short hallway from the door to the hotel's sliding glass doors. The hotel's designers had built the place so that customers, upon first entering the hotel, could catch a glimpse of the shiny mahogany brass bar. The big mirror behind it, the big-screen TV above it for watching sporting events, and a vast array of booze on the double counter below the bar made it an impressive sight. It was no secret that the best profit margins for a restaurant were found in drinks, especially alcoholic drinks.

That son-of-a-bitch is looking this way, thought Igor, able to see the FSB goon looking through the glass entryway doors toward the bar.

Fuck it, he thought to himself. *I must do this.*

Igor grabbed a can of peanuts and emptied about two handfuls into a bowl. He did the same with a bag of potato chips.

He took the two bowls—one in each hand—and placed one between Marco and Jake, and the other between Marco and Hennadiy.

"Grazie!" said Marco.

"My pleasure, Mr. Conti," said Igor.

Igor turned around to grab the three napkins. He also grabbed a pen from the drawer and quickly wrote down a message on one of the napkins.

"The doorman is watching you."

He turned around again toward the bar, and as he began to place the three napkins on the bar, he quickly glanced down the hallway toward the front doors. Igor could see the FSB guy still looking through the glass doors. The FSB man, seeing that Igor had glanced toward him, quickly disappeared from view.

Igor placed the three napkins on the bar in front of his three patrons. He placed the one containing the message directly in front of Marco Conti.

Marco saw the message's words immediately. He nonchalantly placed a bunch of potato chips on top of it. Jake thought he saw some writing on the napkin, but could not read what it said before Marco smothered it in chips. Hennadiy noticed nothing.

Five minutes later, when Marco and Igor again made eye contact, Marco gave Igor a quick nod of acknowledgment.

After about ten minutes of uninterrupted conversation among the three wine salesmen, Marco started sniffling. With his last chip gone, he took the napkin, pretended to slightly blow his nose on it, wadded it up, and stuck it into his pocket.

CHAPTER 80
LET'S GO FOR A SMOKE
September 2024

"IGOR, YOU GOT ANY CIGARETTES OR CIGARS BEHIND THIS BAR?" asked Marco Conti.

"Of course, Mr. Conti. Which would you prefer?"

"I'll take three cigars if you have that many," said Marco.

I haven't smoked a cigar since I married Sara, thought Jake. She hates the smell of those things. But hell, if Marco says we're smoking cigars, I'm in.

"Sure thing, *signore,*" said Igor.

Igor went over to a drawer just below the rows of booze and pulled out three Cuban Punch cigars. He also pulled out three packets of matches to go with each cigar.

"How much are they?" asked Marco.

Igor quoted Marco a price half of what the cigars sold for in the bar. And Marco knew it. Marco gave him enough Russian ruble bills to cover four times the price Igor had quoted.

"Thank you for your trouble," said Marco, handing the bills to Igor.

"This is too much," said Igor.

"Not for me," replied Marco.

"*Cazzo,* let's go for a smoke," said Marco to Jake and Hennadiy, speaking every word in Italian.

Marco—by using the code word *cazzo* (the "f" word in Italian)—caused Jake's and Hennadiy's ears to perk up. Jake and Hennadiy had briefed Marco about the use of the word when one of the team members was under some kind of duress or had discovered something threatening. Jake, Manny Alvarez, and Hennadiy used the same word during their Calabria expedition over two years prior.

One could plug the Italian "f" word into a sentence almost anywhere, just like the Italian soldiers did that Jake had served with. For example, "what the *cazzo*," "who the *cazzo*, and "why the *cazzo*" were all acceptable in the Italian military lexicon.

"A smoke sounds like a great idea," said Jake, again, in Italian.

Marco stood up, pulling the napkin out of his pocket and uncrumpling it, as if to blow his nose again. He "blew" his nose three times. Before he crumpled up the napkin again, he looked down at it and tilted it toward Hennadiy, so Hennadiy could see the words on it.

"Man, the stuff that's been coming out of my nose lately has been nasty," deadpanned Marco.

He then folded up the napkin again and said, "Before we go out for a smoke, I need to go to the bathroom. In the meantime, Hennadiy, think of something to chat up our doorman friend about when we leave the building for a cigar break. Keep it short. I just want him to know how well you speak the local lingo. That should confuse the hell out of him."

We have to control the narrative and stay two steps ahead of that goon, just like Jake said during training back in Tuscany, thought Marco.

Marco pivoted and headed for the bathroom, located just off to the side of the bar. Once in the bathroom, he went into the sit-down stall, sat down, and flushed the paper down the toilet.

Appearing back at the bar, he said, "Let's go smoke these cigars. Hennadiy, please lead the way."

The three men headed for the hotel's automatic brass-embellished sliding glass doors.

Hennadiy led the group through the doors and addressed the Russian goon who was standing by his podium. The FSB agent was thrown back on his heels to see one of the three men he was keeping tabs on head straight for him. Jake and Marco kept walking, headed for a park bench about 100 yards in front of the hotel. It was situated in a pedestrian walkway, just above the Don River.

Before walking on, Jake said to Hennadiy, "*Ci vediamo presto* (We'll see each other shortly.)

Hennadiy responded, "*Si, ci vediamo presto*" in perfect Italian.

Jake and Marco continued walking, speaking loudly in Italian, as if they were having an argument about some nonsensical matter.

Hennadiy stayed behind and turned back toward the doorman. Hennadiy stopped in front of the Russian and took a minute to nonchalantly light his Cuban cigar.

"Been a helluva long day, hasn't it?" asked Hennadiy in Russian, right after lighting his cigar. "I saw you out here when I left this morning."

"It's not been a bad day," said the doorman in Russian, with an obvious Muscovite accent. "I've had longer days."

"Oh, ya? How long?" asked Hennadiy, trying to be annoying.

"Well, more than twelve hours, I'd say," said the man.

"No shit? That *is* pretty long," replied Hennadiy. "Damn, twelve hours on your feet must be rough. You ever work in a wine vineyard?"

"Uh, no, I haven't," said the man.

"Well, I've worked in one. And some days go from sunrise to sunset, especially during harvest time. Now that is a long ass day, ya' know what I mean?" asked Hennadiy, grinning and taking a wild-eyed puff of his cigar.

"Where did you work in a vineyard?" asked the man, who already knew Hennadiy was an Italian wine salesman.

"In Italy," said Hennadiy.

"Why is your Russian so good?" asked the FSB agent.

"Is it *good?* Well, hell, thank you. Then I should do super well with my new job selling wine here. But to answer your question . . . my parents were Russian and left Russia in the mid-1990s, when that dumbass Boris Yeltsin was in charge of the Kremlin. They hated that son-of-a-bitch and the instability he caused for Russia. Man, do you remember when Yeltsin was so drunk he peed his pants in public? *Son-of a-bitch . . .* was that guy ever *not* drunk? Yeltsin stunk up not only the Kremlin but the entire fuckin' Russian economy. Even though they were in Italy by then, my parents cheered like crazy people when Vasily Puchta got elected in 2000. Hell, they're even thinking about moving back to Russia since Puchta's been kicking those Ukrainian Nazis' asses. What d'ya think?"

"What do I think about *what?*" asked the man.

'What do you think about them moving back here? Should they *do* it?"

"Uh, well, ya', I think they should," replied the man.

"Hmmm." He seemed to consider the advice. "Well, thanks for chattin,' *amico* (friend)," replied Hennadiy, turning to walk toward Jake and Marco.

"Sure," replied the man, dumbstruck. "Any time."

CHAPTER 81
SMOKE 'EM IF YOU GOT 'EM
September 2024

THE THREE MEN SAT ON THE PARK BENCH, facing the beautiful setting sun. The Don River and the small, wooded area on the other side were also fully in view.

It was one of the oldest personal security moves in the book: walk to a safe area where there are no listening devices, where nobody expects you to go, and where no remote listening devices are trained on you from some nondescript van or hotel room. Even better, go somewhere where your trackers are not expecting you to go, and with a good reason to go there, like smoking smelly Cuban cigars.

"Smoke 'em if you got 'em!" Jake said, recalling stories of his father's service in the old army, when troops would do a twelve-mile road march and smoke whatever they had during their "smoke breaks."

Both men smiled at Jake's enthusiasm.

"Dang, these Cuban Punch cigars are good," said Hennadiy.

"This is maybe the third or fourth cigar I've had in my life," said Marco. "But it tastes rather strong to me."

"I love 'em," said Hennadiy. "What you call strong, Marco, I call *spicy*. This would go great with a Ukrainian vodka. Do you think the doorman would crap his pants if I yelled at the top of my lungs, 'I need a Ukrainian vodka!'"

"No, but I might," said Marco.

All three chuckled.

Hennadiy recalled that Jake was not aware of the napkin-delivered message.

"Jake, the reason we're out here is because of a note Igor handed to Marco on that napkin. You didn't see the note, but I did."

"Aw, crap, I thought we were coming out here to just smoke some good cigars," replied Jake. "What did it say?" asked Jake.

"The doorman is watching you."

"*Shit,*" responded Jake. "Not good."

"Nope," replied Hennadiy.

"What's our next move?" asked Marco.

"Well, whatever it is, I say we make it within the next twelve to twenty-four hours," said Jake. "Bad news does not get better with age. Right now, we have knowledge and initiative on our side. The guy does not know that we know who he is. And if we play this right, we can buy enough time to get lost inside of Russia—and get out of Russia with those boys—before the Ruskies know what we're up to and try to locate us. But you, Marco, you need to get out of Russia on the first thing smokin' . . . preferably tomorrow morning."

"I don't want to leave you guys," said Marco, "but my mother and father—and Margarita—would never forgive me if I ended up in a gulag or worse."

"So, ya,' Marco, you *gotta* roll tomorrow," said Jake. "Early. As early as possible."

"It's still early in the game, and my impression is this FSB guy doesn't yet know if we're legit wine salesmen or not," continued Jake. "The store visits we made the past two days were a credible ruse. I think we still have legitimate cover. So, we do have some time to make our moves. But that window could close overnight."

"Indeed, Jake," said Hennadiy. "We need to compress our operational timeline."

"What are our next steps—besides me getting out of Russia as soon as possible?" asked Marco.

"Marco, Georgiy needs to pick you up early tomorrow, before the goon gets to his little podium," said Jake. "Do you think Georgiy could do that? Is he trustworthy? I say he meets you a couple of blocks from the hotel."

"I do think he's trustworthy," said Marco. "Over the past five years, I've taken really good care of the guy, and he's let it slip that he thinks Vasily Puchta is taking the country in the wrong direction."

"Good," replied Jake. "Obviously, we won't check out of the hotel. Igor is clearly on our side, too, so we will tell Igor tonight, before he closes the bar at 11 P.M., that we'll be having a long day tomorrow. We'll tell him, Marco, that you had a family emergency and need to leave soonest. We—meaning Hennadiy and I—will tell Igor that we'll be picking up the slack in working the wine sales business after your departure. We'll also tell Igor that we'll be visiting four stores tomorrow and then meeting some store managers in the city for dinner tomorrow night. We don't expect to return to the hotel until midnight tomorrow. At some point in a couple of days, when Mr. Goon Man knows we are no longer at the hotel, he might ask Igor some questions. So, we want Igor to be able to tell the guy exactly what we told him."

Hennadiy and Marco nodded in acknowledgment.

"And then, thanks to Manny's work with Blake Conners, who is still owed some favors from his days with the Pack, we'll put our logistics and transportation plans into action," added Jake.

"We didn't talk about those plans in any detail," said Marco. "The *Pack?* What is that?"

"We didn't talk about it for good reason," replied Hennadiy. "What you *don't* know can save your life. Forget I even mentioned it. Like we said back in Tuscany, it's better that you have absolutely no idea of what our next moves will be. That way, if you—God forbid—get rolled up by the Russians, you won't know a thing about our plan and you won't be lying when you say 'I don't know.'"

"Understood," replied Marco.

"And Marco, before your head hits the pillow tonight, you need to book the earliest flights out tomorrow. By the time the goon takes his lunch break, you should be on your flight from Moscow to Munich, or any other flight that is available to an EU airport: Budapest, Helsinki, Munich, Prague, Rome, Tallinn, Vienna, Warsaw . . . you name it. It doesn't matter where, as long as it's out of Russian airspace and into the European Union-controlled airspace, and to a safe Central or Western European city. *Capisci?* (Understand?)"

"*Si, capisco* (Yes, I understand)," he replied.

"When the jackass FSB guy starts wondering if something is up, it will be day after tomorrow at the earliest, when he comes in for work and realizes we've left the building, so to speak. IF—NO, *when*—we properly execute our plan, we'll have the kids on Ukrainian soil by then. Now—if you guys agree, let's take a few minutes out here just shootin' the shit, and then go back into the bar."

"I can think of or worse places to go!" said Hennadiy, laughing out loud.

CHAPTER 82
THE BACK DOOR
September 2024

THE MEN REENTERED THE HOTEL. SUBTLY, THEY RECONFIRMED that only two security cameras watched the front entrance.

They walked to the barroom and retook their seats at the mahogany bar.

"The drinks are on me," said Marco to Igor.

"Wow, thanks, boss," said Jake. "What put you in such a good mood?"

"We've had a great visit to this city," said Marco. "And we still have a few more stores to visit over the next couple of days."

Marco said it just loud enough to make sure any of the nearby patrons, if they were listening, could hear it.

Igor successively placed three napkins down on the bar, one for each drink he was about to bring.

Per the plan the team finalized before returning to the hotel, Jake nonchalantly wrote the question on his napkin. He subtly rotated it 180 degrees, so Igor could read it as he brought Jake's drink, "a whiskey coke without the whiskey."

Jake knew the trio would have a zero-dark-thirty wakeup, if they slept at all. More alcohol would make him less sharp.

"Does the bar have a back door to the street?" wrote Jake on his napkin.

Igor brought Jake his Coke, without rum, and "one cube of ice." Igor briefly eyed the message as he placed the drink on the bar.

"*Si,* (yes)," he responded to Jake's question.

"I didn't know you could speak Italian," responded Jake.

Igor winked at Jake.

"Can you leave it unlocked tonight?" wrote Marco on his napkin.

Igor went back for Marco's drink and Hennadiy's drink, one in each hand. He placed Marco's drink in front of Marco and read the message.

"*Assolutatamente* (absolutely), *signor,*" replied Igor.

"Do the side stairwells have security cameras?" Hennadiy had written on the third napkin.

"No. Only the front," whispered Igor.

With everyone having their drinks, Marco—like an Italian boss—picked up his Conti Vineyards red wine and toasted the group.

"Here's to a great week, gentlemen! Conti wines will make a big comeback in Russia!"

"*Cin-cin* (cheers)!" replied Jake.

"*Salute* ('to your health'; pronounced 'sa-LOU-tay')!" responded Hennadiy!

After twenty-five more minutes of chit-chat between themselves and with Igor, mainly about which countries had the best national soccer teams, the men bid Igor *buona notte* (good night).

From the bar area, they walked to the central elevator. They had never observed security cameras on the floors, and Igor had denied they were there, but one could never be too sure. So, they did what anyone would expect them to do: take the direct and most logical route back to their fifth-floor rooms.

***

At 4:20 A.M., Marco departed his room for the side stairwell. Back in Tuscany, Jake told him that a room nearest a stairwell was "better than a room near an elevator."

"Less noisy, less traffic, and depending on the hotel, during a fire, it's closer to a better route down than the elevator."

Even though he would not be a part of it, Marco felt good about the team's plan as he reached the ground floor, walked through the bar's unlocked front doors, and approached the bar's back door. He cracked the door open, just like Jake had told him. He checked his field of view. There was nobody in sight. He calmly stepped out and pretended to lock the door from the outside, in the off chance that somebody was looking out from a nearby window or happened to suddenly pass by. Marco walked toward his 4:30 A.M. agreed-upon rendezvous point with Georgiy.

At 4:25 A.M., Georgiy reduced his SUV's speed as he approached the roundabout. He was twenty yards from their rendezvous point. Georgiy spotted an easily accessible, curbside parking spot near the agreed-upon pick-up point. He guided his vehicle to it. Within ten seconds after parking, Georgiy saw Marco approaching from the dark clump of nearby trees, which had been hiding Marco from the nearby streetlights.

Marco, carrying only his backpack, opened the door and got in the SUV's front passenger seat. Georgiy did not yet know where he was taking his friend. He knew only that Marco would "need his services from 4:30 A.M. to noon." Marco wanted to be sure to account for Georgiy's driving time back from the distant airport to Rostov.

Marco trusted Georgiy, but not to the point of trusting Georgiy with his life. In Puchta's Russia, one could never be sure who was who. If anybody had become suspicious of Marco and his "new employees," he did not want to telegraph in advance his early morning trip to the airport.

Marco's directive to Georgiy was direct and simple.

"I've had a family emergency. Please drive me to Krasnodar Airport, my friend."

"Will do, sir," replied Georgiy.

At 4:30 A.M., Jake and Hennadiy, in their individual rooms, slipped on their Russian military look-alike boots. The two wisely broke in the boots during the intervening three months since they'd purchased them. They packed all of their fancy Italian business stuff into black plastic bags and put on casual-looking jeans, t-shirts, and light zip-up jackets. Not wanting to look like Frick and Frack, they purposefully chose different colored jeans and jackets.

Jake rechecked the three Russian *buterbroty* (whole grain bread, salami, cheese, and cucumber slices) sandwiches he and Hennadiy purchased the day prior at a sandwich shop not far from the hotel. Two water bottles were in the backpack, too.

At 4:45 A.M., Jake and Hennadiy replicated Marco's path to the hotel's bar, taking the side stairwell and to the ground floor. From there, they walked through to the bar and its unlocked front door. Upon entering the bar, the back door was reachable in several seconds.

The two men met just inside the door. They cracked the door to check for any outside traffic—pedestrian or vehicle—before stepping out into Rostov-on-Don's dimly lit, pre-dawn streets. Their walking direction away from the hotel was the opposite of Marco's.

Where Marco headed north by northwest from the hotel, Jake and Hennadiy walked southeast toward the nearby *Voroshilovsky* Bridge. The roughly 300-yard-long bridge and its pedestrian walkway would lead them to the south side of the Don River and on to the parking lot of the Rostov Arena. Their walking time to the Arena's parking lot was expected to take just over a half-hour.

Manny Alvarez's advance logistics work with Blake Conners assured that a *Lada Niva* 4x4 SUV was awaiting the two men in the Rostov Arena (*Stadion Rostov*) parking lot. The arena seated over 45,000 spectators and was used during the Soccer (FIFA) World Cup hosted by Russia in 2018.

On the way to the bridge, they threw the black plastic bags with their fancy Italian attire and shoes into a dumpster. They reconned the dumpster during the previous two days' trips to and from the hotel.

As the men got to the bridge, they were thankful that the lighting on the pedestrian walkway was not that great.

"Since leaving the army, the only time I get up at 4 A.M. these days is to go fishing," quipped Jake. "6 A.M. is much more to my liking now."

"I think I could get used to later wakeups, too," said the newly-retired colonel who spent thirty years in a Ukrainian Air Force uniform.

As the two men neared the center of the bridge, a vehicle entered the bridge from behind them. It was headed in a southerly direction across the bridge. In the dinged-up sedan were two twenty-something Russian punks, looking to shake down an unsuspecting local citizen or tourist—preferably drunk—for some quick cash.

The Russian economy's sharp downturn had made Russia's streets meaner than they were in the preceding years. And, as the BBC reported on September 30, 2023, Russia's police officers were "burned out, disappointed and demoralized." Many had left, and more were leaving, police duty as they realized they could earn more by working in a supermarket than by risking their lives for their towns, cities, and country.

As the vehicle with the slightly tinted windows slowed down to get a good look at the two pedestrians, it slowly came into Jake's curbside peripheral view. Hennadiy, to Jake's right, soon saw it as well. Both men fearlessly and simultaneously looked at the car.

"I can make out two of them in there," said Jake. "The guy on the passenger side looks like a teenager."

"I can't see shit," replied Hennadiy, "but if it's only two, and they're not armed, we should be fine."

Jake stopped abruptly, looked at the car, and slowly shook his head side-to-side. He unzipped his jacket about halfway down and put his hand in the jacket and over his heart, as if to draw a gun. Both Jake and Hennadiy shook their heads at the car. Their intended message was simple: "Don't even think about it."

The person who could be seen on the passenger side turned his head as if saying something to the driver. Although the vehicle had almost come to a complete stop, it again picked up speed and kept driving across the bridge. The deterrent gestures by Jake and Hennadiy had worked.

"If they had brought out the guns, we could have been in deep trouble," said Jake calmly, and then chuckling.

"No doubt," replied Hennadiy. "Trying to ignore them when it was obvious they were checking us out would have conveyed fear on our part. Sometimes you gotta do some crazy shit to get out of a jam. Although we need to keep our eyes open for them to make sure they don't set us up for something on the other side of the bridge."

CHAPTER 83

OUR RIDE

September 2024

JAKE FORTINA SPOTTED THE LADA 4 X 4 SUV just before Hennadiy did.

"That looks to be our ride," said Jake.

Jake understood this was the most critical point thus far in the men's "trip," at least for Jake and Hennadiy.

Thank God, thought Jake, feeling relieved that the vehicle was where Manny said it would be.

Hennadiy had the same thought.

Jake knew that without that vehicle, their only backup was to rent one or, in the worst-case scenario, steal one. Renting one would add a whole host of issues for completing their operation, including leaving electronic and personal identity traces of their locations as well as providing law enforcement with a quickly identifiable source of their vehicle, just based on the license plates alone.

As the two men approached the vehicle in the semi-darkness of the stadium parking lot, with all lamp poles *fortunately turned off,* thought Jake. Jake discerned a barely visible human figure sitting behind the steering wheel.

Jake glanced around to make sure there was nobody else nearby. The stadium parking lot's vastness and the adjacent city's grey light allowed him to see much farther than he'd expected at a few minutes after 5 A.M. He didn't spot another soul or vehicle in the parking lot.

Jake, still cautious, calculated that the figure in the vehicle could call in reinforcements rather quickly if needed. But he wasn't sure the dark figure in the vehicle had spotted him and Hennadiy yet.

"There is someone in there," said Jake. "Did Manny tell you there'd be anybody in there waiting for us?"

"W-T-F, over," said Hennadiy to Jake, mimicking a short-range radio transmission to Jake as the two men eyed the driver. Kovalenko had heard the salty acronym from Jake before. "What now?"

The two men stood about forty yards from the vehicle. They didn't dare take their eyes off the apparently male figure seated in the driver's seat.

"We don't have a lot of choices," said Jake. "The guy's obviously waiting for us . . . or he just fell asleep. But the way he's sitting upright, I doubt he's sleeping. If he wanted to kill us, he'd be hiding in the back seat. But the son-of-a-gun is just sittin' there, staring at us, like a statue."

"Did Manny say anything to you about us meeting someone when we took possession of the vehicle?" repeated Jake. "This was not on my bingo card."

"Nor mine," replied Hennadiy.

Both men noticed slight movements by the silhouette in the front seat.

"Screw it," said Hennadiy, "I see no other choice but to approach the vehicle. It's our—and the boys'—ride outta here. Our plan B is way too risky, not to mention that it will throw us off our timeline."

"Agreed. Let's keep walking," said Jake. "You break left toward the passenger side, and I'll head for the driver's side."

The two men slowly approached the vehicle.

Suddenly, the silhouette made a move. The driver, about six-feet-two-inches tall, got out of the vehicle and faced Jake and Hennadiy. In an instant, all doubt about whether the man had spotted Jake and Hennadiy was gone.

The man's "Buona sera (good evening)!" pierced the damp early morning air.

"More like '*Buongiorno*' (good morning), no?" countered Jake reflexively, in perfect Italian.

"*Si, si,*" said the man, chuckling and nodding his head. "Buongiorno. It's been a long night."

Still on edge, with the man's "Buongiorno," Jake and Hennadiy simultaneously elected to keep moving toward the Russian and to keep speaking to him in Italian. The Russian walked a few paces in front of the vehicle toward the men . . . and stopped.

The man then reached into his partially unzipped jacket.

"Woah, woah!" said Jake, putting his arm out and not knowing what else to say to the man who seemed to be pulling out a gun.

"Don't worry," said the man, now brandishing something glistening in the pale light. "I just wanted to make sure Conners gets this bottle of vodka."

Jake and Hennadiy were speechless. Knowing he and Jake were unarmed, Hennadiy came up just short of seeing his life flash before his eyes.

"Oh, hell yes," responded Hennadiy. "We'll make sure he gets it."

The former Russian special forces soldier and former Wolf Pack member—now freelance criminal—was happy to meet someone who knew Blake Connors.

As a retired US Army senior sergeant, Connors had done a mercenary hitch in Italy with Anatoly Roman Volkov's now severely degraded and disjointed private army. With Volkov and his Mr. Fix-It Chief of Staff, Boris Stepanov, both languishing in an Italian prison, the man holding the bottle of vodka continued to operate with Russian black marketeers and transnational criminals as a "logistics man for hire."

But the man had no idea that Conners—after the American had turned himself in to the US embassy in Rome to cooperate with the American and Italian governments—had severely compromised the Wolf Pack organization and its operations in Italy. The man also did not know about Blake Conners' turning on the Russian oligarch and his private army. The man only knew that he owed Blake Conners a big favor for saving his bacon during a major theft in Italy, a warmup for the epic art heist in Rome.

The vehicle and the things it held were the man's payback to Conners. It was pure gravy when Conners told the man the used vehicle and its contents also came with a 40,000-euro (roughly $42,000, with daily exchange rates varying) bonus. Since it was a favor to Conners, the man would have been happy with half that amount, which he had already received by international wire. Hennadiy Kovalenko provided the money to Manny

Alvarez, and Alvarez laundered it through Conners and on to Conners' Russian buddy.

Hennadiy never told Jake what the Lada and its contents had cost. The vehicle's contents were more costly than the vehicle itself. The 40,000 euros was a bargain for both buyer and seller. Hennadiy had given Manny a 75,000-euro budget, so Hennadiy was getting money back from the deal.

As Jake and Hennadiy's means of transportation, the Lada SUV was the perfect choice. It was a popular car brand manufactured by AvtoVAZ, a Russian state-owned company. Lada vehicles—mainly the compact *Lada Vesta*—were driven by Russian government bureaucrats throughout the country.

Although the vehicle and its contents were a "payback" favor to Blake Conners, the Russian did not turn the bonus money down, considering it a major win-win. Now, his only objective was to meet the men who knew his former buddy and partner in crime.

"So, you guys knew Conners?" asked the man, continuing in Italian.

"We sure as hell did," replied Jake in Italian, as Hennadiy nodded enthusiastically and replied with a confident "Yep."

"Blake was a real badass," added Jake, knowing that if he dropped Conners' first name, it would prove Jake's connection with Conners. "I served with him in the green fucking berets. He was the best of the best."

"He sure was," replied the Russian. "I never in my craziest dreams thought I'd be working with an American soldier in Italy. But he was a real good shit, that Blake Conners, and I'll never forget him. I wouldn't be standing here if it weren't for him."

"That doesn't surprise me," said Jake.

The man handed the vodka bottle to Jake.

"I'm sure Blake will love this," replied Jake.

A slight pause ensued.

The man struck a serious, business-like tone.

"Gents," said the man, stepping back from the vehicle and shining his cellphone light on the SUV's side, "how do you like the paint job?"

On the Lada's side, in official Cyrillic Russian lettering, it read, "Border Police." The man then shined the flashlight on the car's hood.

Jake looked at Hennadiy for his assessment.

"Looks legitimate," replied Hennadiy. "Well done."

"And gents," said the man, walking them to the car and opening the back driver's side door, "it's all here, under the back seat."

The man reached in and grabbed the top of the back seat. He jerked it forward. He shined his cellphone light in the space behind and under the seat.

"There they are: two (Russian) border guard uniforms, one with a colonel's rank, the other for a captain," said the Russian. "These are the camouflaged tactical uniforms. I matched the sizes to what Conners requested. The boots are there, too."

Jake and Hennadiy both nodded in the darkness.

The man focused his cellphone's light on another spot.

"Here are two clean burner cell phones and two sets of night vision goggles. They (the cell phones) are good shit, made in the West. There are two pistols and eighty rounds of ammo, too. He said you wouldn't need more than that, because if you did, you'd be fucked anyway."

Throwing his head back, the Russian cackled.

Sounds like something Conners would say, thought Jake, grinning.

"There are also two sets of black overalls and black skull caps. Oh, ya, and I forgot about the tarp, the extra gas can, and the dozen water bottles. They're in the back. And the keys are in the ignition. Sounds like you guys are gonna do some fun shit, no?" he asked.

"Maybe," replied Jake, smirking in the dark. "Just maybe."

"What about the military ID cards? And the orders?" asked Hennadiy.

He nodded in confirmation as he handed the papers to Hennadiy.

While Hennadiy checked everything, Jake took up some small talk with the man. Their conversation centered on the arena and the man's favorite soccer team.

Hennadiy, meanwhile, checked that the supplies were there as stated, and then jumped in the vehicle driver's seat and placed his backpack on the front passenger seat. He turned the ignition. The vehicle started immediately. He could see the "full" reading on the gas meter. He shut the vehicle off.

Hennadiy opened his backpack and grabbed the two envelopes. They had been stuffed inside each one of his boots until this morning, when he put them on.

Hennadiy got out of the vehicle and walked up to the man, interrupting his and Jake's chit-chat.

"Here's the rest," said Hennadiy, handing the man the two envelopes. "Each envelope contains what you asked for. Go ahead and count it."

The man opened each and thumbed through the stacks of 200-euro bills.

"Looks good," he said. "Nice doing business with you."

The man turned around and began walking across the parking lot toward the Don River bridge. The morning's first grey light began to make its appearance.

"Oh, ya," said the Russian, turning around after several steps. "There is an extra key in the glove box. And don't forget to give that vodka to my American comrade!"

CHAPTER 84
YOU GOT A FIFTY IN THERE?
September 2024

GEORGIY HEARD THE SIREN BEFORE HE SPOTTED THE RUSSIAN PATROL CAR in his rearview mirror. At 6:20 A.M. on the two-lane country highway, he and his passenger were well over halfway to the airport.

Angry with himself that the cop snuck up on him, Georgiy noticed that the police vehicle contained only the driver, and nobody on the passenger side.

Good, he thought. *Better chance of making a donation.*

The cop was driving more aggressively than the average Russian police officer. But in 2024, with many leaving the police forces for better-paying jobs, one never knew what to expect.

The jackass is practically in my trunk now, he mused, looking in his rearview mirror. *He's trying to scare me in hopes of a bigger tip. But it's not going to work.*

Marco Conti sat in the back seat, trying to relax.

They've got nothing on me, he thought. *I have broken no laws.*

With Rostov-on-Don's Airport and the airspace above it closed due to its proximity to Mariupol and the combat zones in Ukraine, Georgiy made this trip from Rostov to the Krasnodar Airport a couple of times per week. He felt much more relaxed than his backseat passenger.

Georgiy understood that along his route to the airport, some of the small-town police officers would come out to the highway to earn some—and in some cases, a lot—of extra cash. Depending on the time of day or night, it happened to Georgiy about once a month, somewhere along the three-hour trip.

Georgiy felt like he had perhaps twenty to thirty seconds to pull the vehicle over before pissing the police officer off to the point of aggravating the situation. Georgiy searched the road's shoulder ahead of him for a spot to safely pull over. It wasn't easy, as the forest on both sides of the road encroached on the road's rather narrow shoulders.

But at least traffic has been light, he thought, with one car coming from the opposite direction on the old highway about every three minutes or so.

"Mr. Conti, do you have any euro bills with you?" he asked, looking in his rearview mirror at Conti while slowing the SUV down.

"I do," replied Marco.

Marco and his two international buddies had made a point of being sure to have sufficient cash for their mission, needed for when you least expect it.

Georgiy, still looking in the center rearview mirror, observed Marco reaching into his breast pocket. Marco pulled out a small, thin leather wallet that contained three credit cards and five fifty-euro bills.

"You got a fifty in there? Or maybe two twenties?" asked Georgiy.

"I've got a fifty," said Marco as Georgiy pulled the vehicle to a stop.

"Mind if I make a donation with it?" asked Georgiy.

"Not at all," said Marco.

Georgiy extended his right hand—with his palm up—behind the seat. Marco put a folded fifty-euro bill in Georgiy's palm.

Georgiy grabbed it and, in one motion, reached for his glove box. He opened it. He grabbed the purpose-built plastic envelope containing his registration and proof of insurance out of the glove box.

He and Marco both heard the police vehicle's car door slam.

Georgy slipped the fifty-euro bill into the envelope and between the registration and insurance documents.

The last time Georgiy got stopped by a straight cop was in 2022. Georgiy was ready for that possibility, too. If the cop challenged or questioned Georgiy about the money in the envelope, he'd simply say, "Aw, shit, I forgot that bill was in there. That was a big tip from one of my international patrons."

In 2022, it worked like a charm.

Georgiy rolled his window down just before the late-middle-aged, portly police officer walked up to the car.

The cop practically leaned into Georgiy's window.

"What the hell is your hurry, son?" asked the officer.

Georgiy thought he might have heard a slight slur in the man's speech, but he couldn't smell any alcohol.

"I run a transportation service, and I have an important West-European businessman in the back seat. We are headed to the Krasnodar airport. He's had a family emergency. Sorry if I was going too fast," said Georgiy.

"You sure were," said the police officer.

"Where is your important passenger from?" asked the officer, now bending down to look into the back seat.

"Italy," said Georgiy.

The officer held the envelope, not yet looking at it.

"What the hell is he doing here?"

"He sells wine," said Georgiy.

"Hmmm," replied the officer.

"Is there any wine in the trunk?"

Georgy had met a few corrupt police officers, but he was surprised by how bold this one was.

"Nope. There's nothing back there. Just the passenger in the backseat."

"Well, that's too bad," said the police officer.

He looked into the envelope and, without fanfare, grabbed the euro bill and stuffed it into his breast pocket. He handed the envelope back to Georgiy.

"Listen, son, you need to slow the hell down. This time, I'm not going to write you a ticket. But next time, you might not be so lucky. Could cost you a hefty fine. Understand?"

"Yes, sir," replied Georgiy.

CHAPTER 85

"WE HAVE A MISSION TO DO"
September 2024

STANDING OUTSIDE THE VEHICLE WITH THE FRONT DOORS OPEN and the interior dome light disengaged, the two men immediately put on their border guard tactical uniforms. It was gradually becoming daylight, and Rostov was slowly waking up.

Hennadiy got behind the steering wheel, and Jake climbed into the passenger seat. It was wartime, and it was not uncommon to see Russian military members of all stripes wearing camouflaged tactical uniforms this close to Ukraine's border, in a city with a major Russian military headquarters.

They decided in Tuscany that Hennadiy would be the colonel and Jake would be the captain. Hennadiy's Russian was indistinguishable from that of the educated Russian speakers who came from Moscow and served in the officer ranks of Russia's armed forces. And it was understood by both men that whenever they passed through military checkpoints, it was the driver who, about ninety percent of the time, got questioned. Hennadiy was the only choice for the job.

But there was a problem: a colonel normally did not drive with a captain in the vehicle. That typically was the captain's job. So, Manny Alavarez helped the duo cook up a story: the captain had twisted his driving ankle the day before playing soccer, but he had to come on the trip because he knew a lot about Luhansk, their destination, before crossing the border into Ukraine.

Hennadiy wheeled the vehicle out of the stadium parking lot and headed for Konstantinovsk, a town of roughly 18,000 inhabitants situated on the Don River. It was about a two-hour drive east by northeast of Rostov. Having cleared Rostov's city limits after about thirty miles, Jake felt he was in familiar terrain.

"Feels a lot like Michigan or other places in the US Midwest," said Jake as the bright morning sun made its appearance. "A lot of open spaces, some farmland, forests in between, and a small village here and there along the way. The Don River no doubt has provided this area with plenty of water for agriculture and sustenance over the centuries."

"It's a big river," said Hennadiy. "The fifth largest in Europe. It starts up in central Russia, not far from Moscow, and dumps into the Sea of Azov."

Hennadiy continued. "You know, Jake, this kinda reminds me of home, too. And I have no doubt there are some good people working and living in these rural areas. It's too bad that SOB in Moscow has fooled so many people in this country. But you and I have a mission to do, and we are going to get it done."

"Amen, my brother," replied Jake. "Amen."

CHAPTER 86
THE HIDE AREA
September 2024

"THERE'S OUR LANDMARK," said Jake.

While Gazprom was a well-known, big Russian natural gas company, its lesser-known subsidiary, Gazprom Neft, was a retail supplier of gas for automobiles and trucks throughout Russia. Out in the middle of the southwestern Russia countryside, just off the highway, Jake was surprised at just how modern and clean the Gazprom Neft gas station was.

Heck, that's as nice as any gas station we have back home. Too bad we can't run in there and grab an espresso and a sandwich, thought Jake.

Not knowing if the station had security cameras, Jake and Hennadiy didn't want to take the risk to their operational security by getting themselves recorded on a security videotape.

Jake and Hennadiy kept driving about a mile past the station, took a left turn off the main thoroughfare onto a forested two-track road, and drove about 100 yards into it.

They had reconned the area using Google Maps and Margarita's description of the area surrounding Konstantinovsk, an area she had twice visited.

"This spot will do just fine, don't you think?" asked Hennadiy, referring to a parking spot in the trees off the road.

"It's perfect," replied Jake. Plenty of natural concealment and easy access out of here at night."

Jake got out of the vehicle, walked around the back, opened the hatch, and grabbed the 20-liter (5.3-gallon) gas can. He emptied its contents into the SUV. He walked about forty yards through the trees and found several small branches on the ground. He covered the gas can with the branches and other small deadfall.

CHAPTER 87
THE HOUSE
September 2024

AFTER DARK, THE TWO MEN MADE THEIR MOVE. Their fourteen-minute drive to the wooded area behind the boys' house was uneventful. Wearing their night vision goggles to prevent people from seeing their headlights, they pulled off the hard surface road and drove forty yards into the trees. They backed their vehicle into their final spot. Backing in allowed for a quick, "tactical departure," should one be needed.

Calmly putting on their black overalls and skull caps, Jake and Hennadiy left their vehicle. After walking about ten paces, they realized there was enough ambient starlight that they would not need their night vision goggles. Positioning themselves in the wood line forty yards behind the house, they had a perfect view into the boys' bedroom.

Jake briefly put on his night vision goggles and increased the magnification.

The window, thought Hennadiy. *Thank God.*

Hennadiy was thankful the boys' window, rolled from the bottom up, was open by about an inch. That would make access much easier. From their position in the trees, both men were thrilled when the boys' bedroom light came on. But Hennadiy was very surprised when he saw Sergiy. Gleb was harder to make out, with only the top of his head coming into view as the boys began to get their clothes off and their pajamas on.

"Is that them?" whispered Jake, knowing this was a very critical moment in their mission.

"It is," whispered Hennadiy. "But Sergiy has grown maybe a foot since I last saw him."

Indeed, it had been over three years since Hennadiy had seen the boys.

The men waited until Sergiy, now twelve years old, turned out the overhead light. It instantly became obvious to both men that the boys had left a smaller and less luminescent light on, perhaps on a nightstand or chest of drawers. They couldn't be sure until they got to the window.

Once Sergiy was sure that Gleb, now eight years old, fell asleep every night, Sergiy would turn off the light. On some nights, Sergiy would pass out right after Gleb did, and the light would remain on until the morning.

***

Jake and Hennadiy waited an hour, and then Jake moved off to the side to get a better view of the master bedroom. From their position facing the back of the house, the room was on the left side. Jake watched the bedroom window for about forty-five minutes, until the lights went out. Jake silently returned to Hennadiy's side.

"The lights are out in the main bedroom," Jake whispered.

Per the mission rehearsals, he and Hennadiy waited another half hour and then decided to make their move.

What the two men did not know was that Kira had left a half-drunk Dimitry sleeping on the couch. Before she'd crawled into bed, Kira had taken her ritual, strong sleeping pill. Once she crawled into bed, she put in earplugs, offering some refuge from Dimitry's wall-shaking snoring. A severely depressed Kira believed Dimitry when Dimitry said, "I will kill you the next time you try to stop me" from hurting the boys, so any thought of Kira coming to the boys' rescue had long passed.

Hennadiy led the way to the bedroom window, with Jake right behind them.

The rehearsals called for Hennadiy to climb into the room first, with Jake following. If Gleb happened to be awake and spotted the first intruder, it was anybody's guess what would happen. That was a risk both men decided was acceptable.

On the other hand, if Sergiy spotted Hennadiy first, then Hennadiy was ninety percent sure that Sergiy would recognize him. That was also a ten percent risk that both men were willing to take.

Fortunately, the windowsill was about chest high for Hennadiy and Jake. But the heavier Hennadiy would need a boost from Jake. Again, it was something they had practiced before the mission. As both men stood at the window, Jake got on his hands and knees. Hennadiy stepped up on Jake's back and peered into the room.

Hennadiy could see that the small light was not on the nightstand between the two beds but on the chest of drawers, where the sole electrical outlet for the room was located, in the far-right corner of the room.

"Thank God," thought Hennadiy, knowing he would not have to crawl over the nightstand and the light to get in the room.

Hennadiy grabbed the bottom of the window slowly and raised it all the way up. As he did, the widow made two audible squeaks. Sergiy, whose head was just to the right and below the windowsill, began to stir. But he was not fully awake. Gleb slept on the other side of the nightstand, with both boys' heads at the window side of the room.

Sergiy mumbled something—*perhaps in his sleep,* prayed Hennadiy. Hennadiy froze. He did not want either boy to wake up until he and Jake were fully in the room.

Hennadiy half-pulled himself and half-crawled through the window, headfirst. He landed with a slight thump on the floor after his torso and lower legs bounced off the nightstand. He quickly recovered, stepped back, and Jake came through the window right behind him. Jake's was a better "landing."

The plan was to quietly wake up Sergiy first, and then Gleb. But what happened next was not part of the original contingency planning or rehearsals.

"Uncle Hennadiy!" cried out Sergiy.

Little Sergiy, who was not so little anymore, didn't know if he was in a wonderful dream or reality.

Hennadiy and Jake both put their fingers to their lips to signal and say, "shhhhh, be quiet." But it was too late.

Down the hall, from the living room, a half-asleep and more than half-drunk Dimitry heard Sergiy's voice. He was finishing a bag of chips and about ready to head to bed when he heard the commotion.

Still seated on the couch, Dimitry yelled "What the fuck!" as loud as he could toward the boys' bedroom.

Kira, in her sleepy refuge from the hell her life had become, heard none of it.

Jake immediately pointed and whispered to Hennadiy, "Stand in the corner." The corner was opposite the window and would be to the left of the old man's peripheral vision if he entered the room. Jake added, "Turn off the light." Hennadiy, standing between the chest of drawers and the wall closet, turned off the small-shaded lamp atop the chest of drawers.

Jake immediately got into bed with Sergiy and pulled the sheet over both himself and Sergiy.

Within seconds, they could hear the old man shuffling toward the door and grumbling to himself as he tried to get his belt off.

The door opened, and the man turned on the overhead light, about to scream at the boys and make them wish they'd never cross him again.

Jake hesitated for two seconds, making sure Dimitry was fully inside the room. In one swift motion, Jake sprang from the bed holding the sheet wide with his arms stretched out and threw the sheet over the top of the old man before he knew what hit him. Jake instantly put a chokehold on the old man.

Dimitry had no idea what kind of Twilight Zone he had ventured into. All he saw was a big white sheet coming toward his face, with no clue as to who or what was behind it when it enveloped him.

Jake held his choke hold long enough for Dimitry to pass out, but not long enough to kill him. As Dimitry began slumping to the floor, Hennadiy helped Jake ease Dimitry down to a lying position, on his side, on the floor. Jake and Hennadiy wanted to do their best to ensure Dimitry had no long-term or debilitating injuries, despite his treatment of the boys. Falling and hitting his head on the floor might do that. Placing Dimitry on his side so that if he threw up during the night, the drunken man, who smelled strongly of vodka, would not choke in his vomit.

Gleb slept through it all.

"What can I do?" whispered Sergiy.

"Dang, I like this kid," whispered Jake to Hennadiy.

Looking at Hennadiy as he pulled two zip ties out of his pocket, Jake quipped, "Is he related to you?"

"Damn right he is," replied Hennadiy.

Jake zip-tied the unconscious man's hands at his wrists. He then took the man's unbuckled, half-out belt and cinched it down on Dimitry's ankles.

"Sergiy," said Jake. "Please hand me your pillowcase."

Sergiy removed the pillowcase from his pillow and handed it to Jake.

Jake took the pillowcase, twisted it several times to form a makeshift rope, and tied it around Dimitry's mouth. He checked Dimitry to make sure he could still breathe through his nose. Jake tied off the pillowcase on the back of Dimitry's head.

"Do you have any belts?" Jake asked Sergiy.

"Yes, I do," replied Sergiy.

"Good. Give me the one you like the least."

Sergiy went to the closet and pulled out an old belt.

Jake took the belt and grabbed Dimitry's zip-tied wrists. He pulled his wrists a few inches toward the corner leg of the bed and, with Sergiy's belt, tied Dimitry's zip-tied wrists around the corner leg of Gleb's bed.

"Is your mother a light sleeper?" whispered Jake.

"She's not my mother," replied Sergiy. "My mother is dead. But Kira, no, she is not a light sleeper, at least not anymore."

"Good. Well, it's time to wake up Gleb," said Jake.

CHAPTER 88
WE'RE GOING HOME, BOYS
September 2024

ON HIS WAY TO THE FRONT DOOR, JAKE WALKED BY THE MASTER BEDROOM DOOR. Through the door, he could hear Kira snoring. Jake continued to step lightly toward the front door.

Reaching the door, he unlocked it from the inside. He ground his boot soles into the cement floor and small area rugs, leaving slight, black scuff marks. The ruse was intended to throw investigators off their trail or at least slow them down enough to consider not one, but two or three scenarios when trying to piece together the evening's events.

Jake grabbed the boys' two pairs of tennis shoes from just inside the front door.

He returned to the room, where the boys had finished putting on their "favorite"—as directed and helped by Uncle Hennadiy—clothes and jackets from the closet. Jake shut the door behind him.

Hennadiy and Jake knew it was time to leave.

"Let's go," whispered Hennadiy. "We're going *home,* boys."

Gleb had a question.

"Is it OK if I take my Spider-Man pajamas, Uncle Hennadiy?" asked Gleb.

Hennadiy looked at Jake. Jake nodded.

"Of course it is," replied Hennadiy, smiling.

Gleb snatched his pajamas off the bed.

Jake went out the window first. Hennadiy handed each boy through the window to Jake. Hennadiy came through the window last, assisted by Jake from the ground. Once on the ground, Hennadiy again stood on Jake's back and lowered the window back down within an inch of the windowsill. The entire time the duo spent in the room with the boys was eleven minutes, large parts of it taken up by the boys pulling their clothes out of the closet and getting dressed, as well as getting a knocked-out Dimitry situated on the floor.

***

Standing in the darkness at the back of the vehicle, Hennadiy did all the talking.

"Ok, boys, we're going on a trip, a trip back home."

"Yaaaay!" whispered Gleb.

Sergiy smiled hugely.

"So, if you gotta pee, do so before you get in the back. We're going to cover you with this tarp. Sergiy, it's your job to make sure there is plenty of space at the end, up near the back seats, for air to get in. We'll do a little test before we leave, OK? Got it?"

"Sure thing, Uncle Hennadiy," replied Sergiy.

Hennadiy felt like he was talking to a different person than the one he had last seen at a family reunion in the summer of 2021.

He has the confidence and presence of a boy three or four years older, thought Hennadiy. *Remarkable for what he's been through.*

"If we get stopped, you guys need to be super quiet. But before we head to the Ukrainian border, we'll be able to stop for a few hours and get some sleep, if you haven't fallen asleep already. And if you need water, just say so. By tomorrow morning, we will have you back in Ukraine, OK?"

"And we will be able to see our father then?" asked Sergiy.

The question crushed Hennadiy's heart. His mind scrambled for an answer.

"When we get to Ukraine, we can talk about that, OK?" answered Hennadiy, not wanting to crush Sergiy's spirit with the truth before starting their journey.

"OK, guys, go pee, and we'll get you in the back," said Hennadiy.

The boys stepped a few paces away and did their business, and Jake and Hennadiy got them situated in the back. Gleb took his Spider-Man pajamas and made a pillow out of the lump of clothes. Sergiy took off his puffer jacket and did the same thing. Within seconds, Hennadiy and Jake quietly pulled the SUV out of its hide area.

"Are you boys comfortable back there?" asked Jake.

"Yes, we are!" replied Sergiy with enthusiasm.

Both boys felt like they were on the adventure of their lives, with no thought of the danger that both Jake and Hennadiy knew was ahead.

Minutes later, Hennadiy pulled the vehicle over to a wooded area, just off the highway they'd come in on. Jake got out of the vehicle, went to a middle-of-nowhere wood line, and walked about thirty yards into it. He covered his and Hennadiy's black overalls, skull caps, and extra zip ties in a small pile of brush.

They kept their pistols and night vision goggles under their seats, just in case.

Before Hennadiy pulled away from the wood line, the presence of Jake and Hennadiy, now wearing their border guard tactical uniforms, the warmth inside the vehicle, and the safety the boys felt for the first time in over two and a half years lulled the boys into a deep sleep. It was well past their bedtime.

CHAPTER 89
THE CHECKPOINT
September 2024

NAUTICAL TWILIGHT WAS SLOWLY MAKING ITS GREY, EARLY MORNING APPEARANCE. It was 5:13 A.M. Hennadiy drove along the E58 coastal road west of Rostov and along the northeastern shore of the Sea of Azov. Sunrise was in fifty-five minutes.

At Primorka, the coastal town of 3,800 inhabitants and only sixty miles from the border with Ukraine, Hennadiy took the two-lane, narrow country road due north through the tiny rural villages of Pokrovskoe, Ryasnoe, Mateev Kurgan, and Alexseevka. Each village was just a few miles apart from each other and within a few miles of the Russia—Donetsk region border.

Thank God for those satellite photos, thought Hennadiy.

As a colonel in the Ukrainian Air Force, nobody batted an eye when Hennadiy entered the top-secret area in the Ministry of Defense and asked to see the overhead satellite images covering the areas east and north of Mariupol. The human intelligence reports coming out of the Donetsk area, some 100 miles north of Mariupol, were also very helpful in planning Hennadiy's and Jake's mission to rescue the boys.

"We're within six miles of the border with Donetsk," confirmed Hennadiy after passing by the village of Alexseevka, just a few miles inside the border.

"Roger that," replied Jake.

Hennadiy lowered his driver's side window about two inches. He smiled at hearing the morning songbirds announce their pre-dawn presence from the trees just off the road. Hennadiy knew it would not be much farther until the first major test of the day for him, Jake, and the boys.

Driving thirty miles per hour on the now unpaved, gravel road, he saw it: it was right where the satellite photo showed it to be, about 300 yards ahead.

"There it is, Jake," he said redundantly, as Jake had spotted it the same instant as Hennadiy. "The first checkpoint."

The boys were still sound asleep in the back of the SUV, oblivious to the fact that this "first major checkpoint" would be the first major hurdle in determining if they would be able to return to Ukraine with their uncle . . . or not. Unbeknownst to the boys, their new life, if they got that far, would be with Hennadiy and Mila Kovalenko, and not their father.

"You got this," said Jake. "*We* got this."

Per the plan, they took out their identity cards and had them ready.

As they approached the checkpoint, Jake and Hennadiy's heart rates picked up. But deep down inside, they knew they had excellent cover by wearing Russian border guard uniforms, being inside an authentic-looking border guard vehicle, and hopefully, carrying legitimate—or at least legitimate-looking— border guard identification cards. Manny had paid the Russian criminal a hefty price for those cards, as well as their military orders, sending them to Donetsk.

As they slowly approached the manually operated gate, at about 150 yards out, Hennadiy reduced his speed to about twenty-five miles per hour. Jake remembered why they picked this crossing point for going into Donetsk, the former Ukrainian Oblast region now occupied by the Russian Army. Vasily Puchta "annexed" (meaning seized and made part of Russia) the Donetsk region on September 30, 2022. On the same day, he "annexed" three other Ukrainian border regions with Russia: the Kherson, Luhansk, and Zaporizhzhia oblasts. Jake realized that in ten days it would be the second anniversary of those annexations.

Fortunately, about one quarter of the region is still occupied by Ukrainian sympathizers and partisans, thought Jake.

As they rolled up to the checkpoint's barrier, a young Russian soldier on Hennadiy's side of the vehicle cradled his rifle in his right arm and held out his left hand, the vehicle to stop.

The twenty-year-old soldier had been drafted from the fringes of Irkutsk, a southern Siberian city of about 550,000 people nicknamed "The Paris of Siberia" because of its wide streets and stylish buildings. Irkutsk is situated about 150 miles north of the Russia-Mongolia border.

The young soldier was 5,800 kilometers (about 3,500 miles) and five time zones from home. But he was lucky, very lucky. He was not at the front where Russian boys and young men were dying by the thousands.

Having been at his post for only two months, the Russian Army private had seen only logistics and supply vehicles come this way through the checkpoint, from both directions.

Civilians were rarely allowed to cross at the military checkpoint, and he'd never seen an official government civilian vehicle come through the checkpoint. The white SUV with the big blue lettering on its hood and side was a first for him.

As Hennadiy stopped the SUV at the barrier, the soldier looked at his buddy on the opposite side of the vehicle. His buddy was a bit more worldly and militarily experienced, but only by a few months. He approached the SUV from the right side of the windshield and saw the two passengers.

The one driving the vehicle is clearly a senior officer, the older soldier thought, *and the individual in the driver's seat is an officer as well.*

He gestured to the younger soldier, and the two had a quick conference.

"Look," said the older soldier, conscripted from St. Petersburg, "the guy behind the wheel is a senior officer, in uniform. You don't need to check his ID card. Just waive them through."

"But the sergeant said to check everybody," said the younger soldier from Irkutsk.

The two chatted some more. And then the soldier from St. Petersburg did what every young soldier does when he's in doubt: he goes to his sergeant for guidance.

About ten minutes later, the soldier from St. Petersburg came back from the nearby guard shed, this time with his sergeant, a twenty-three-year-old man from Moscow. The sergeant had been woken up by his soldier forty minutes before his regular wakeup time, and the sergeant was not happy.

He came around the front of the vehicle and approached the driver's side window. Hennadiy had rolled down his window the instant he stopped at the barricade.

The sergeant stepped up to the window.

"Good morning, sir, I'm sorry I have to ask you this, but do you have any ID?"

"Sure thing, sergeant," replied Hennadiy in perfect Russian, fully aware of Russian military ranks.

"We don't get many vehicles like this coming through here, sir," added the sergeant.

"I understand," replied Hennadiy, handing his ID card to the soldier.

The moment of truth, thought Jake, praying the ID card looked legitimate.

The soldier took it and gave the ID card's front side a quick look. He then flipped it over, giving it an even quicker glance.

"Thank you, sir," he replied. "I'm sorry I have to tell you this as I am sure you are already aware . . . but we've been instructed to state this to *everyone* who passes through this checkpoint."

The younger soldier had what the sergeant was about to say written on a piece of paper, still stuffed in his uniform pocket. But the sergeant had the message memorized perfectly.

"You are about to enter the Donetsk Oblast. It is part of Russian Territory, but small parts of it are still illegally occupied by the Nazi enemy from the west. So be aware and proceed at your own risk."

"I understand, sergeant," replied Hennadiy. "Good job."

The sergeant saluted the Russian border police colonel, and Hennadiy returned his salute.

"Lift the gate up and let them pass!" shouted the sergeant, still angry that the young private woke him up early for something so unimportant.

Hennadiy stepped on the accelerator and drove on.

Illegally occupied, my ass, thought Hennadiy.

Jake knew there was no time for celebration, only prayerful gratitude. Another big hurdle to getting the kids to freedom and safety had been overcome. But Jake knew there was more danger ahead.

CHAPTER 90
THE BORDER
September 2024

"THERE IT IS," SAID JAKE, WHO SPOTTED THE BUILDING FIRST. It was more impressive than the Russian Army guard shack and "screening" checkpoint they had just driven through a few kilometers back.

Hennadiy spotted the physical structure an instant after Jake did. Having done their intelligence homework, from information provided by Ukrainian human intelligence sources (spies) still located in the Donbas region, they understood the purpose of this outpost at the former Ukraine-Russia border. It was mainly used to monitor crossings into Donetsk, which Russia had seized and was now considered by the Kremlin to be within Russia's greater geographic borders.

Just a month prior, Vasily Puchta mandated that all Ukrainians—roughly twenty to twenty-five percent of the remaining Donetsk region population—apply for Russian citizenship, "or be deported." If deported, this would mean their homes and all possessions would be seized and forever lost to Russia. Many decided to stay and continue to risk Russian authorities.

On January 21, 2024, roughly nine months prior to Jake and Hennadiy's imminent arrival at the border, twenty-eight civilians were killed, and at least thirty others were wounded in an artillery strike on a Donetsk city market. Both sides denied involvement. Since then and even earlier, Ukrainian partisans were in the area doing whatever they could to disrupt Russia's attempted stranglehold on their Ukrainian homes and fellow citizens.

Hennadiy slowed his speed to 15 mph as he entered a series of barricaded "S" turns. They were intended to dissuade any vehicle-borne suicide bombers from taking a direct, top-speed shot at the crossing and its adjacent cinder block building. Ahead, Hennadiy and Jake could see a border guard junior sergeant wearing the same uniform as Hennadiy and Jake.

Completing the "S" turn, Hennadiy stopped the SUV right where a sergeant stood waiting. Hennadiy lowered his driver's side window.

"Good morning, Colonel!" began the sergeant, saluting Hennadiy.

"Good morning, sergeant," replied Hennadiy.

In the back, Sergiy was awake under the tarp.

The loud voices had awoken Gleb, too, and Gleb began to stir. He mumbled something as he slowly came out of his slumber.

Sergiy knew he must act.

"Gleb . . . shhhhhh," he whispered gently.

With a little light entering under the tarp where the boys' heads were—opposite the back hatch and closer to the back seats—Sergiy could see Gleb facing him and that Gleb's eyes were open.

Sergiy held his finger to his lips again, in the universal signal for "Be quiet."

Gleb's eyes widened, acknowledging he'd received the message.

From the front, Jake had heard the commotion from the back of the vehicle, but fortunately, the Russian border guard did not react, obviously not having heard it. Nor did Hennadiy react, but Hennadiy had clearly heard it, too.

"Sir, I must ask you for your ID card and the other passenger's card, as well," said the sergeant.

Hennadiy extended an open palm toward Jake to take Jake's Russian border guard ID card, and Hennadiy added his own to it. He handed both ID cards to the young sergeant.

Jake's card had yet to be given the "seal of approval" by the border and military authorities.

Given they were in a Russian government vehicle that was essentially leaving Mother Russia to travel into a dangerous, "wild west" part of annexed Russia, the guards at this border crossing were more concerned about traffic coming *out* of annexed Donetsk and into Russia. And Jake chose to focus on that thought.

"Here you go, sir," replied the sergeant, handing the cards back to Hennadiy.

Hennadiy and Jake were relieved.

But as Hennadiy handed Jake's card back to Jake, and an older sergeant—*at least ten or fifteen years older than the young sergeant,* reckoned Jake—seemed to step out of nowhere. He walked up to Hennadiy's side of the vehicle. Through the opaque, bulletproof window behind the young sergeant, the older sergeant had seen the official vehicle pull up. He was instantly curious who this colonel might be, why he was driving the SUV instead of the other passenger, and what he was doing coming into the Donetsk region.

Just as Hennadiy was about to take his foot off the brake and onto the accelerator, the older sergeant spoke.

"Wait, sir," said the older sergeant. "Don't you have a driver?"

"I do," Hennadiy shot back, "but my captain hurt his driving ankle playing soccer two days ago, and he said the driving makes him very uncomfortable. What a pussy. They don't make captains like they used to!"

Hennadiy threw his head back in a wild-eyed laugh.

The old sergeant grinned.

"I have no response for that, colonel," replied the senior sergeant, also thinking it was funny.

Jake thought *that* should *get us off the hook.* It didn't.

"Sir, are you headed to Donetsk City?" continued the sergeant.

It's the only place that made sense to the sergeant for this senior Russian border guard colonel to be traveling to.

"Yes," replied Hennadiy.

"Might I ask, what your business is there?"

"If you can prove to me that you have a need to know, sergeant, I'll tell you," replied Hennadiy. "My mission is straight from the Kremlin. Do you need to know more than that?"

If the sergeant pressed his case or went to get the senior-ranking person at the crossing, a young captain, Hennadiy was ready for a response: "To perform a reconnaissance for a location to conduct a prisoner exchange with those fuckin' Ukrainian Nazis."

And if the senior sergeant went total jackass on him, Hennadiy had the letter, still in the glovebox, which—hopefully—would prove it to the sergeant.

The senior sergeant considered his responses and nodded.

"Understood, sir," replied the senior sergeant. "Be safe as you travel up to Donetsk city. The route is safer than a year ago, but it's still dangerous territory. The lettering on the side of your vehicle could make you a big target if the wrong people see it."

"Will do," replied Hennadiy. "And by the way. I appreciate you doing your duty."

The sergeant saluted Hennadiy, and Hennadiy returned his salute.

Hennadiy took his foot off the brake, eased it onto the accelerator, and slowly drove away into the Donetsk countryside. Being this far southwest in the Donetsk region—and close to the Russian border—was still quite safe. With the border post in Hennadiy's rearview mirror, about 300 yards behind them, Hennadiy and Jake relaxed.

"They don't make captains like that anymore?" quipped Jake. "Gotta say, I resemble that remark! Even in the real world, you outrank me, and you're doing all the driving!"

The retired US Army lieutenant colonel and his newly retired Ukrainian colonel friend laughed out loud.

Sergiy piped up from the back.

"Uncle Hennadiy," said Sergiy.

"Good morning, Sergiy!" replied Hennadiy. "What's up?"

"Are we safe now?" asked Sergiy.

"Not quite," replied Hennadiy. "Almost, but not quite. You guys are going to have to wait a little longer. Stay under that tarp."

Hennadiy continued to drive toward the town of Starobesheve when Sergiy piped up again.

"Uncle Hennadiy, I gotta pee," replied Sergiy.

"I gotta pee, too!" added Gleb.

"Me three!" replied Jake.

Sergiy, who was within months of turning thirteen, chuckled.

Hennadiy nodded his head.

I need to make a communications check, anyway, he thought.

"OK, guys, we'll find a safe spot in the forest to take care of business," replied Hennadiy.

CHAPTER 91
WAIT!
September 2024

AS JAKE AND THE BOYS WERE TAKING CARE OF BUSINESS, HENNADIY pulled out his burner phone. He typed in the simple text message: "ETA 0900–0915 (9:00–9:15 A.M.)."

"Artem," the Ukrainian partisan leader who would serve as the foursome's contact for traveling out of the Donetsk region and back into Ukraine, was expecting the text. He was not sure what number it would be coming from. The plan had called for Hennadiy to acquire the burner phone in Russia. But Artem understood he would not know what the number was until Hennadiy contacted him. He knew only that Hennadiy would contact him sometime between 0600 and 0800 to confirm their linkup time.

Located in Vuhledar (population, 14,000), Donetsk Oblast, about forty miles southwest of Donetsk city, Artem shook his head when he received the message from Hennadiy.

"Wait!" Artem texted back. "Change ETA to 1730 -1800 (5:30–6:00 P.M.). Situation fluid."

When Hennadiy departed from Munich just a few days prior, he knew the situation southeast of Donetsk city—although the locations and frontlines of Russian Army and Ukrainian Army forces seemed to be stabilizing—was still "fluid." However, Russian Army forces were probing for Ukrainian Army and Ukrainian partisan forces, and vice versa.

Sometimes, the opposing forces were less than two or three miles apart, almost playing a game of chicken. However, what Hennadiy did not know was that the Russian Army forces were within two weeks of mounting a major offensive to seize Vuhledar and disrupt the Ukrainian defenses of the area, so a gradual Russian Army buildup was taking place.

Hennadiy also did not know that this morning, Artem and his team had sent out a small drone into the no-man's land east of Vuhledar. They spotted some Russian tanks kicking up a dust trail about eleven miles from their hideout. This was a first for the Ukrainian partisans. Previously, while they had observed light Russian reconnaissance vehicles, they had not observed any heavy tanks closer than twenty miles away.

To get to Vuhledar, Hennadiy would have to drive through the rear of those tank lines, through their front lines, and on to Vuhledar.

If he gets stopped by Russian soldiers, I hope he's a damn good actor when he tells his story, thought Artem.

***

With Jake and the boys back at the vehicle, Hennadiy let Jake in on the new information.

"We've been held up. Our contact just texted me to set a new ETA (estimated time of arrival), to around 5:30–6:00 P.M. Sunset is around 6:30 P.M. We will proceed from here at 4:00 P.M. It should take us about ninety minutes to drive. If all goes well, we'll arrive at Vuhledar right at 5:30 P.M., maybe 5:45. I'd rather be early than be late," said Hennadiy.

"I completely agree, my friend," replied Jake.

"And Hennadiy," added Jake, "I think it's time we grabbed our weapons."

"Roger that," replied Hennadiy.

Jake thought back to his days as a US Army Special Forces A-Team leader in Afghanistan.

At least there, it was better than a fair fight. I could call in artillery, Apache helicopters, air strikes . . . most anything we needed to get us out of a jam. Here, it could get tricky.

Jake opened the rear passenger door, pulled the seat back, and grabbed the two Russian Army pistols.

Sergiy and Gleb were sitting in the back, ready to get under the tarp again when told to do so. Sergiy's eyes widened.

"You got one for me?" asked Sergiy, thinking he'd had enough summer military training to be helpful.

"Sorry, pal," replied Jake. "There are only two pistols here. Maybe next time. But we have some sandwiches for you and Gleb."

Jake took his extra sandwich out of his backpack and gave it to Sergiy, and Hennadiy followed suit with his sandwich, giving it to Gleb.

"Thank you!" said Sergiy, then Gleb.

CHAPTER 92
CLEAR SHOT
September 2024

HENNADIY AND JAKE COULDN'T BELIEVE IT. With their loaded Russian Army MP-443 "Grach" (9 mm) pistols between their legs, and extra ammo clips in their pants pockets, they had just driven in a westerly direction from Novotroits'ke, Donetsk Oblast, and through the Russian Army's rear encampments and logistics areas. The main TO509 country road was completely open. All the Russian military positions were at least 200 yards away from the road. Every single tank they had seen was facing west, *as they should,* thought Jake.

The Russian Army had decided to keep the road completely open to be able to move vehicles and equipment efficiently through the area.

Well, they must have learned at least a few tactical lessons, thought Jake.

The Russians had learned—or at least it seemed so to Jake— that any Russian Army traffic jams would make for excellent, big-bang-for-the-buck targets for the Ukrainians to attack. In the preceding two and a half years of war, the Russians had lost tens of thousands of soldiers and billions of dollars' worth of vehicles and equipment, *because of stupid, War 101 tactical errors,* thought Jake.

Tactical errors like allowing vehicles to get bunched up— sometimes even bumper to bumper—or stopping on a road for even short periods of time had caused tremendous losses of soldiers and equipment to the Russian Army.

As Hennadiy continued to drive the SUV down the narrow, supposedly two-lane hard surface road, Jake broke the silence.

"Looks like we've got a clear shot to home," said Jake.

A slight pause ensued.

"But this feels like it's been too darn easy," said Jake.

Hennadiy nodded.

"I hear ya," responded Hennadiy.

With two young family members of Hennadiy's lying under a tarp in the back of the SUV, both men felt the immense gravity of the moment. However, they were grateful that the big "Border Police" letters on the side of their vehicle seemed to dissuade most anybody from coming after them. Besides, the soldiers were far more worried about the enemy "Ukrainian Nazi's" than they were about a lone Border Police vehicle that was on their team.

Jake wanted to say it, but decided to keep his thoughts to himself.

I hope I didn't just jinx us with that 'too easy' comment.

CHAPTER 93
ENEMY FORCES AHEAD
September 2024

JAKE AND HENNADIY LET OUT A SIGH OF RELIEF but said nothing. They had just passed through Stepne, a Ukrainian village of a few hundred people in the Ukrainian steppe area. There were no trees or shrubs as far as the eye could see. Only open, green fields. Some fields were plowed; some were not.

This looks like open tank country, thought Jake, *where Russian tanks can see and engage their targets from over two miles away.*

Hennadiy could almost taste the freedom and safety he, Jake, and the boys, especially the boys, would hopefully soon experience. There were twelve miles to go, across open steppe terrain (*feels like Iowa or Nebraska,* thought Jake). At the end of the twelve miles, they could hug Artem and his brave Ukrainian partisan teammates.

After driving two and a half miles past Stepne, they approached the village of Solodke. The sun was slowly making its downward exit, just on the horizon to the west. And it was directly in Hennadiy's eyes. The Solodke village was entirely situated on the left side of the road, with completely open terrain to the right.

The blinding sun caused Hennadiy to slow his speed. As he did, a phantom appeared on the road, silhouetted by the sun from behind. The phantom held its rifle in its right hand with the palm of its left hand extended out toward the "Border Police" vehicle.

Where the hell did he come from? thought Jake.

A young man in a camouflaged Russian uniform stepped around to Hennadiy's side of the vehicle and approached Hennadiy's driver's side window. Through Hennadiy's window, Jake could see a BRDM, a Russian reconnaissance vehicle, about fifty yards away. It was tucked up next to a small, wooden house.

In his early days at the US Army Infantry School, Jake had memorized the profile of the BRDM, along with other former Soviet military vehicles. Beside the armored and wheeled troop carrier, he could see two soldiers seated on the ground. They were eating some military rations out of cans. A fourth soldier was in the vehicle's cupola. His rifle was at the ready position, observing what was taking place at the SUV.

Jake's militarily experienced thought was instant.

We surprised them. They are in the middle of eating their evening chow, and one soldier came away from the BRDM to do his duty, while another soldier put himself in an overwatch position in the vehicle's cupola.

Hennadiy rolled down his window.

Standing outside the window, like a highway patrolman about to have a chat with a driver, was a young, lanky, twenty-four-year-old Russian Army lieutenant.

Given his drooping eyes and tired look from months of deadly cat and mouse games with Ukrainian partisans, Jake and Hennadiy thought the lieutenant was at least thirty-five years old, not twenty-four.

"Good evening, lieutenant," said Hennadiy in perfect Russian, wisely conveying—and pre-empting—that this Border

Guard colonel behind the wheel recognized who he was speaking with.

"Good evening, sir," replied the young officer, having served just over eighteen months in the Russian Army. He had read the lettering on the side of the vehicle, and he recognized the colonel's rank immediately.

"Um, sir, are you . . . perhaps . . . lost?"

Jake folded his hands over his crotch, ready to grab his pistol if needed. But there was no reason to expect that this young lieutenant suspected anything unusual about a perfectly legitimate-looking Russian Border Guard vehicle.

"Why do you ask that, lieutenant?" Hennadiy inquired. "I know *exactly* where I am. We just passed the village of Stepne, and we are now at Solodke, correct?"

"Uh, yes, sir, that is correct," replied the lieutenant. "But you should know that if you keep heading west down this road, I can't guarantee your security. Those enemy Nazi bastards are unlikely to be in the next village. We've been keeping a constant eye on the village. But Ukrainian partisans and regular forces are highly likely to be in the village after that."

"I *know* that lieutenant," said Hennadiy. "And that is why I'm here. Listen to me, son. You've heard that we have conducted a couple of prisoner exchanges over the past year with those Ukrainian sons-a-bitches, correct?"

Hennadiy could see the lieutenant's mental gears shifting. As a Russian Army cavalry scout, the lieutenant had bravely volunteered to lead a tip-of-the-spear Russian Army reconnaissance platoon. His platoon served as the "eyes and ears" of the Russian commanding general and his staff, who were ten to twelve miles behind him. The scout lieutenant and his men were trained to observe and report enemy activity while ensuring they remained unseen and did not engage the Ukrainian enemy, unless, of course, they had no choice.

But *this* was something the lieutenant had not been trained for.

"Yes, well, I have heard of *one* exchange, a few months back," said the young man.

"Well, before we mount our big offensive in a couple of weeks, and seriously kick some Ukrainian ass, we are going to conduct another prisoner exchange. And it's going to take place not far from here, within a few days. I'm on orders from the Kremlin to confirm the right spot to do it. It needs to be a relatively neutral and open area, and that terrain ahead of us, about five miles down the road, is the spot the Kremlin is considering for the exchange," said Hennadiy, lifting his left hand and pointing down the road.

Hennadiy continued.

"It's a perfect place for a prisoner exchange, at least from what the map says. My job is to confirm it by doing a personal, on-the-ground reconnaissance. We can't just trust the map for these things. I think you know something about personal, on-the-ground reconnaissance . . . don't you, lieutenant?"

The lieutenant, far less skeptical than he was before Hennadiy gave his explanation, nodded affirmatively.

Pensively, the lieutenant looked down the road in the direction Hennadiy had pointed.

"OK, sir. But are you sure you don't need an armed escort to do this? I have a BRDM nearby, at the ready. And there is another one on the other side of the village behind me that I can call forward, too."

"You are a brave son-of-a-gun, young man," replied Hennadiy. "If I could, I'd pin a fucking medal on you right now, just for volunteering to drive out into no man's land with me and my captain. But . . . here's the thing. My job is also to link up with somebody when I get there. I can't tell you who that is. But I imagine you can understand that some trust and guarantees must be established before doing a prisoner swap, so that is part of my mission . . . to establish some trust. And if I come rolling up to my Ukrainian contact with a badass, armed to the teeth BRDM right behind me, that's not going to do a lot for building trust, is it?"

"No, sir," replied the lieutenant.

"What is your name?" asked Hennadiy.

"Ivan Rodchenko," came the reply.

"Well, Lieutenant Ivan Rodchenko. You are a damn good soldier. Keep taking good care of your men. But now, I have a mission to perform. You have a safe evening."

Hennadiy, without saying another word to the lieutenant or waiting for his permission, rolled up his window and pressed on the accelerator.

After about fifty yards, Hennadiy looked in his rearview mirror. He could see the lieutenant still standing there.

Jake and Hennadiy did not say a word to each other. They knew they had just dodged big trouble. The lieutenant could just as well have told the men to stop until he got clearance from his superiors to let the Border Police car proceed beyond friendly Russian lines. But that did not happen.

Dusk was slowly casting its shadow on the area. In a few minutes, they would pass by the rural settlement of Vodyane. The settlement was situated roughly four miles northeast of Vuhledar, their final destination.

About two miles from Vodyane, with their heart rates having settled down, Jake spoke.

"That was an Oscar-worthy performance, my friend."

Hennadiy smiled.

"I hope it's the last one we'll need."

CHAPTER 94
VODYANE
September 2024

"CAN YOU MAKE OUT SOME OF THE VILLAGE LIGHTS?" asked Jake, having spotted them about a mile ahead. It was twilight.

"I sure can," confirmed Hennadiy. "We'll take a left at the 'T.' It's about four miles after that to our link-up point. I will call Artem when we are within a mile of the village."

Jake and Hennadiy felt good. But they were still cautious. They still had to link up with Artem and his men in Vuhledar. Just as there were pro-Ukraine partisans in the area, there could also be pro-Russia partisans in this area of mixed, grey, and shifting allegiances.

As Hennadiy wheeled up the SUV to the "T," to make a left turn, Hennadiy could see that a country two-track dirt road continued ahead to the rural settlement of Vodyane.

He slowed to a rolling stop and then took a left turn, toward Vuhledar.

He barely had a chance to pick up speed when three men, armed with rifles, emerged from the wood line. Each man had various versions of hunting or old military uniforms, with no rank or insignia. One man continued to the middle of the road, while the other two covered him with their rifles pointed at the SUV. The lead man signaled the vehicle to stop.

"Shit," muttered Hennadiy.

The lead man approached the vehicle from Jake's side. He signaled Jake to lower his window.

Jake gripped his pistol with his right hand and, reaching across the front of his torso, activated the electric switch to lower his window. Hennadiy gripped his pistol, still between his legs.

The man uttered something to Jake. Jake could only make out a few Russian-sounding words. He looked at Hennadiy.

"Fuck, you guys spooked us," replied Hennadiy instantly, in Ukrainian.

The lead man, with a full beard and now leaning in the window, had a wry smile on his face. Hennadiy had understood every word the man said.

"Sorry," replied Artem. "We can't go into Vuhledar. We cannot go north from here, either. Too many Orks in the area."

Jake had heard the term Ork once or twice but didn't fully understand its meaning. Hennadiy knew it instantly. It was the pejorative Ukrainian term for Russians, meaning "a member of an imaginary race of humanlike creatures, characterized as ugly, warlike, and malevolent."

"Orks" also appeared in Tolkien's *The Lord of the Rings.* They were a brutish, aggressive, and evil race of monsters.

"What's our Plan B?" asked Hennadiy.

"We must drive about two miles down the road toward Vuhledar and take a right into the farmland. The turnoff is about a half mile before Vuhledar. We will then follow some two-track roads to Bohoyavlenka. We know Bohoyavlenka is firmly in Ukrainian hands. We have two vehicles, and I have five men with me. I will lead from the front with the two men who are with me now, and my second vehicle will be right behind you, with three men in it. Bohoyavlenka is about nine kilometers (about 5.5 miles) north of us. Should take about fifteen minutes to get there. Questions?"

"No questions," replied Hennadiy.

"Are you the Italian?" asked Artem in Italian, looking down at Jake.

"Close enough," replied Jake, also in Italian, with a wink.

Artem returned Jake's wink with a grin.

"Wait till we get the two vehicles out of the wood line, and as soon as the lead vehicle gets in front of you, we move!"

Artem and his two men returned to the wood line.

"I kinda like that guy," said Jake, chuckling.

"I do, too, amico (friend)," replied Hennadiy. "I do, too."

Hennadiy and Jake did not know it, but "that guy" was one of the most adept, competent, and foxlike local Ukrainian partisan commanders in the Donetsk region. The Russians had promised a huge reward to anybody who killed or captured him.

The Russians had added a "50% premium" on the reward if Artem were to be captured and turned over to the Russian Army alive. His potential intelligence value—if he ever confessed— was far more valuable to the Russians than a corpse.

When the Russian Army tried to completely subdue Donetsk in early 2022, "Artem" (not his real name) had been away from his humble home when Russian troops stormed his house. The Russian soldiers raped his beautiful wife, Oksana, repeatedly and then killed her and Artem's six-year-old son. Artem's son had "seen too much," according to the Russian squad (about ten men) leader who headed up the atrocity.

Thirty years old and looking ten years older, Artem had dedicated his life to restoring Donetsk to its rightful owners, the Ukrainian people. He had long since accepted that a violent death was a strong possibility for him.

CHAPTER 95

BOHOYAVLENKA

September 2024

HENNADIY PULLED THE VEHICLE INTO THE BARN, located in the center of Bohoyavlenka.

Along the way, Jake thought he had not only observed a few Ukrainian citizens in the town, but there was the occasional Ukrainian soldier, too. On their trip along the two-track roads, they had passed what looked to be Ukrainian military positions. But it was hard to discern if the area was covered only with Ukrainian Army troops or a mix of Ukrainian Army troops and local partisans. It would soon be clear that it was a mix of both.

Once Hennadiy stopped in the barn and its main doors were closed behind them, he and Jake got out of the vehicle. They came around to the back of the vehicle and lifted the back hatch. They both pulled back the tarp.

"Boys, we are now safe!" said Hennadiy.

Little Gleb let out a "yaaay!" and hugged his uncle Hennadiy. Sergiy hugged Jake, calling him "Uncle Jake." Jake blinked back a tear.

After lengthy hugs between the four of them, Gleb spoke up.

"I gotta pee!" said Gleb.

"Me, too!" said Sergiy.

"Me three!" replied Hennadiy.

One of the partisans, overhearing the conversation, led Hennadiy and the two boys through pitch-black darkness about forty yards to an outhouse.

The two partisan vehicles remained outside the barn. But after a few minutes, Artem walked in, followed by two of Artem's men. They were carrying a big pot of vegetable and oatmeal soup. Four plastic bowls, some spoons, and some black bread accompanied the soup.

Looking at the side of the "Border Police" SUV, Artem laughed.

"That vehicle is going to need a new paint job!" he told Jake.

"I kinda like it," replied Jake. He chuckled.

"God, I never thought I'd say that about anything the Russians made."

When the trio came back from the outhouse, Sergiy had a question.

"Uncle Hennadiy, when do Gleb and I get to go back to Mariupol . . . to see our Dad?"

Hennadiy looked at Sergiy and Gleb. He knew it was time to tell them both something he had dreaded telling them. He decided it was better to tell Sergiy first, and then Hennadiy and Sergiy would both tell Gleb the sad news about their heroic father, and that Mariupol was now completely in the hands of the Russian Army.

But Hennadiy wanted to be in a private place, where only he and Sergiy could talk together.

"Sergiy, let's make sure we all grab a bottle of water, and then you and I can chat. Maybe we'll talk inside the car?"

"Sure thing, Uncle Hennadiy," replied Sergiy. "Sure thing."

CHAPTER 96
DISNEYLAND PARIS
June 2025

GLEB KOVALENKO AND GIACOMO FORTINA-SIMONETTI WERE ECSTATIC and full of pure, boyish glee. They were wearing their Spider-Man shirts as they rode through the popular Spider-Man W.E.B. Adventure at Disneyland Paris. Sergiy was seated between them.

Sergiy was having fun, too. At thirteen years old, he still thought Spider-Man was cool, but he no longer had the fervent admiration for Spider-Man that he once had as a nine-year-old. He'd learned too much about movie-making.

For the Disney trip, Sergiy was given the "mission" by Hennadiy to "help take care of the boys." As always, Sergiy shouldered his brotherly responsibility with love and pride.

Hennadiy, Jake, Mila, and Sara rode behind the boys. They were on the opposite side of the same car and facing opposite directions. As parents, they considered themselves very blessed. Sara had conceived Giacomo in her late thirties, when Jake was newly forty. Mila dearly missed her sister, but felt privileged to be a mother to her sister's sons at this later stage in her life, especially when she'd never been able to have children herself.

Riding in the next car were "Uncle" Marco Conti and "Aunt" Margarita Conti.

Their wedding, held just two weeks earlier in Siena's magnificent *Il Duomo di Siena,* graced by works from Bernini and Michelangelo, was spectacular. Given how much bigger it could have been with the Conti family's exceptional wealth, it was a relatively small event for 150 people.

Jake, Sara, Hennadiy, Mila, all three of their children, and Anna, Margarita's friend from Russia, were in attendance. Cute-as-a-button Giacomo served as one of the ring bearers. A four-year-old girl, Maria, from the Conti side of the family, accompanied Giacomo as the flower girl.

After the wedding, Margarita and Marco took their ten-day honeymoon in the City of Love, Paris. And now, they were gratefully spending three more days in Paris with people they had both fallen in love with.

"It's not only our love story," said Margarita to Marco. "It's a love story about the boys, too."

Following the Spider-Man ride, at a Disneyland Paris ice cream shop, Hennadiy spoke with Jake.

"Look at us, Jake. Nine months ago, we didn't know if we could get the boys home. How did we get here, my friend?"

Jake looked at Hennadiy with an empathy and love—if often going unspoken—that follows men who committed to risking their lives together for something greater than themselves.

"You want my two cents?" asked Jake, grinning.

Hennadiy smiled back. "Absolutely."

"Faith and love, my brother. Faith and love. And Divine providence."

Hennadiy looked down at his coffee and nodded his head.

"And some pretty darn good acting, too, Mr. Oscar Winner," added Jake.

Hennadiy threw his head back in laughter.

AFTERWARD

Since June 2023, the European Union has led political efforts attempting to protect the children of Ukraine. Sweden and other members of the EU have been tirelessly fighting for accountability and an end to Russia's forced relocation of Ukrainian children. To that end, the Swedish Prime Minister Ulf Kristersson, on behalf of the Leaders of the Nordic Baltic Eight, released a statement on August 16, 2025, demanding that "Russia urgently returns children who have been abducted from occupied territories, as well as prisoners of war and civilian prisoners."

If you wish to learn more about how the war in Ukraine is affecting the lives of the people there, especially the children, please see the list that follows. This is just a small number of good resources to learn about the Ukraine-Russia war and the illegal abduction of Ukrainian children from the cities and towns of Ukraine to Russia.

20 days in Mariupol, written and directed by Mstyslav
Chernov, aired on February 24, 2022, on PBS, now
available on Amazon Prime Video
https://www.amazon.com/gp/video/detail/amzn1.dv.gti.4d8
69a16-27d4-4340-ad78-
23c53d6a4fc0?ref_=imdbref_tt_ov_wbr_ovf__pvt_aiv&tag
=imdbtag_tt_ov_wbr_ovf__pvt_aiv-20.

This documentary has won multiple awards, including the Academy Award for Best Documentary Feature Film, 2024; the Directors Guild of America Award for Outstanding

Directing, 2024; the BAFTA Award for Best Documentary, 2024; the Peabody Award for the Documentary category, 2024; the Shevchenko National Prize in Journalism and Opinion Journalism, 2024; and the Sundance Film Festival Audience Award for Best Documentary, 2023; among others. The documentary tracks a team of Ukrainian Associated Press Journalists who are trapped in Mariupol as they try to document the atrocities of the Russian invasion.

Sarah El Deeb, Anastasiia Shvets, and Elizaveta Tilna, "How Moscow Grabs Ukrainian Kids and Makes Them Russians," *AP News*, March 17, 2023, https://apnews.com/article/ukrainian-children-russia-7493cb22c9086c6293c1ac7986d85ef6.

Mick Krever, "The Russian Official at Center of Alleged Scheme to Forcibly Deport Thousands of Ukrainian Children to Russia," *CNN*, February 15, 2023, https://www.cnn.com/2023/02/15/europe/russia-ukraine-children-maria-lvova-belova-intl/index.html.

Anna Holligan & Diana Kuryshko, "Ukraine's missing children tracked down in Russia by digital sleuths," *BBC*, February 9, 2024, https://www.bbc.com/news/world-europe-68249102.

"Inside a Russian summer camp where kids are trained for a life in the military," *SBS Dateline* (Australian Public Broadcasting Service) 2023, available on YouTube, https://www.youtube.com/watch?v=w2z26CVQ-JE&ab_channel=SBSDateline.

Anton Starikov, "'Field Wife': Officers Make Life Hell For Women In Russia's Military, A Female Medic Says," *Radio Free Europe*, March 30, 2023, https://www.rferl.org/a/women-russian-military-field-wife/32342221.html.

Margaret Brennan, "Ukrainian children recount horrors of being kidnapped by Russian soldiers," *CBS News, CBS Mornings*, February 27, 2024, https://www.cbsnews.com/news/ukrainian-children-kidnapped-russian-soldiers-united-nations/.

Olesya Gerasimenko, "Russia police crisis: Burned out, disappointed and demoralized," *BBC*, September 30, 2023, https://www.bbc.com/news/world-europe-66924404.

US Embassy Georgia, "Russia's 're-education camps' hold thousands of Ukraine's children, report says," February 23, 2023, https://ge.usembassy.gov/russias-re-education-camps-hold-thousands-of-ukraines-children-report-says/.

"Ukraine fires MLRS artillery at Russian positions near Bakhmut," *The Sun*, 2023, https://video.search.yahoo.com/search/video?fr=mcafee&p=when+did+Ukraine+get+MLRS&type=E210US105G0&guccounter=1#id=4&vid=0e994bddf79c3677501685826f8c24da&action=vie.

Ulf Kristersson, "Joint Statement of the Leaders of the Nordic Baltic Eight on Ukraine," Government Offices of Sweden, accessed August 17, 2025, https://www.government.se/statements/2025/08/joint-statement-of-the-leaders-of-the-nordic-baltic-eight-on-ukraine/.

Volodymyr Zelenskyy, "Thirty-Eight Countries, Together with the Council of Europe and the EU, Urged Russia to Immediately and Unconditionally Return Ukrainian Children," President of Ukraine Official Website, accessed August 19, 2025, https://www.president.gov.ua/en/news/tridcyat-visim-krayin-razom-iz-radoyu-yevropi-ta-yes-zaklika-99337.

Acknowledgments

The author wishes to acknowledge Rachael Rhine Milliard's exceptional collaboration in editing, formatting, and preparing *Vital Mission* for publication.

ABOUT THE AUTHOR

RALPH R. "RICK" STEINKE is the award-winning author of a memoir, *Next Mission: US Defense Attaché to France* (2019; to be republished in late 2025 or 2026). He is also an award-winning author of the Major Jake Fortina series, which includes *Major Jake Fortina and the Tier One Threat* (2022), *Jake Fortina and the Roman Conspiracy* (2023), and *Change of Mission: A Jake Fortina Series Novel* (2024). All Jake Fortina books have received awards, individually and as a series.

Steinke has spent a lifetime in US national security roles, including twenty-eight years in the US Army and fourteen in the Department of Defense. His official duties have taken him from the US Military Academy at West Point to over thirty countries on the Eurasian landmass, including Afghanistan and Ukraine. Steinke holds master's degrees in West European studies and diplomacy from Indiana and Norwich Universities, respectively, as well as post-graduation certificates in national and international security affairs from Harvard and Stanford Universities. His personal passions include faith, family, fly fishing, and travel.

SOCIAL MEDIA
Facebook: Rick Steinke Author 2
LinkedIn: Ralph "Rick" Steinke
AUTHOR'S WEBSITE: https://ricksteinke.com/